MONEY, POWER & GREED

AJ HOLLAND

DEDICATION

My name is AJ Holland. I have written the following book inspired by stories told to me by a dear friend, known in this work of fiction as Hector James Parker. A smart, witty man with a generous heart, Hecky was a furious businessman but always fair. He did not deserve the end he received from people he had spent a lifetime supporting, both financially and emotionally.

Hector was born in 1948 to two loving parents. His father was a mathematician, and his mother was a school-teacher, so Hector came from a well-educated, middle-class family. From an early age, his life was always full of how-to-do-this and how-not-to-do-that, reflected in one of his favourite sayings: 'I would rather do business with a person who can tell me exactly how they can solve a problem rather than someone that has to take reference from a book.'

Hector was a good cricketer, tennis player, and billiards player. Most notably, Hector was a philanthropist who had one plan in mind after his passing. At his end, he would have put in place many financially well-structured organisations that would benefit people from all walks of life in Australia for many years down the track.

He was totally committed to getting to live to see his ultimate cricket century, but others put an early end to his dreams.

PROLOGUE

'No, Leonie, no more green juice. *Please*—I don't want to die. I want to stay here with you.'

Leonie shook her head and mentally rolled her dark eyes. She towered over Hecky. He seemed so small now. Hector Parker used to be such a strong, handsome man. She had once been in love with him, in love with the excitement of their secret tryst, and in love with the notion of being with someone who was more than her.

'Doctor's orders. He said sleep will make you feel better.'

Hecky began to cry.

'Don't be pathetic. It's too late for tears.'

Leonie continued to prepare the morning dose of morphine that would send her former lover into a deep sleep that she hoped one day would never end. She flexed her fingers, cold from clutching the chilled morning hit of Chardonnay, which she slugged from the special porcelain cup hidden in the tennis club's freezer. She'd had a few hits of Dutch courage this morning.

'Just hold still and stop your crying!'

As she pushed on the syringe, a look of hopelessness came over Hecky's face. Leonie threw the empty syringe into the bin beside his bed, then—without any compassion—she shoved him back onto the pillow. He didn't resist; the morphine had started to take effect. She still had to change his damned incontinence pad before she could leave. It was soaking wet and should have been changed hours ago. She roughly rolled Hecky onto his side and ripped the pad out from under him. *Not much longer,* she thought. It wouldn't be long before she would have everything he had worked hard for.

The disgusting ablutions finished, she regarded him with contempt. He was fast asleep, his mouth wide open, his eyes twitching in dream. He looked a bloody mess.

PART ONE

CHAPTER ONE

The planets align

The pressure was on, and with two wickets in hand and only two overs left to play, we were six runs short of beating St Michaels for the senior GPS cricket championship. My parents were sitting together on the grassy hill at the northern end of 'the common'—as the oval we were playing on was called. Mum was becoming quite vocal as I faced the next fastball from a tall, red-haired boy who had been relentless in his efforts to bowl me out; but she knew I would not let my school down.

Wow, that was close. I snicked it, and almost got out on a caught behind, but the keeper failed to catch it, and the ball went through to the second slip. No runs, still six behind. The wicketkeeper was giving me a bit of lip. As the bowler set himself up, the keeper continued calling, 'Hecky, hey Hecky, how do you like it now?' He must have had the irrits with me because I'd been shit-stirring and heckling him when I was keeping behind the stumps during St Michaels' batting innings. I knew heckling was distracting when you're facing a competent fast bowler, especially a lefty. It looked like we were in for a fight to the finish. My batting partner and I were endeavouring to keep me in play as I was further up the order giving us a better chance of getting the six runs needed to win the match. Down he came … bang! I had to block. No runs. The same result for the next five balls of the over. Of course, that meant that Hendo, my batting partner, had to face the first ball of the last over. The red-headed bowler was going to double up and serve up the final six balls, as he had the best figures for the day and had a spare over left to bowl. John 'Hendo' Henderson and I met in the middle for some discussion about how to hit a six off the last over and totally stuff up St Michaels' year in the blistering sun. We decided that there was only one way out of this for a victory: if the opportunity arose for either of us, then we should have a crack. The boundary line was set at fifty yards and scoring a six wasn't impossible. A big call, but what the hell? As we both went back to our creases, I heard Hendo call out to the red-haired bowler, 'Is that the best you can do?' That really pissed off our bowling opponent. *Well, that will be it*, I thought. Hendo set himself, and I got ready to run like hell if Hendo happened to fluke an edge or something. Down he came at Hendo, who half-stepped forward and centred the ball, hooking it hard towards the northern boundary. We were running our hearts out, hoping to get a couple of runs. As I was running back for my second, I stole a glance at Big Red, who had his face in his hands. Hendo's ball had gone over the boundary. The only six of the day. As the umpire raised both his hands, I ran over to Hendo, almost knocking him down. Our fellow teammates rushed madly onto the field, and our coach, Mr Stevens, congratulated us on our success. Hendo was very calm about the whole event. I knew Hendo's philosophy—it's not the dog in the fight but the fight in the dog that wins every time.

I never forgot those words.

Both teams lined up and shook hands. As I shook hands with Big Red, he looked me straight in the eye and said in a determined voice, 'Great game, Hecky.' I gave him a grin.

Our team gathered into a circle, arms over each other's shoulders. As the team captain, I called for the Southside war cry and we screamed, 'Aquila, aquila, blue, red, blue, aquila, aquila, blue, red, blue.' We sped up the rhythm, stomped our feet, screamed the chant even louder, then threw our cricket caps into the air.

It may only have been the under-seventeen GPS final, but it was undoubtedly one of my most memorable wins, and I now had a nickname: 'Hecky' Parker.

We joined some of the parents who had been lucky enough to see our win. A special hug from my mum in front of my mates did not phase me, and a shake of the hand from my dad. As the sun dropped into the western sky, my folks and I enjoyed the chance to sit in the afternoon shadows and absorb the wonderful ambience that the school offered, with its beautiful boarding houses to the south, the seemingly endless abundance of immaculately kept ovals to the east. It all gave me a sense of pride. *I belonged here.*

My days at Southside Grammar School were filled with tennis, cricket, and study. I joined the debating team—little did

I know that the skills I developed in arguing, mainly about politics, would develop a firm view of the importance of the Australian Labor Party, a for-the-people party. I once had a heated debate with Russell Munze, a student who came off the land. Russell was totally committed to the National Party with its policy for the rural sector, ensuring that rural Australia got a fair go. He and I agreed to disagree on many things over our four years at Southside. Russell was a big man who played rugby at school, and he ran terror through the minds of some of his opponents when he attacked the try line at full speed ten yards out. Both of us developed great friendships at the school from all walks of life, friendships that would last a lifetime.

I loved music, especially foot tapping and jiggling to The Beach Boys … 'Round, round, get around, I get around, yeah, get around, round, round, I get around.' I was a naturally gifted singer and joined the school choir in my second year, enjoying the emotionally stirring lyrics of songs I would recall in later life, especially in times of the loss of someone close to me. For me, the school chapel was a special place. I joined the school choir in my second year and can remember the words to the school hymn: 'The head that once was crowned with thorns is crowned with glory now; the king of kings and lord of lords in heaven's eternal light.' Again, words that never left me in deep emotional times, and in times of the loss of someone close to me. They are great words of comfort.

I had already dealt with loss. There was a terrible tragedy in my home when my younger brother Daniel passed away. Daniel developed polio at the age of seven and unfortunately, the disease got into his lungs. There was a trial of a new treatment in America, but it was hugely expensive, and Mum and Dad's budget just could not stretch to cover the treatment as well as an overseas trip. This was a huge moral dilemma, and my parents were completely destroyed by Daniel's death. They both took six months off work to properly mourn his passing.

Dad was a mathematician who taught at his office in the Hibernian Building in north Brisbane. He had a strong following of young land surveyors who were working for large surveying firms to achieve the practical experience required to qualify as registered surveyors. I looked up to my dad and fancied modelling myself on his career.

I developed a lot of my competitive spirit at home, where my schoolteacher mum would give out little prizes. Mum would have me and my brother racing each other around the outside of our house, and, because I was older, I was put on a handicap. We both loved the challenge because whoever won the race got a special small ribbon. Daniel's death was a tragic blow—I lost my racing buddy—but you move on; you just have to take the time and grieve. At that time, I vowed to myself I would always have choices. And to have choices meant working hard to get ahead financially.

I did well at school. Maybe having professional parents had its advantages. In the final years at Southside, I started thinking about my next journey. I was always going to move on to university, and the discussion was about what degree I would study as I was keen to use both of my key skills of English and mathematics. Southside Grammar was great. The school focused not only on education, but it arranged for special inspiring speakers to visit to the school and give lectures on the responsibilities of moving on through life after Southside. These speakers inspired us to always look out for each other down the track. As the year ended, our group members were well and truly committed to each other. This was a bond that we'd carry into our adult life. I was a Southside boy through and through.

In 1966, our family went camping for three weeks during the Christmas holidays. We had never camped before and we knew the holiday wouldn't be the same without Daniel. Mum had gone back to teaching, but sometimes, when she thought she was alone, I noticed her just standing, staring into nowhere tearily.

Dad packed the borrowed box trailer, ready to leave the next morning for our adventure. We were heading to Rainbow Bay at the southern end of what is now called the Gold Coast. We were going to set up camp right on the beach. Dad borrowed a box trailer for all the camping gear, including the tent. Putting up the tent was going to be interesting, as Dad and I had never pitched a tent. It would be interesting to see Dad in this environment. As a thinker, I was sure he would sort things out.

Usually conservative with our family funds, Dad had splurged and bought a new Ford station wagon. He was insistent its V8 engine would be up to pulling the loaded trailer. He tried to explain the finer details of the car to me, but it all went straight over my head.

We all got up early. Mum packed us morning tea for our trip while Dad and I checked the load to ensure it was secure. We had clothing, fishing gear, camp stove and a tent slung over the top. Dad had tied the load down with ropes, but his knot-tying was a bit suspect. He jokingly said, 'Son, if you can't tie knots, tie lots!' I knew nothing about knots, but Dad seemed confident with his effort.

An hour or so later we set off. Mum was decked out sixties-style. Although she hadn't embraced the full psyche-delic patterns of the time, she embraced the shorter hemlines and the brightly coloured go-go earrings. Always the conservative dresser, Dad wore his best sports jacket. Not exactly camping attire, but appearances were important to Dad. It was going to take about three hours to get there, but it was a beautiful day for a drive. The Ford was purring, and Dad was showing off a bit on the highway. Each time he gave the V8 a bit of extra acceleration, Mum would hit the panic button, so he slowed back down to sixty miles an hour. I was sitting in the back seat, my sweaty legs sliding on the shiny vinyl as Dad took the corners. The heat was quite extreme, which sort of took the shine off travelling without air-con, but with the back windows down, the wind almost sucking my breath away, I got my enthusiasm back. We passed some interesting things as we came into the outskirts of Southport. I saw a sign for a crab farm and wondered what sort of crabs they grew on a farm.

A chip off the old block, I took notice of the way things were made. So going over the Southport Bridge was exciting. It was built from large timber poles, its central arc high enough to accommodate taller boats. As we were going over the peak of the bridge, Dad gave the Ford another spurt of power to give us a bit of a thrill. 'Up and over!' he called out as we flew over the hump. I heard a huge bang. Dad didn't react, so I thought everything was all right. As we hit Burleigh Heads, a horn was blasting loudly behind us. The driver of a small truck was waving his arm, indicating for Dad to pull over. 'He's probably trying to sell us something, Richard,' Mum muttered.

Dad drew into the kerb, got out and walked back to see what the driver wanted. 'Hello there,' Dad said.

'G'day to you, sir. Going camping, are you?'

'We are.'

I looked out the back window. The truckie was a tall bloke, about mid-twenties, messy red hair, surfie singlet, boardies and thongs. Curious, I jumped out of the car and joined Dad at the back of the truck. I picked up a very strong fishy smell – was it the truck or the driver? He had a bit of a chuckle and said to Dad, 'Go round the back of my truck. I think you'll find something that you recognise.'

'Recognise anything?'

Dad and I followed him to the back of the truck.

'That's my tent!'

'Yep. It flew off as you were scooting over the hump on the Southport Bridge.'

The truckie started laughing loudly as he spotted the mass of loosened ropes that were doing their best to hold down what was left of our camping gear. Dad was very embarrassed and explained that it was our first trip. Then Mum joined us to hear what was happening. Seems it was all down to Dad's rope-tying. There was nowhere for Dad to hide, and Mum gave Dad a bit of stick about the knots.

The truckie asked, 'Where are you planning to camp?'

'Rainbow Bay.'

'Well,' he said, 'you're in luck. I'm headed that way.' He held out a strong, freckled hand to Dad. 'My name's Rusty McCloud. I'm a net fisherman at Rainbow Bay. I just dropped off a load of mullet at the Southport Co-op.'

Dad glanced towards the truck, nodding.

Rusty went on. 'I'll re-tie the camping gear still left on your trailer. Maybe leave the tent on the back of my truck. You can follow me down to the Rainbow Bay camping ground. Sound, okay?'

'Very kind of you, Mr McCloud.'

I was a bit embarrassed by Dad's formality. 'Mr McCloud' was probably not much older than me.

'Just call me Rusty,' he said.

Dad introduced me and Mum. 'Rusty, this is my wife, Grace, and my son, Hector. But he likes to be called Hecky.'

Before we knew it, we were busy untying all of Dad's 'if you can't tie knots, tie lots' knots. 'I'll show you how to tie a 'sheepshank' knot.' I asked Rusty why it was called a sheepshank, but he didn't know. He was a patient teacher and even encouraged Mum to get involved in our knot-tying lesson. 'A great knot for a heavy load. I use this knot to put pressure on my fish hauling nets. There's been an unusually wet season down the Tweed, and massive schools of mullet have been washed out of the Tweed River into the ocean just a mile or so south of Rainbow Bay. That's when we pounce, dragging our nets out and around the unsuspecting mullet. Everyone who pitches in to help pull the nets gets a few mullet for their efforts. Why don't you come and join in? I reckon you'd enjoy it.'

He beamed at me, and I was instantly in awe of this giant of a man, so different from anyone I'd ever met.

Rusty hopped back in his truck and pulled out in front of us. He was a steady driver, and along the coastal road we had time to take in the name signs of some of the beach names: Tallebudgera, Currumbin, Tugun, Bilinga, Kirra, Coolangatta. Next stop was our destination, Rainbow Bay. It was a beautiful day, and it was lunchtime when we arrived. Because of all the drama with the tent, the trip down had taken us longer than we had planned.

Rusty helped us pick the best spot for our tent—a grassy patch up off the beach looking east towards Snapper Rocks. We were lucky to get this spot: some other campers had just packed up, so we took over their position. Rusty reversed up to the campsite, unchained the tailgate of his truck, undid the ropes, and then rolled our tent out of his truck. The tent flopped onto the ground, just a pile of disorder that represented our home for the next three weeks.

Rusty jokingly said, 'Well, the rest is up to you people. It has been a pleasure meeting you all. Good luck with the tent.'

I looked over at Dad. 'No pressure, Dad,' I said, tongue in cheek. Dad was very quiet. I don't think he had thought things through. It all looked so simple in the adventure magazine.

We thanked Rusty for his generosity.

'No problems. Hey, Hecky, if you see us netting fish on the beach, jump in and grab a spot on the net rope. We can always use strong young blokes to help pull in tons of angry mullet to the beach.'

'Sure will,' I replied.

So now it was down to us. Mum rolled up her sleeves and started ordering Dad and me around. As it turned out, Mum had put tents like this up several times before on school sports days. Dad suddenly came to life, and Mum became our hero.

'Richard, you get the heavy hammer and get ready while Hecky and I pull and stretch the canvas. We are going to transform this pile of misery into a magnificent, strong structure that will keep the Parker name intact.'

Mum and I oriented the tent towards the beach.

'Okay,' Mum said, 'now that we have the tent positioned, I'll lay out the floor pegs so you can hammer them into the sand. Richard, be careful you don't hurt yourself with that hammer.' Poor old Dad was out of his comfort zone, and he knew it. He started to tap-tap the metal floor pegs through the loops around the outside edges of the square tent floor while Mum and I put the tent poles together. We identified the longer middle support, which ensured the roof had enough pitch to allow any rainwater to run off and down the sides.

Next thing, Dad was jumping around, crying out in pain. He'd hit himself on the little toe with the hammer. 'I told you, Richard,' Mum said.

'I know, *don't hit yourself.*' Dad was bleeding a bit, and we were working in sand, which didn't help. His little toe was a bloodied mess of broken skin, blood, and sand. It was the first time I had seen Dad lose his temper, jumping around and blaming everything and everyone but himself. Eventually, Mum took control of the hammer and away she went. She had a keen eye with the hammer. 'There's a Band-Aid in the car's glove box. Give it a wipe with your hanky. It'll be okay. I need you to put up the poles soon because it will take the three of us.'

'All right, I'll sort out this toe. Don't worry yourself with my problems, Grace; it's only a flesh wound and will probably only take the entire holiday to heal.'

Mum smiled. 'Bravo, bravo, long live the theatre.' Dad finally saw the funny side. Mum was a stern taskmaster and Dad knew he was barking up the wrong tree if he wanted sympathy. Half an hour later, we were moving our camping gear into the finished tent. *Home sweet home*, I thought. After Mum hung a privacy curtain and created two small bedrooms at the back of the tent, I set up my camp stretcher, grabbed a towel, and bid Mum and Dad goodbye. I was going for a swim. 'Be careful!' Mum called out.

'Yes, Mum. I'll stay close to shore.' A friend at school had told me Snapper Rocks could be a very dangerous place if taken for granted. While I was a competent swimmer in the pool, I had never experienced the feeling of sand between my toes before. As I kicked my way to the surf, the dry, fine, pure white silica sand made a squeaking sound beneath my feet. There were a lot of other people in the water, so I felt quite safe. As I walked along the hard sand at the water's edge, I thought I'd take a look at what was on offer at the kiosk at the southern end of the beach. Up to my right, I noticed about a dozen fishing boats set up on large, round wooden rollers. I had no idea how these fishing boats would play a major role in my later years.

Up on the deck of the kiosk there was a stack of black rubber floats. A young, suntanned man wearing a nametag - Jack - asked me if I wanted to hire a surfoplane. This was new to me, so I asked what they were used for. He pointed out to the crowd in the water where about a dozen swimmers were floating on top of the surfoplanes. When a wave came up behind them, they would furiously paddle with their arms and kick their feet, so they were propelled onto the waves and back to the beach.

'Can you swim?' I assured him I had been taught at school and was a very confident swimmer. 'Why don't you take one out for half an hour to see if you like it?'

I was *beside* myself with excitement. I hung my towel on the railing of the deck, thanked him, grabbed a surfoplane, and ran down the beach to give it a go.

'Have fun!' he yelled as I dashed towards my first wave. I was trying to look like an old hand as I entered a whole new world of enjoyment. My first wave was unforgettable, and I was thrilled and breathless as the wave picked me up and drove me hurtling towards the beach.

When I touched the sand after my first wave, I looked back towards the kiosk, where I could see Jack standing on the deck. I gave him a wave, and he waved back. *Another sucker*, he was probably saying to himself. I caught a few more waves and went back to talk to Jack about hiring a surfoplane.

'How much, Jack?'

'What's your name?' he asked.

I replied, 'Hecky Parker.'

'Well, Heck, they are two shillings an hour.'

'I'll go and get four shillings.'

'Are you sure you can go two hours?' he said.

'Yes, I can!'

I ran back to Mum and Dad, who were enjoying a cold beer together outside the tent. 'Mum, Dad, did you see me on those waves?'

Mum responded, 'Yes, we did. I didn't know that you could surf, Hecky.'

'Neither did I, Mum. Have you got four shillings out of my pocket money, please?'

'Of course.'

As she passed over the coins, Dad warned me, 'Don't go out too far. There are sharks in this area, real killers, if you give them a chance.'

I took the money and ran back to Jack.

'Here you are, Hecky. I've pumped extra air into this one, so it will make it easier to catch waves.'

I quizzed Jack on the threat of sharks. He reassured me that if you don't go out too far, you're safe. *How far is too far out?* I was thinking to myself. I stayed in amongst the other surfers; safety in numbers theory, what could go wrong?

The two hours went by quickly and I was totally stuffed. My arms could not paddle out again, and my legs wobbled as I walked back to give Jack his surfoplane.

'How did you go, Heck?'

'Great,' I replied. 'What time will you be opening in the morning?'

'Oh, about nine o'clock.'

'Gee, that's late.'

As Jack was stacking the surfoplanes into his trailer, he explained that he was going dancing that night. 'You never know what mischief you're going to get up to on a Monday night at the Rusty Nail. Tell your mum and dad about the place; they'll enjoy themselves. The food and grog are fantastic, and the local girls are even better.'

'Is it a fancy place? What do they wear?'

Jack laughed. 'There are no rules; providing that you behave yourself, it's open slather.'

'I'll explain things to Mum and Dad. See you tomorrow.'

As I found my way back to the tent, I thought of how friendly and relaxed the locals were.

'How was that?' Mum asked.

'Fantastic, Mum. Can't wait until tomorrow. What are we doing for dinner?'

'Well, Dad and I have had such a lovely afternoon together that we thought we might walk over the hill to Coolangatta. We've heard the Coolangatta Hotel has great food, and it's only a fifteen-minute walk. Are you up to it after your surf?'

'Mum, I could eat a horse on the run,' I responded.

She laughed. 'Dad's having a shower up at the public dressing shed. We'll leave in about half an hour.'

'Okay, Mum. I'm as clean as a whistle after my surf, so I'll just get dressed.'

CHAPTER TWO

The privacy screen worked well, and I was dressed in a flash. I was pumped and looking forward to dinner at the Coolangatta pub. As we walked over Greenmount Hill towards the pub, Dad limping a little, the three of us, arm in arm, Mum was holding court as usual. I think her teaching profession gave her confidence that she could talk on any subject with authority. Sometimes she was so committed to getting her point across I felt she was talking without breathing. All Dad and I had to do was listen and agree, if you get my drift. As we walked into the pub, I noticed a menu board at the entry and beside the menu, to my horror, was another sign: 'Trivia Night'. Mum's face lit up. Dad and I gave each other a look of, *It's going to be a long night.*

'Quick boys, let's sit at that table up the front so we can hear the compere calling the questions.'

As we sat down, a beautiful young waitress welcomed us and presented us with a menu. I did a double take as she looked somehow familiar. *Where have I seen her before?*

Mum was very excited and kept looking around the room to see if she knew anyone. 'No,' she said, 'nobody here I know.' Good, we can relax.

At the top of the menu was steak, chips, and salad. 'What do you think, boys?'

'Yeah, Mum, good idea,' we both responded. Another look from Dad. Mum caught this one. 'Richard, you know that someone has to be in charge, and I think I do a very good job. What do you think, Hecky?'

'Yes, Mum, you do. I don't know how Dad and I get through our day without your direction, Mum.'

As the waitress headed off to deliver our order, I spotted a well-dressed older man moving around the room, welcoming each table, and handing out pencils and paper. As he approached our table, Mum adjusted herself and sat up very straight, ready for our compere's welcome.

'Good evening,' he said, 'and welcome. Will you be joining in tonight?'

Mum jumped in. 'YES, I'm a teacher.'

Dad and I used to have a private line that we kept between us: How do you know if there is a teacher in the room? They'll tell you! Dad gave me a little throat clear and a tap on the leg under the table. I responded with a grin.

'Well,' he said, 'I'll look forward to seeing how your general knowledge stacks up against some of our regulars. Some of them also come from professional backgrounds. And, sir, what is your profession?'

'Well…' Dad cleared his throat, and with half his hand over his mouth, he said he was a mathematics professor.

'Well, I hope there are some equations for you to solve in tonight's questions.'

Funnily enough, the compere didn't ask me what I did. I don't think he was game after Mum and Dad's professions.

The food arrived, thick T-bones, fat golden chips and a tiny side salad. The room was abuzz with laughter and smoke, and you couldn't help but feel happy. This lifestyle was for me. Whatever uni course Mum decided was okay for me, this part of the planet is where I wanted to be.

As the beautiful waitress started clearing the plates, I was still gnawing away at my steak bone. Mum gave me a tap on the arm. 'Hecky, please stop and hand over your plate.'

Reluctantly, I put the bone down on the plate and looked up at the waitress. When we made eye contact, I hoped she didn't notice me blushing. She was very attractive, especially when she gave me a smile that really set the cat among the pigeons. *Where did I know her from?*

Mum was busy passing the paper and pencils around the table, getting ready for the start of the quiz. The compere was now standing with a microphone, a spotlight beaming down on him. A hushed silence came over the crowd. This compere had a certain charisma that grabbed my attention. He introduced himself as 'Sandy Shores', and Mum gave a little giggle. She whispered, 'It's probably his stage name.'

Dad gave Mum a quiet shush. To our surprise, the compere informed the room that they had special guests competing tonight. 'Please make welcome Professor Richard Parker, his wife Grace, and their son, Hecky. Grace is a teacher, so look out, ladies and gentlemen, you have some tough opponents here tonight.'

A few friendly boos came our way from around the room. 'And tonight, I also have a special assistant. As you know, I have a new assistant every month, but tonight I'm especially excited. My assistant is the wonderful Peta Rosé. Please welcome Peta to the stage.'

On that cue, a tall, blonde, large-busted person made her way to the microphone. Some of the men in the room were giving wolf whistles as she sashayed this way and that. She welcomed the crowd and told us her job for the night was to collect the answers and bring them back for Sandy to sort out. You could have heard a pin drop as the crowd processed her deep, resonant voice. *Wow*, I thought, *Peta is a man dressed as a woman*

Mum and Dad were very focused through the night until the last question, which was a tiebreaker between Mum and an elderly lady over to our right. When asked to spell 'hippopotamus', Mum spelled it with an 'ous' at the end and the other lady spelled it correctly. Mum had drunk a couple of beers and told us boys that she was a bit tipsy. We told Mum not to worry, as there would be another time.

Peta took the winner up on to the stage and presented her with a voucher for a free seafood dinner at the Rusty Nail Tavern. Sandy thanked the Rusty Nail owner, Rusty McCloud, for his generosity with the seafood voucher. As the spotlight spun to the back of the room, the three of us looked at each other with amazement. It was Rusty, our friendly tent recovery person!

Sandy went on to thank Peta for her help tonight and announced that she was starring at the Rusty Nail in her female review show. 'Don't miss it,' Sandy said. 'It's a real hot, hot show, full of surprises, so don't miss it.'

The house lights were on again and the crowd were finding their way to the bar, the toilet, or the minority—including us—were heading out onto the street to go home. As we were waiting our turn to fit through the front door, I saw Rusty leaning on the bar talking to three men, one wearing a police officer's uniform. I gave Rusty a quick call: 'Rusty!' He glanced over at me and gave the three of us a warm wave. 'First night in the tent, Parkers. Who oversaw the tent erecting?'

Mum was quick to take all the credit.

Rusty called out, 'Sleep tight,' with a big laugh. 'See you around, Hecky.'

'Sure, Rusty.' I was thrilled he'd remembered my name.

'Hey, Hecky, there is a big chance that some fish are moving through tomorrow. Come and give us a hand with the net.'

'Okay!' I said excitedly. As we found our way back to the tent, I could not help but think that if Dad could tie knots, Rusty and I would never have met. It was a beautiful moonlit night, which made walking through the tents easy, but we had to be careful not to get tangled up in all the ropes of our fellow campers' tents.

We spotted our tent—still up, a miracle. When Mum and Dad agreed to have a nightcap together in their fold-up camping chairs, I thought I would leave them to brush my teeth.

The next morning, I couldn't remember putting my head on the pillow. I had been absolutely stuffed, but I awoke to a beautiful Rainbow Bay morning. Dad was up, and the billy was on the stove; Dad was making Mum a cup of tea. 'How good is this morning, Dad?'

'Sure is, Heck. Mornings like this make you realise how fortunate we are to live in such a wonderful place.'

'I agree.'

'You surfing today?'

'Yeah, the surf is looking good, and Jack's agreed to hold a surfoplane for me. I'll have some Weetabix first if we've got any milk.'

'Yes, in the ice chest. The ice man came around this morning.'

'Great,' I replied. 'I'm going up to the toilet. Morning, Mum.'

'Morning, Heck.' She was wearing the dressing gown I had bought her a couple of years ago. 'Come here and give me a hug; you're not too old to give hugs to your mother?'

'No, Mum, I never will be.'

As I hugged her, I could smell her beautiful Mum-smell in the dressing gown. We didn't hug much since Daniel's passing, but things were starting to settle.

Morning, Daniel, I said to myself.

After breakfast, I put my T-shirt and swimmers on and grabbed my towel. I could see Jack at the other end of the beach, setting up for another tough day at the office. 'See you two for lunch.'

'You be careful.' Dad slipped me some extra cash to take care of any incidentals that came up, so I was feeling independent—a great feeling—as I jogged my way along the beach up to Jack. *What a life*, I thought.

'Morning, Jack.'

'Morning, Heck. Sleep well, did you?'

'Yes, I had a great night with Mum and Dad. We walked over to the Coolangatta pub. How was your night at the Rusty Nail?'

'Fantastic! Danced for hours. There's a new band playing called Moonstones. They play great rock and roll, and the dancing partners line up.'

'I love live music. Not sure about the dancing though.'

'Reckon you'd get to like it,' he said smiling.

'Jack, I've got ten shillings.' I pulled the loose change out of my pocket. 'So can we keep a tally on how much I've spent on surfoplane hire at the end of each day?'

'Okay, Heck, I'll sort it,' he said. 'There's plenty of activity in the water today, so grab a surfoplane and go hard.'

Jack squinted into the glaring sky. 'Hey, Hecky, here's a tip: keep your T-shirt on and you'll need some white zinc for your lips and nose. Wait here.' He reached for a big bottle of white zinc. 'Put some of this on now before you get wet. I don't want one of my paying customers getting sunstroke on me; it's bad for business.'

'Thanks, Jack.' Jack and I studied the waves to identify the best spot to paddle out. 'The surf is a bit bigger today, more fun,' Jack said. 'Try to get out the back.'

I ran down the beach towards the area he'd pointed out. A couple of giant waves smashed me on the paddle out, but I kicked hard and soon got out the back. It was a hoot of a surf and again I surfed until I couldn't paddle out anymore. I sorted things out with Jack and headed back to the tent to make a late lunch sandwich. But forget the sandwich. Mum and Dad had gone over to the Coolangatta pie shop. Dad said that the pies were great, and they were still warm enough.

'Fantastic. Mum, where's the pie shop?'

Dad jumped in with a laugh. 'It's in the middle of the main street, and it was called the "chew and spew".'

Mum gave a little tut. 'Richard, you know that is not its real name.'

'Well, when I asked that young surfer where the pie shop was, that's what he called it!' I could see Dad was really getting into the holiday swing.

'Hey, Mum, what are we doing for tea tonight?'

'Dad and I were wanting to try out Rusty's place, the Rusty Nail. After all, he was very kind to us during our little mishap with Dad's rope-tying episode.'

'Now come on, Grace, let's put that behind us. You know I was embarrassed.' Dad went on to say, 'I would like to move a family motion.'

'What's that, Dad?' I asked.

'Well, I would like to move a motion that we bury the rope incident and all move on.'

Mum and I looked at each other with a smile. 'Well,' I said, 'we should leave that motion in abeyance until we arrive back home with *all* of our camping gear.'

Mum agreed and said, again with a smile, 'Richard, you're not off the hook yet.'

'Any further business?' I asked.

Mum moved a motion that we should all have tea at the Rusty Nail, and further to that, Dad had to pay the bill. 'All those in favour?' All hands raised. 'Then it's carried,'

Mum said. The three of us had a great laugh and moved on to the rest of the day, *rest* being the operative word.

I woke to the sound of a car horn: three short blasts, followed by two more. I was a bit bleary-eyed but could see what looked to be Rusty's truck parked on the dry sand, pointing out to sea. Out in the water in front of Rusty's truck was a rowing boat with two rowers pulling their hearts out on the oars. The rowers were being directed by the varying number of horn blasts. What seemed to be a net was being held at one end by two men from another truck parked further along the beach to the north. The rowers were doing it tough, pounding their way through the enormous waves. When the horn blasted three times, the rowers pulled harder on their right-hand oars and headed back to the beach. The cork-floated net was still pouring out of the rowing boat. Rusty was now running down to help sort out the boat as it hit the beach. The net had created a half-circle around a dark mass in the water, and the boat had been dragged up the beach a bit, out of harm's way.

Rusty spotted me and yelled out, 'Hey, Hecky! Come down and give us a hand. Bring your dad.'

Dad and I jumped to attention and ran down to help the others drag the net line. Dad was still struggling with his sore toe, but at least he had given up complaining about it. That was a bonus.

'Get in, fellas, and get into our rhythm. When I yell "PULL!" give a short sharp pull. Got it?'

Dad and I were into it. Pull, two, three, four; pull, two, three, four; pull, one, two, three, four. The other end of the net was being given the same effort as ours. More of the holidaymakers had joined in, and Rusty yelled the count again, As the net half-circle became smaller, hundreds of fish started jumping into the air, trying to escape the inevitable. Rusty was yelling again. 'Keep pulling and start working your way towards each other.'

Rusty settled a bit, but as the two pulling teams came closer together, his intensity lifted again. The trapped fish were going crazy, and the net was becoming heavier with each one, two, three, four. Finally, the two teams of net-pullers were about twenty yards apart. 'Okay,' Rusty yelled out. 'Now we stop going sideways but keep our rhythm: one, two, three, four, that's good.' The net circle was now chock-a-block with mullet, some dead and some still fighting. 'Okay,' he yelled. 'Let's go, big effort, get the rhythm. Let's get it up onto the dry sand.'

There must have been tons of fish in the net.

'Success!' Rusty yelled out as the last circle of the net was dragged up to the dry sand. We were all totally covered in salt spray and fish scales. What the hell was Rusty going to do with so many fish? As if on cue, a large, dark green military-looking truck came onto the beach, and we all joined in the process of throwing the mullet into the bin of the truck. I guessed it would be taking the mullet to the Southport fish market.

As we were all working together, Rusty brushed past me. 'Well done, Hecky. You too, Richard. Couldn't have done it without you two.'

The exhilaration of Dad and me pulling on the net together was fantastic.

When the large truck was full, we started to load two smaller trucks that were waiting on the beach. 'Okay, all the team that helped with the net, thank you for your teamwork. Those that pulled, please take a few mullet, and I hope you enjoy them. Thank you again.'

Then Rusty called out to the truck driver to put a tarp over the fish in his tray and tie it down securely.

'Hey, Hecky, can you and your dad give the truck driver a hand to tie off the load?'

'Yes,' I said without hesitation. 'Come on, Dad, let's show Rusty what we Parkers are made of.' The tails of the tarp ropes were hanging down both sides of the truck, ready to be tied off. 'Okay, Dad, put the end of the rope through the rail of the truck, make a half-hitch with your left hand, then tuck the loop in your right hand into the half-hitch. Let go with the left hand and slowly pull down with your right hand.'

I hadn't noticed Rusty standing behind us. As I pulled down the rope with my right hand, the truckie's knot engaged. 'Well done, Richard. Well done, Hecky. It's like riding a bike; you'll never forget it.'

Dad, visibly relieved, picked up two mullet and so did I. Mum was sitting in her camp chair with a tall XXXX beer. 'Okay, you two, off to the showers.'

'Let's have a beer before we have a shower.'

'What, Hecky as well?'

'Yes,' Dad said.

Funnily enough, Mum didn't resist. Dad called out, 'Bartender, two beers, please.'

Mum stood up, went into the tent, and returned with two beer glasses. And there I was, having my first beer with Mum and Dad. I didn't think much of the beer taste. Little did I know that I would consume thousands of glasses of XXXX in my future life. Other than feeling a little light-headed, I felt very refreshed.

The three of us were deep in conversation as the camper from behind us walked past carrying several mullet. 'Wasn't that exciting?' he said. 'Fresh mullet for dinner.'

'Us too, if we knew how to fillet them.'

'Well,' he said, 'if you give me a hand, I'll show you how to fillet mullet. It's easy.'

'Thanks.'

'I'll be back in a few minutes with my fish scaler and filleting knife. We can walk over to the beach rocks and deal with the mullet there.'

'Hecky.'

'Yes, Mum.'

'We'll have an early dinner here tonight and look at going to the Rusty Nail tomorrow. Is that all right?'

'Suits me, Mum. I'm feeling a bit tired; I think all this relaxation is wearing me out!'

When our neighbour came back with his filleting gear and a bucket, we introduced ourselves. His name was Lesley. 'People call me Les for short.'

'Where are you from, Les?'

'Brisbane,' he replied. 'Graceville, in the western suburbs.'

'I know it. We're from Holland Park.'

'How are you enjoying your holiday?'

'Great,' I replied.

As we trudged through the soft sand, it was hard going. It was a full moon, so the tides were at their highest, swallowing all the hard sand.

'Here's the rock where I usually clean my fish.'

'Does Rusty pull his nets regularly?'

'Yes, the mullet are running early, and he is full-on with his mullet netting. Do you know Rusty?'

'Yes,' I replied proudly. 'He's a good bloke.'

Les agreed. 'He's certainly the man around here. Have you been to the Rusty Nail Tavern yet?'

'No, we were going to go tonight, but fresh mullet took preference.'

'You'll enjoy the tavern; it's so full of excitement that you don't know what will happen next. Now, let's sort out dinner. You walk down and fill up the bucket with fresh saltwater. Make sure you don't get sand in the bucket; sand will spoil the party. We don't want any unhappy customers with sand in their mullet.'

I filled the bucket to the brim.

'Okay, this is the scaler.' He showed me a tool with a round metal piece connected to a small wooden handle. One of its edges had small teeth.

'Hold the mullet with your left hand and, with your right hand, scrape off the scales, like this.'

'Got it.'

'Make sure you take off all the scales; then I'll do the filleting.'

'Easy,' I said.

We were all set, and some of the wash from the surf was swirling around our feet. *This is the life*, I thought.

Les was an expert with a filleting knife. 'Just watch me, and you can give the filleting a go next time.'

I finished scaling my last mullet, and Les still had a couple to fillet. 'We'll keep some of the mullet backbones for sandworm bait tomorrow.'

'Okay,' I said, having no idea what Les was talking about.

The fish were finished, and we were on our way back to the campsites, the full moon rising behind us. As we walked back, Mum and Dad were still in the same spot that I had left them.

'How'd you go, Hecky?'

'Oh, it was so great, Mum. Fish for dinner.'

'The frying pan's ready to go for you, son. I'll finish preparing the salad in a tick.'

Dad didn't move. He was relaxing, enjoying his glass of beer, and watching the moon as it rose over Snapper Rocks. Les put our eight fillets on a plate on our camp table. 'Enjoy your fish,' he said.

'Thanks, Les. See you tomorrow.'

'Sure. I'm going to catch some sandworms tomorrow, and on the low tide, I'll find a suitable surf gutter to catch some summer whiting. I'll look out for you. Night.'

While the frying pan heated on our metho burner, I put some plain flour into a bowl, adding splashes of beer and whipping the mixture until it was quite thin. I coated the mullet strips, and when the oil was hot enough, I cooked all eight fillets, two pieces at a time until they were crisp and brown. Dad was ready at the table with his plate, knife, and fork, and two pieces of fresh white bread bought from the chew and spew this morning. I had put a couple of pages of newspaper on the table to put the cooked fish on to soak up some of the dripping. We would eat any fish left over for lunch.

Well, forget fish for lunch tomorrow. We ate the lot. Mum and Dad were over the moon with the fresh mullet, Dad commenting, 'The flavour of fresh mullet is a taste you don't forget.'

After the delicious dinner, I was off to have a cold shower and then get myself off to bed.

'Night, Mum. Night, Dad.'

'Good night, Heck.'

'Thanks for this holiday. I love you both.'

'We know you do, Heck, but it is good to hear those words; you know what I mean.'

'I do, Mum.'

Lying on my camp stretcher, I started thinking about our night at the Coolangatta pub and the waitress that served us came into my mind. I was racking my brain trying to think of where I'd seen her before and then it clicked: the end-of-year interschool debate! She'd been the final speaker for the St Saviour's team that had torn our argument apart. The topic was something about values, ends justifying means, or something like that. How funny to see her out of school uniform and working here, at the Gold Coast. I pictured her in my mind again and I started to get aroused but thought better about it, with Mum and Dad outside the tent. At eighteen years of age, I'd had many sexual encounters, but thus far, I hadn't had anybody join in with me. I dreamed of sharing sex with a beautiful girl my own age. The waitress would be my target, but how do I set it up without Mum and Dad catching on? *A work in progress.*

Another beautiful Rainbow Bay morning. I called out to Mum and Dad if they wanted a cup of tea. 'Yes please,' they both called out. As I was waiting for the water to boil, I looked out to sea. Several of Rusty's fishing boats were heading into shore after a night's fishing. This place was action stations every day. The waves were still quite big, and I watched as the boats took turns negotiating the surf break.

After drinking my tea, I went down to give them a hand along with about thirty or forty other people who had gathered to help get the boats into position above the high tide mark. Once the boats were safe, the weary fishermen started to unload their huge catches into cane baskets. I had not seen this type of fish before. As they were being unloaded, I overheard one fisherman say that the fish were snapper, caught from a spot off Cook Island. I had seen Cook Island from up on top of Point Danger and I knew from history classes that James Cook had named both places on his *Discovery* trip in 1770.

When a fisherman yelled, 'Anybody want to buy some snapper?' he was mobbed by the excited crowd. I ran to the tent and asked Mum if she wanted any fish. Mum thought about it but said she was keen to get Dad's wallet out and go to the Rusty Nail tonight. She was looking forward to having a meal and seeing the show that was starting its season tonight featuring Peta Rosé.

Great idea, Mum, I thought. I was hoping to invite the beautiful waitress to come with us; that would surprise both of my parents. What the hell did I have to lose? I planned to go over to the pub in the afternoon and see if she was working.

Meanwhile, I went back to the fishing boats to see if they needed a hand. The crowd had dissipated, and I noticed that one boat had a piece of canvas tucked over a large mound in the front compartment. There was no activity around the boat as they were not selling their catch and I noticed a man sitting in the boat, looking a bit edgy. Rusty wasn't around, but I could see his truck parked up in among the pandanus palms. Every now and then, the man in the boat would furtively pass a box to one of his mates, who would then take it up and load it into Rusty's truck. No one else seemed to notice. I could make out the markings on one of the boxes: 'Whiskey, Scotland'. *Why would they have boxes of whisky? What was going on?*

I went over and paid Jack for three hours of surfoplaning, then hit the water. I was still a bit puzzled by what I had seen. In fact, I felt intrigued. What surprised me the most was that they were doing it in broad daylight, using a few snappers as their cover.

I had a great surf, then made myself a sandwich. Mum had left me a note to say that she and Dad had gone shopping for a new dress and that Dad better have a big wallet to match her new dress for tonight at the Rusty Nail. Mum was going all out for the Rusty Nail.

I went over to the Coolangatta pub to see if my waitress was around. I was on such a high I jogged over to the pub. I spotted her as she finished taking the order from a table of four, I waved my arm to get her attention. She looked puzzled at first but gave me a beautiful smile, came over to me and said, 'Hi! What are you doing here?'

All the bravery was starting to dissipate, but I managed to get out, 'Are you working tonight?'

'Yes, I am. Why?'

'Well, I hoped you would come with me and my family to the Rusty Nail. It's opening night for Peta Rosé and her cast; should be a hoot.'

She hesitated and then said, 'I think I could get my friend Beth to take my shift. What time are you going?'

'About six o'clock.'

She said she could meet us at the Rusty Nail if that suited. She was staying in a flat just up the road in Beryl Street, a short distance from the Rusty Nail.

That would be perfect! As she half-skipped away, I called out to her, 'What's your name?'

'Rhonda, what's yours?'

'Hecky.'

She blushed a little—God she was gorgeous—and then asked, 'Hecky, did you used to go to Southside Grammar?'

'Yes.'

'You were in the debating team?'

'Yep.'

'You were the lead speaker in the interschool debate, weren't you? We were debating "Do the means justify the ends" and you were on the affirmative?'

'So, you remember too!'

'Oh yeah, I was so impressed with your confidence and passion for the Australian Labor Party. I'd love to talk some more about that—just wondered if you really would lay aside your morals to achieve what you wanted.' She raised her eyebrows. Was she challenging me?

'But I can see my manager giving me the evil eye. I have to get back to work. See you tonight, Heck.'

My heart was thumping. My first date and she was beautiful. Mum and Dad were going to be surprised. This time, I ran back to the tent, bursting with all sorts of new feelings.

Mum and Dad were sitting enjoying a cup of tea.

'Well now, where have you been?' Mum asked.

Fortune favours the brave. 'Well, you both may as well know now. I have asked the waitress from over at the pub to come with us tonight.'

They both seemed a bit shocked. Mum tried to soften the waitress situation by saying that she looked beautiful and was probably a nice enough girl, but a waitress … 'I had bigger plans for your first girlfriend.'

'I know, Mum, let's see how it all goes.'

'Okay, no problem. We'll make her welcome.'

'Great, Mum. Thank you.' Dad gave me a look of *you little devil*. I was still numb with what I had achieved in such a short time.

'Mum, I'm going for—'

'Let me guess,' Mum jumped in. 'Another surf?' She laughed.

'Yes, Mum. Les is a past surf life saver, and he is teaching me body surfing so that I can catch some waves.'

'Well, be back by four o'clock. We'll be leaving early so we get a top seat, and you'd better be looking your best. Dad bought me a new dress from Edna Harrison Fashions. I love it.'

Dad piped in. 'Almost broke the bank!'

'Oh sure, Richard. I was a bit embarrassed when you stepped forward to pay for my dress and pulled out your handkerchief to take the money from the corner of the hanky.'

'Very funny, Grace.'

We all cracked up.

The drive over the border to the Rusty Nail was only a five-minute trip, and I was as nervous as a cat on a hot tin roof.

'Settle down, Hecky. Your leg jiggling is driving me crazy.'

'Sorry, Mum.'

The carpark was almost full. 'Hope we get a table,' Mum said. We were standing in line waiting to be taken to our table when, over the top of the early patrons, I got a glimpse of Rusty. I put my hand up and gave him a hello. He saw me, and before we could blink, a short, stocky man had me by the arm and escorted us to a table for four—great seats.

'Okay,' I said, 'I'll go back to the door and wait for Rhonda.' And there she was, beautiful. She killed the boho hippy look with flair and confidence and I wanted everyone to know she was with me. I gave her a quick kiss on the cheek, and she accepted it as if it was our one-hundredth date. That settled me a bit. Next hurdle, Mum. 'Mum, Dad, this is Rhonda.' Dad jumped to his feet and shook her hand.

'Pleased to meet you, father of Hecky.'

'Oh, sorry, obviously you don't know our surname; it's Parker. This is Grace, and I'm Richard.'

'Very pleased to meet you both.'

Mum was first to move in for the kill. 'Hecky told us that you live not far away from here.'

'Yes, I'm renting a flat and have been working at the pub to build up some money for me to live on this year.'

'Oh, are you going travelling?'

'No, I've been accepted into the University of Queensland, and even though I've got a scholarship, I'll need funds to live on throughout the year.'

Mum, taken aback by her statement, sat up and gave Rhonda her undivided attention.

'Oh, and what are you studying?'

'Medicine,' she replied.

Mum's jaw almost hit the floor. 'Richard, quickly order some drinks before the waiter comes and takes our order for dinner.'

Too late. The waiter arrived at our table with four tall glasses fizzing with bubbles. The waiter said, 'These are on the house from the owner, Rusty. The drinks are called "Rusty Nails". Welcome.'

Mum was still trying to get her composure from Rhonda's statement about uni. The place was abuzz, the band playing soft dinner music that gave us a chance to get to know each other with the help of a Rusty Nail each. Both Rhonda and I hadn't been able to get a word in, but it didn't seem to worry her. She was extremely confident and could hold her own in any conversation that was thrown at her. Of course, that debating experience had value.

'Mum, it turns out that Rhonda and I have sort of met before.'

'Really? Where, Hecky?'

'At the interschool debating comp last year.'

'Ah.'

She was processing.

Dinner was a huge mixed seafood platter for four people—oysters, cracked mud crab, snapper fillets in breadcrumbs, some crumbed squid rings, and potato chips.

Rhonda just fitted in easily. Then the tables were cleared, getting ready for the show to start. The lights dimmed, and a spotlight flooded the centre of the stage. It was Peta Rosé, dressed in full costume—a tighter-than-tight glittering dress and a headdress of peacock feathers. She looked stunning. Dad had to be convinced that she was a *he*; he could not believe it.

Peta made her way through the tables until she was standing in front of Dad. She was belting out a Nancy Sinatra hit, 'Hey Big Spender'.

At 'big spender', Peta suggestively ran her hands down over Dad's balding head, and the crowd went wild. Peta moved on to the other tables and teased some other customers. What a great opener. Rhonda was laughing loudly, and Dad was still glowing with embarrassment. Mum was in a state of uncontrolled laughter, referring to the dress-paying episode at the shop today. Dad was starting to settle, but when he brought out his hanky to wipe his mouth, it started Mum laughing again. The rest of the show did not leave us short of laughter. The show lasted two hours, including half an hour for intermission, where all the actors came out into the fully lit room and introduced themselves. When the show finished, Mum and Dad got up from their chairs and excused themselves.

'It has been a pleasure meeting you, Rhonda, and I hope we get to see you again.'

'I'm sure you will,' she responded and gave me a little squeeze on the leg.

'I'll walk you home, Rhonda.'

'That'd be nice,' she said.

I pulled back her chair and waved good night to Rusty. Rhonda grabbed my hand as we walked back to her flat. 'Would you like a cup of tea, Hecky?'

'That would be great.'

Rhonda's flat was basic, but, as she was quick to point out, it was a means to an end, and she would probably move closer to the university by the beginning of term. 'I've enjoyed working at the pub. You learn a lot about people.' She paused. 'How old are you, Hecky?'

'I just turned eighteen, and you?' I asked.

'The same.' As she passed me my cup of tea, our eyes found each other, and she whispered, 'Are you still a virgin?'

When I told her my story about my sexual experiences so far, she had a good laugh and said that she was also a virgin. I was very aroused by this time, as I'm sure she could see.

'How about this for a plan? Let's aim to see each other a bit more and see what happens?'

'I can live with that.' And although I was certainly up to the task, Rhonda was a special gift, and I was prepared to wait till next Christmas if I had to. To kick things off, I gave her a full-on kiss on the lips. Like me, she had not done much passionate kissing, but we certainly made a go of it. My heart was racing ten to the dozen and a change of subject was in order.

She picked up her tea. 'What are you going to study at uni, Heck?'

'Science,' I replied.

'Good choice. You can take up a lot of opportunities with a science degree.'

'Yes. My father's a mathematician and he privately teaches maths to lots of trainee surveyors throughout their early days of trigonometry. If I have the time, I would like to work in the field of surveying and along the way do my science degree.'

'Sound plan,' she said.

'Yes, I'm definitely an outdoors person and surveying is a way to not be stuck in the office.'

'Looks like we both have years of study ahead of us!'

'I'll say.'

She paused.

'Well, Heck, do we have a deal?'

'Yes, we do.' And we sealed it with another kiss. This time, the kiss was long and slow.

'I'm working in the morning,' she said. 'Pop in and say hello if you get the time.'

'I will.' I stood up and did my best to conceal what was obvious.

'Good, I look forward to seeing you,' she said.

As the door closed behind me, I felt complete. The way Rhonda carried herself was a testament to her commitment to not throw away her most valuable possession cheaply. Our arrangement suited me perfectly.

It was about two miles back to the tent. I started to jog; then I moved it up to a slow run; with nearly a half a mile to go to the tent, I sprinted. I was feeling on top of the world. I think running is an excellent way to release emotion.

Mum and Dad were out in their camp chairs having a nightcap.

'Well, lover boy, you certainly are a surprise.'

'Yes, Mum. I'm a lucky man.'

Dad agreed. 'Rhonda is a delightful young lady. Good luck with it all.'

'Thanks. Dad. I'm off to bed.'

Our holiday took an entirely different focus, and Mum and Dad had to take a back seat with me, as I was spending a lot of my time with Rhonda. We discovered we both had similar interests. We body surfed and jogged together and shared similar political views.

Unfortunately, our family holiday had to end. We were leaving the next day and Dad was looking forward to the challenge of packing the camp trailer and securing the load with Rusty's knots that Dad now had down pat. I asked Dad to drop me over at the Rusty Nail so I could thank Rusty for all he had done for us. Our holiday would have been nothing like it turned out to be, thanks to him. When I got there, Rusty was sitting having his lunch. As I walked towards him, he gave me a Rusty-smile and I smiled back. He called to one of the barmen, 'Ginger beer and ice for Hecky.'

'Thanks, Rusty.'

'Well, how was your holiday?'

'That's why I'm here—to thank you not only for your help but for your kindness and friendship.'

'Yes, it has been my pleasure,' he said. 'Heck, can I ask you a question?'

'Yes, of course.'

'Well, it's about the other day over at Rainbow Bay when my fishing boats returned from fishing.'

'Rusty, we don't need to go any further. Your business is your business. You can trust me to keep quiet.'

'Okay, thanks, Heck. I thought that would be the case. Oh, and well done with Rhonda; she's a keeper. Some of the local lads have put in a lot of work to get her to go out on a date, but she is rock solid and insists that she is seeing someone. Well done. I'm heading over to Rainbow to deliver some fishing gear to one of my skippers, so I'll drop you off. Let's go.'

As we were driving over to Rainbow Bay, Rusty invited me to stay in touch. 'I have a small flat out the back of the Rusty Nail, and you and Rhonda are welcome anytime.'

'I might take you up on that. Rhonda and I will both be studying at UQ, and I expect we'd enjoy a seaside break occasionally.'

'What are you studying, Hecky?'

'Rhonda's doing medicine and I'm doing science. I'm also aiming to get into surveying like my dad.'

Rusty stroked his chin. 'Mmm, you might be quite handy to have around, and I know you can be very discreet.'

'Let's keep in touch.'

When we reached the camping grounds, Rusty hopped out of the truck, looked me straight in the eye and firmly shook my hand. 'Good luck, Hecky.'

'Good luck to you, Rusty.'

As I waded through the soft sand back to Mum and Dad, I reflected on my future with Rusty. There possibly were going to be times when I would have to walk a fine moral line, perhaps not to my parents' standards.

'Care for a beer, son?'

'Yes please, Dad.'

As I sat down on the warm sand, I pondered about a change in the way Mum and Dad were communicating. It gave me great heart to see them in this happy state, as if they had found each other.

And I had found my love, Rhonda.

PART TWO

CHAPTER THREE

Still enjoying our love for each other, Rhonda and I were committed students. I was burning the proverbial at both ends, having started my cadetship as a land surveyor while taking my degree. I planned to start a further course in town planning, so that once I completed all my studies, I would be a qualified surveyor with a double degree in science and town planning. I yearned for the financial wherewithal to support my loved ones if they needed help. But more than that, I wanted to leave my mark on the world. I didn't know what that would look like, but I just knew that I wanted to do good things.

Rhonda was living in the university dorms, which was convenient, and Mum and Dad had set me up in a small flat near to the university. We were totally in love and our commitment to each other was complete. When we spoke, it was always about our future together. We had everything you could wish for in a loving relationship. It was cricket in the summer and tennis in the winter, and we both excelled at university, and I had started to spread my business wings.

I was innately ambitious and, thanks to the strong relationships I built through high school and uni, I was well-connected. While I was studying, I was looking for ideas to use my future credentials and I stumbled across an opportunity to purchase some land north of Brisbane. I tossed around the idea of rezoning the parcels of land and invited my banking and accounting student mates for some taxation and financial advice. They assured me the land would be far more valuable after rezoning, and further, they suggested I use a company name to keep my identity secret. Of course, I would make sure my advisors benefitted.

My future plan was to marry my extremely beautiful and very smart Rhonda. In the early stages of our relationship, I was keeping her in the dark with any of my financial dealings. Once I had complete confidence in myself, I would involve her as director of some of the completed projects. Rhonda being a director wasn't illegal, just a way for me to keep doing deals and increasing my fortune, and also continue expanding my business contacts. I had another plan, and that was to join the Australian Labor party. I planned to secretly convince many of my university contacts to do the same; but we would all be seen to be independent of each other. Construction and land deals would be my focus.

Rhonda and I travelled down to the Tweed most weekends and stayed in the flat at the back of the Rusty Nail which was going gangbusters. The Peta Rosé review had become a bigger-than-big live show, the stars of the show being treated like royalty around town. Most of the locals accepted that the actors in the show were men dressed as glamorous women. The shows were a sell-out every night while the alcohol and cigarette sales were huge. Rhonda and I were treated as if we were part of the Rusty Nail family, but every Sunday, after we had dinner, we would pack up our clothes and drive back to Brisbane. I had bought a work truck, which was rough but reliable and driving it made me feel like a real builder.

During our stays, I came to know Rusty better and felt he trusted me. I slowly started to understand Rusty's sideline operations—drugs, cigarettes, whisky, and rum. I was staggered at the scope of his operations and just a bit unnerved about Rusty's comfort with bending the rules. Sometimes I wondered if he was going a bit too far with shifting illegal contraband. Like me, Rusty was well-connected, but in a different way. He was well set up with many local politicians, police and men that wouldn't take *no* for an answer.

Because the tavern was situated on the Tweed River, it opened up operational opportunities to use his fishing boats as the perfect front. When the weather allowed, his snapper boats would go out to sea. Of course, fish wasn't the only thing that the boats brought home. Rusty's boats would meet up with large freighters that were travelling north to Brisbane, and, under the cover of darkness, the ships would release their floating merchandise. Rusty's men would pluck the packages from the water, then continue to fish to complete the smoke screen. He had total control of his operation. All his men understood the meaning of the words, 'Don't fuck with Rusty … if you value your dream of living to be an old man, don't fuck with him.' His control was total.

At the end of each uni year, Rhonda and I spent the Christmas holidays at the Rusty Nail. After a wonderful extended holiday, we headed back in the truck for our final year of study. Rhonda would have to complete her medical degree with a couple of years of internship at one of the hospitals, and I would move forward with all of my plans. I shared a little about my plans with Rusty who was very encouraging.

As we drove back for the start of term, I was thinking about Rusty and how important he had become in my life. Rusty was ten years older than me and kept himself very fit, enjoying ocean swimming and soft sand jogging on Kirra beach in bare feet. Although Rusty drank a lot of beer, he always ate well and kept himself as a 'lean mean fighting machine' as he used to put it. Of course, he had lovers, but he kept his social life private, probably because of his business activities.

There was always a bit of mystery about Rusty's private life. He had an unusual relationship with the local Catholic priest, whose residence was a few hundred yards upriver from the Rusty Nail at a place known as Monastery Hill which overlooked the Rusty Nail. Father Brian O'Reilly, always dressed in his clerical rig in public, had explained his life's journey to Rusty on the day they met over a cup of tea. He explained to Rusty that in his years before coming to Tweed Heads, he had lived in China. He had not chosen any religious faith until he started studying kung fu in a Buddhist temple in the Shaolin Monastery. After three years at the temple, he became a student of Buddhism. His skills as a kung fu student enabled him to travel extensively throughout China practising the Buddhist ways and achieving master kung fu status, before leaving China to return to Australia after the passing of his father. He moved back into the family home with his mother, who was a devout Catholic.

So, at twenty-five years of age and in the physical prime of his life, and of course a vegetarian, Brian O'Reilly was searching for a continuation of his Buddhist beliefs. His mother and father had both smoked, and it had worn both of them down. With his dad gone, his mum's resistance to depression was at its lowest, so Brian started to take his mum to Sunday mass. Brian was impressed with the way the church looked after his mother and committed to following the Catholic faith by joining the priesthood.

Because of his Buddhist beliefs, transition to the brotherhood was easy; he was already committed to a life of abstinence, and he had a true belief in Jesus Christ. His life as a Catholic brother began in a seminary at Manly in Sydney's eastern suburbs where he studied for four years and when he graduated, he was assigned to the parish of Tweed Heads at Monastery Hill, under the watchful eye of an ageing Father Bourke. The beautiful old building was once occupied by an order of monks. It was a magnificent piece of architecture but had fallen into disuse until it was revived by its Catholic occupants. At the completion of the restoration, the monastery was renamed Sacred Promise. An order of nuns and a housekeeper lived in one section of the monastery, while Father Bourke and Father O'Reilly occupied the other half of the building. It worked well.

Father Bourke encouraged his young protégé to build a beautiful garden, and with the help of some local parishioners, the community project created a piece of Buddhism paradise. Father O'Reilly included a large lotus pond, home for many large multicoloured carp. He erected a roof over one corner of the garden, which provided relief from the scorching summer sun, and there was a bird aviary filled with canaries. This all added to the feel of the garden, which had been transformed into a sort of heaven on earth.

Father O'Reilly had not let on to any of his parishioners his plan of starting a two or three student kung fu dojo. He did not rush into any early selections, but continued on with being an effective Catholic priest, getting to know everybody connected with the local church. He knew the special kung fu students would come into his life as he moved forward with his priesthood.

His first student was a blond-haired boy called Jacob, who was living with an elderly lady in a house in Coolangatta. The lady wasn't Jacob's mother, but she had looked after him since he was born. Jacob was twelve, but you would think he was several years older with his confident approach to life.

Jacob had been volunteering in Father O'Reilly's garden and when Father O'Reilly pointed out that he needed a timber floor under the roof of the dojo, Jacob suggested they approach a builder parishioner to construct the dojo floor. A couple of weeks later, the floor was completed, and that was the start of their kung fu life together. Poor old Father Bourke was a bit hesitant but allowed Father O'Reilly's plans to go forward. He and Jacob started training three afternoons a week and then came Saturdays as well. Jacob was a natural kung fu student, very supple and as quick as a whip. Several nuns started morning tai chi classes with

Father O'Reilly, and morale at the monastery was at an all-time high. Father O'Reilly wasn't in heaven yet, but he had found complete happiness.

When old Father Bourke died, Father O'Reilly stepped up. He thought if he could approach his role as 'a person of the people', he would have achieved everything he had sworn to do. He would achieve this by blending into the community, attending every local cake stall, holding confession whenever called upon, not letting any of his flock die a lonely person. That was his plan.

Rhonda and I were in town for the annual blessing of the fishing fleet which was a major part of the maritime calendar at Tweed Heads. This occasion involved the entire population of the town. It was a beautiful morning, and the flotilla of fishing boats was decorated to impress; judging was Father's duty for the day. He was a bit taken aback by one of the boats, which sported five unusual looking scantily clad sailors. Rusty was standing beside Father O'Reilly, taking the salute and the young priest didn't know which way to look as the unusual crew turned around and showed the large crowd their bottoms! Rusty gave Father O'Reilly a nudge on the arm and said in a whisper, 'Bless the Rusty Nail.'

Father O'Reilly had asked the nuns to be the judges. They were all excited and took their role very seriously, with Sister Angela casting the deciding vote to the five outrageous sailors. The crowd went wild with agreement. After that, they enjoyed a wonderful seafood lunch. Father had a light beer and his flock each enjoyed a couple of gin and squashes. Rhonda and I had the time of our lives at lunch, and, to his surprise, Father O'Reilly had to present the winning prize to the unusual sailors. This is when it dawned on him, they were the cast of the all-male review that entertained the Rusty Nail family. Father O'Reilly did a great job with the presentation speech, with his tongue firmly planted in his cheek.

Jacob was seated next to Rusty at our table, deep in conversation and they were completely oblivious to what was going on around them. Rusty had been quizzing Jacob about his age and where he lived. Then, suddenly, Rusty became somewhat emotional.

Rhonda whispered in my ear, 'What's going on with Rusty?'

All the guests became quiet as Rusty just sat and looked at Jacob, then glanced down the table where the nuns were seated. It looked like Sister Ann was in tears. Father O'Reilly went over to them and discreetly asked Sister Maria if she would swap seats with Sister Ann so she could sit near Rusty and Jacob. Slowly, the penny dropped for the guests. The only one of the three that hadn't caught on yet was Jacob, then moments later, Jacob also broke into tears. The family was complete: Sister Ann, Jacob, and Rusty.

In a quiet and compassionate way, Father O'Reilly stood and addressed our table. 'Life,' he said, 'can take many twists and turns. I'm sure that life will be easier now for our three dear friends.'

Later in the afternoon, Rusty asked Rhonda and me to step out onto the deck away from the crowd that had settled into an afternoon of drinking, laughing, and having a good time. 'Bring your drinks with you. There's something I want to tell you.'

We wandered into a shady spot under a towering poinciana tree.

'Sister Ann and I … well, there's no easy way to put this. We were once lovers.'

I looked at Rhonda.

'Ann Kelley and I both went to Tweed River High. I was two years ahead of her but we both were in the athletics team and kept bumping into each other, and well, we became close.'

'How close?' Rhonda said.

'Really close. We loved each other and one thing led to another.'

'What did her parents say?'

'It was just her mum, and I really don't know how she missed all the signs. She was very trusting of Ann and made it clear she only had one dream for Ann, and that was for her to become a Catholic nun after she'd finished high school. Ann had promised her mother that she would try the Catholic convent to see if it was the life for her. But unfortunately, halfway through third year high, Ann fell pregnant.'

'Oh no. What did her mum say?'

'Well, Mrs Kelley was furious and banned me from seeing Ann. You see, Ann wasn't yet sixteen, and I was eighteen. So, I could hardly make a fuss about what happened next.'

'What happened?'

'Mrs Kelley arranged for Ann to take refuge in the local Catholic convent in Murwillumbah, not far from Tweed Heads, until the baby was born. The nuns took great care of Ann who helped around the convent in exchange for free board. It wasn't easy for young, single mums in those days. Ann felt she couldn't return home with a newborn and expected to be pressured to put the baby up for adoption.'

'God, you must have been going crazy with worry.'

'Oh yeah, and it was all kept very hush-hush. I got the courage to visit Mrs Kelley around the time the baby was due. She hadn't been around town much, and I needed to know Ann was okay. When I knocked at her front door, there was no answer. I thought I saw a curtain twitching, so I called out to her, begging to speak with her. She whispered through the door to come around the back and we sat on the back deck. She said I had a hide to even ask about Ann and I broke down, telling her how much Ann and I loved each other.'

'Oh, this is so sad, Rusty.'

'I know, Rhonda. Anyway, she finally softened and shared their plan. She had been lying low so that when she suddenly appeared with a newborn, town folk would assume she had been "resting" and the baby was hers. Ann had agreed to her mother raising the baby as her own child.'

'Oh, perfect. Saved the baby having to be adopted by strangers.'

'Yes, Hecky. It also gave Ann some space to make up her mind. She could decide to come home to Tweed Heads or continue on at the convent as a novice and then come back to Tweed to join Father Bourke at the monastery.'

Rusty's shoulders seemed to relax a little. 'A month later, Jacob was born at the convent. Ann chose convent life. Mrs Kelley raised the baby, and I wasn't allowed to see him. Until today.'

'Ah, I understand now,' said Rhonda. 'How absolutely wonderful for you to be finally reunited.'

'Yeah, it all seems a bit unbelievable but it's true. For the three of us to end up together is the answer to my prayers. Ann has always been the love of my life and I will do whatever I have to for this family to work.'

Rhonda and I could see the tension disappearing from his face. He leaned across the table and gave us a hug, thanking us for our constant support.

We were all so emotional. Rusty called out to a nearby waiter to order us some stiff drinks. I noticed the waiter was also teared up. He must have heard Rusty's confession. As he reached across the table to clear an empty glass left by a previous patron, Rusty put his hand on the waiter's arm and softly said. 'Danny, what you just overheard stays right here. Got it?'

'Of course, Rusty, right here.'

Rusty went back to the table and shortly after, Rusty, Ann and Jacob left the Nail to visit Mrs Kelley to let her know the news.

Our last year of study was a wonderful experience as we both achieved honours. Rhonda still had years of internship ahead. After I qualified as a registered surveyor at twenty-four, Rusty approached me and asked if I would work on a 'special' survey job. It involved creating a new title deed for the land the Rusty Nail was situated on by changing the measurements that were marked in chains, roods, and furlongs on the original plan to metric measures. Rusty assured me that this was common practice, and any person checking the newly marked title deed would not pick up the additional fifty-metre land grab along the waterfront that would be achieved in the transition of the measurement changes. Rusty also assured me that there would be no reprisal from any government officials. He went on to explain that his move to occupy the newly acquired land would be a slow process. Rusty wanted me to resurvey the land using the adjusted measurements and have new survey pegs installed to reflect the new boundaries. 'Hecky, make sure that you drive the new boundary pegs well into the ground so that they don't bring attention. Currently, the additional land is parkland.'

I was a bit taken aback by the request and needed some time to consider it. I felt I needed to keep my reputation squeaky clean. 'Okay, Rusty, give me a week to think on it. I want to check that this move won't affect anyone else. I'll assess what's required, and if we go ahead, I'll need the old title deed. Do you have it?'

'Yes. I don't owe any money on the property, so I'm entitled to hold the deeds. And Heck, this won't affect any-one else, I promise you.'

I nodded. 'Yes, Rusty, if you hold the only copies of the new deeds, then there won't be a problem.'

'Oh, and Hecky, I'll be paying you well for your services.'

'Actually, Rusty, I would prefer that you consider bringing me in as a silent partner. Let's say twenty-five per cent of the profit on any deals that we do together.'

'Twenty-five per cent?' said Rusty as a grin came over his face. I was quick to remind him I was putting my name to the new deed, and that down the track there would be deals that I would bring to the table. 'I want to stay at arm's length, so I think twenty-five percent is a fair cut.'

Again, Rusty smiled, put out his hand, and told me that this handshake was all we needed to have between us. 'Heck, trust won't need to be mentioned from this handshake forward.'

Again, as we shook hands, we made eye contact. 'A good day, Heck.'

'Yes, I agree. A good day.'

Several months later, Rhonda and I married at the monastery, followed by a wonderful reception at the Rusty Nail, then a short honeymoon at Byron Bay. After the dust settled, we purchased a large block of land adjoining a large public parkland in Holland Park—a suburb of Brisbane. I liked the comfort of staying in my own back yard as I had grown up in Holland Park and felt secure there.

We had plans to build a large home with a swimming pool and grass tennis court. Once completed, this investment would create the image I needed to build my image as a trusted surveyor and land developer. Therefore, a solid address was important.

Unfortunately, not much later, Dad passed away from a heart attack; it was totally unexpected—here one day, gone the next. Mum and I were, of course devastated and it brought Rhonda and Mum very close.

We had a very hectic life with the day to day running of my surveying and town planning business, as well as me being away on extended field trips to central Queensland surveying coal deposits for the Australian government.

While I was away, Mum and Rhonda usually went down to the Rusty Nail together for company and Rusty of course, made sure that they were looked after. Peta Rosé and Mum had a lot of fun shopping for Peta's costumes from the clothes designer, Sammy Harrison. Sammy's husband had also passed on and she was a social number one in the Tweed area, mixing with the wives of influential people, which was good for business.

But things were far from perfect for Peta Rosé who attempted suicide. When Rusty rang and told us, Mum and Rhonda packed a bag each and left for the Rusty Nail. Peta had survived the attempt on her own life and was still in hospital. Apparently, the love of Peta's life—Howard, a psychologist—had taken off with a young Brazilian boy. Rusty came to Peta's rescue by organising her recovery in a secure health facility in the Currumbin Valley. Mum and Sammy Harrison teamed up together to support the remaining cast of the show.

The show had to go on and good old Sandy Shores took the reins as the compere of the review at the Rusty Nail. He sang Sinatra really well, but unfortunately, some of his jokes were a bit risqué. Thank God the remaining cast had a broad outlook.

To keep the show going, Mum and Sammy had to deal with everything from a broken nail to saggy tits—a great time that filled a big gap in Mum's life after Dad's passing.

CHAPTER FOUR

Geoffrey

There was a lot going on in Australia in 1967. Our troops were still fighting in Vietnam; Gough Whitlam defeated Dr Jim Cairns and Frank Crean to lead the ALP; and a national referendum gave indigenous Australians the right to be counted in the national census. It was also the year I was asked to join the Queensland Cricket Club, and I jumped at the opportunity. It did not take long for me to be elected to the board which was looking for fresh young blood. I had a keen interest in turf management and loved the game of cricket, so I took a great interest in the wicket preparations. The grass tennis court I had built at home in Holland Park was my pride and joy, and to extend my interests into the Gabba wicket was fantastic. Unfortunately, some of the other cricket board members were not happy with my involvement in the wicket prep. I had no intention of letting go so I needed to parachute in a dummy green-keeper to make it appear that I was in the back seat.

I mentally cast around my contacts for someone who would be a capable front man but who would acquiesce to my directions. It came to me as I drove into the Gabba car-park early one morning. Geoffrey Pike, the maintenance guy. I'd had a couple of chats with him during his smoko breaks when he'd disclosed that he took this job after leaving the army. He'd served in Vietnam with the heavily armed crack 3SAS Squadron, a ten-man fighting ambush patrol operating in the thick, mosquito-infested jungle. Burnt out and exhausted, Geoffrey had returned to his home in the sleepy town of Nimbin in northern New South Wales but found himself restless, too young to retire. So, Geoffrey had picked up the low-profile cleaning and maintenance role at the Gabba. He didn't mind the two bus trip rides to and from work as it gave him time to relax.

When I asked Geoffrey if he'd be willing to pose as the new Gabba ground manager, said, 'Why not? Nothin' to lose.' He was quick to point out to me that the only grass that he had ever grown was the type that you smoked. I thought to myself that he was perfect for the job. I would just put him on one of the wicket rollers and I would have total control of the wicket preparation.

So, I set up a press conference at the Gabba to introduce Geoffrey Pike as the new curator of the wicket. He certainly looked the part—a strong, hard man who other men literally had to look up to. Geoffrey was impressive in his first encounter with the press, respectfully deferring to me when the questions were tricky.

Geoffrey met me at the wicket each morning and we would discuss what was going to happen that day. After a couple of weeks, I noticed Geoffrey was starting to play more of a role in the day-to-day goings on at the wicket, and much to my concern, on a couple of occasions, Geoffrey actually contradicted me in front of the other groundsmen. I didn't quite know how to handle the situation. With the West Indies cricket team now on Australian soil, a hiccup with Geoffrey's removal as head groundsman wasn't an option. So, I had a little chat to Geoffrey on the quiet. That did not go well as Geoffrey stood up to me and told me in no uncertain words that *he* was head groundsman, and—looking down at his wrist—as it was now four o'clock, it was knock off time.

I stepped back, not wanting to rock the boat because the West Indies-Australia test was due to start in fourteen days. The wicket was in outstanding condition. It had no green top and would suit Australia's bowlers better than having green grass showing. The West Indies had a devastating line up of fast bowlers that would create havoc on a grassy wicket.

Ten days to go until the first innings and a press conference was called to inspect the wicket. I had been out of town for a couple of days and arrived late to the conference. Geoffrey was holding court, and the press were laughing, their cameras were going wild. I looked down at the wicket and, to my horror, saw it had been completely swamped with water. I was enraged, and the press were quick to pick up on my anger. I fell to my knees and pounded my fists into the wicket. 'You bastard, you bastard!' I called out. I looked up at Geoffrey with horror. 'What have you done?' I exclaimed.

Geoffrey was quick to point out that as head groundsman he had made a decision to flood the wicket and was confident that it would be perfect for the first day's play, and on that, he again looked at his watch, said that it was four o'clock and he had a bus to catch, excusing himself from the meeting. I found my way to my feet and faced a barrage of questions about my selection of head groundsman. I also excused myself and went straight to the members' bar, where I got well and truly drunk and had to be driven home.

I woke up feeling very hung over as Rhonda pulled back the curtains. 'Come on,' she said in a humorous way. I tried to explain to her what had happened to the Gabba, and she cut me short and said that the whole saga had been on the morning news and that the head groundsman had been interviewed. He was showing the camera crew his technique of bogging up the wicket with his bare feet. I was horrified. 'Oh,' Rhonda said, 'the phone has been ringing off the hook and I just told them you hadn't had time to think about the wicket as it was in good hands, and that you wouldn't be available for comment as you had pressing business to attend to.'

I went underground, keeping a low profile, trying to find a way out of the debacle. I could not help but to turn on the evening news every night and get an update on Geoffrey's progress. Fortunately, the weather was hot and dry with the humidity at twelve percent. Each night, Geoffrey would appear on the news surrounded by the press, answering questions about the wicket as if he were a fifty-year veteran groundsman. I was livid that Geoffrey was the centre of attention. I was a man who had earned respect. I deserved better publicity than I was getting.

Each night that went by, the reports on the condition of the wicket were more promising, and I started to think that maybe Geoffrey was onto something. With four days to go, I wondered how I could get in on the publicity and gain some credit. Geoffrey was certainly the man in charge, and the thought of me eating humble pie was unthinkable. But … maybe I had to. My intention was to attend all five days of the upcoming test. How could I just sit in the members' stand with my friends and not have an explanation of why I wasn't involved? *Okay,* I thought, *where can I buy a humble pie?* Yes, the answer was to go to a pie shop, go down to the Gabba cricket ground and sit down with Geoffrey out at the wicket.

My timing was perfect. I found Geoffrey on the big roller, and he acknowledged my arrival with a nod. Shutting the wicket roller down, he dismounted the massive machine. 'I've been expecting you, Hecky.'

'Yes,' I said. 'I've come to apologise to you for my behaviour last week.'

'Mate, I understand your concerns about my ability. Coming from toilet cleaner to head groundsman was quite a leap, especially with such an important cricket test looming. But you have to know that I take responsibility very seriously. What's in the paper bag?'

'It's a pie.'

'Ah,' he said. 'I do enjoy a fresh, tasty pie.' And with a smirk on his face, he asked me what type of pie it was. I looked into his eyes and said that it was a humble pie. Geoffrey offered his handshake and as he hoed into his pie, we inspected the wicket.

'Magnificent,' I said. 'No cracks, a small, very short green tinge.'

Geoffrey explained that the moisture content was around fifteen percent; that fine, hot weather was forecast with a humidity expectation of around twelve percent; and that the three percent variance between the wicket and the daytime humidity would keep the wicket intact. His confidence completely humbled me. What could I say, other than well done?

When Geoffrey suggested I should come back after lunch and maybe get involved, I jumped at the opportunity.

'I'll keep the big roller free for you. Just put on a big hat and hop up on the roller as if it is business as usual.'

I cannot put into words how emotional I felt, although I did not show it. I went back after lunch and the entire grounds staff were all full-on into the final wicket preparation.

'G'day, Heck,' was his welcome and I felt an instant sense of camaraderie. I cranked up the big roller and worked away with the other staff to bring Geoffrey's dreams to reality. The press arrived later in the afternoon to go through the progress, and Geoffrey made sure that, in the press question time, he acknowledged my arrival back to the Gabba, after several days of urgent business meetings. It was good to have my experience back on board, he said. Strangely enough, all that were present gave me a stirring show of hands. Geoffrey and I shoulder-armed each other, and the photographers went wild. On the front page of the next day's *Telegraph* headline: Bring on the West Indies—the wicket is perfect.

On the first day of play, the city was abuzz with excitement. Geoffrey ordered the wicket covers to be left on till the last minute to help keep its moisture—more moist than dry.

His decision was perfect. Australia won the toss and went in to bat and it was considered to be a batsman's wicket. So, taking the advantage, Australia had a brilliant match and won the first test by one hundred and five runs. This was a great start for Australia, who went on to win the series three games to two. Well done, boys; well done, Geoffrey.

We continued on as close friends until Geoffrey retired from his role at the Gabba several years later and went back to his hometown of Nimbin, where he found some local work. Geoffrey was the cinema manager at night and during the day he managed an old backpacker hostel that he had built using old railway sleeper carriages. The hostel was so successful and popular with Israeli backpackers that he built a giant tepee on the property. The Israelis would all bunk up together in the tepee. Geoffrey told me he didn't know what went on in the tepee, but he could only assume from the volume of their music and the large amount of smoke that came up through the hole at the top of the tepee that life was a big dream in the big tepee.

I caught up with Geoffrey several times at the Rusty Nail for lunch. It was a handy halfway point for us to meet. We had a lot to laugh about from our earlier life. On one occasion, Rusty joined us at lunch. Rusty, never one to let me down without a surprise, introduced us to Simon Woods, a motorbike rider who wore full leather and sported a painted club badge on his leather jacket. Simon 'Splinter' Woods was a giant of a man with a skinhead, but quietly spoken. Our discussion was about normal things—family, his motorbike, his trips up and down from Sydney, how he travelled at night, no traffic, just a blood rush from Tweed Heads to Sydney. When I asked him how long it took, he grinned and said, 'Nine and a half hours, with one fuel stop in Newcastle.'

'That's fast! What about the police? Don't they ever pull you over?'

'What police?' he replied.

'Oh.' I moved the conversation to another topic.

After Geoffrey had headed back to Nimbin, I quizzed Rusty. 'So, tell me, why does Simon travel to Sydney?'

'He's one of my three cocaine movers. They can safely fit eighty kilos of coke in their saddle bags, and we have our bases 'covered' with the cops, if you know what I mean. Splinter rides like hell to Kings Cross in Sydney where he collects around fifty thousand dollars and returns here the following night.'

'How long have you been doing this for?'

'About six months. The only problem is what the hell to do with all the cash. Can you give some thought to me funding some of your land developments? Not all of them, just a couple of million dollars a year.'

'A couple of million!' I was feeling pretty uncomfortable at this point.

'Yep. You can handle that. Why give it to the banks and pay full tax? I'll happily take some of your developed land as part of the repayment, which will keep your tax bill down. A bit of moving and shaking. We'll sort it out; we always do. A bit of cash left over is always handy. The only downside to cash is trying to get comfortable on your cash-filled mattress. The real comfort is in knowing how much cash you have, and no one knows about it.'

'Let me think about it.'

My Christian upbringing was cringing in the corner, yet my entrepreneurial streak was tickled pink. Excited by the proposition, I agreed to go forward.

'Hecky wherever you can, use your cash and launder it. Cash is king in the building game.'

Truer words were never spoken, I thought. I couldn't wait to get back to Brisbane and start planning my next subdivision. Brisbane, compared to Sydney and Melbourne, was still a big country town. There was plenty of opportunity to develop large volumes of land and sell it, not only to the government for housing commission stock, but to everyday residents wanting to live the dream and build their first home. I thought the best way to launder Rusty's cash splash would be to have the land development costs buried in the construction costs. It would make his money laundering job a lot easier by paying the builders a large percentage of building costs in cash. And of course, I was helping Rusty move money at the same time. I thought I should probably charge Rusty a percentage for moving the cash, but then thought better of it. I wasn't paying interest to the banks and interest rates were about six percent. It was a fair deal; not having to provide all of my assets as equity to borrow money also gave me greater flexibility.

I found renewed vigour and moved forward to purchase three large parcels of rural land that I subdivided. It wasn't long before I had not only land sales happening, but the added opportunity to bury cash into the costs of house building. I had a group of hard-working builders I trusted. Like Rusty's business associates, they knew I was also not to be messed with. Some of my trips back from the Rusty Nail carrying sometimes up to one hundred thousand dollars was a bit challenging. There was always a strange-looking suitcase in the car boot. Rhonda never questioned it. I just took it into my office, where I had built a false panel into the desk. It worked well, and I knew a time would come when I would find a trusted person to count and distribute the cash. That would also give me more arm's length protection. You never know what is around the corner in a business like this.

Then Rhonda miscarried. We both wanted a child, but the miscarriage left her unable to fall pregnant again. 'Devastated' just does not even go near to describing how we both felt. It took a while for her to settle, and she gave up her medical practice to become more of a stay-at-home person. She made it very clear she wanted nothing more to do with me in the bedroom. But as the man around town, I somehow found myself not only laundering money but being unfaithful to Rhonda. Further to that, one of my mistresses, Leonie, fell pregnant and had a son. I silently vowed to make sure that he got the best education while Leonie and I vowed to keep him a secret.

How money can change things.

Rhonda and I agreed to stay together and find happiness in our own ways. She got totally involved in charity work, mainly for disadvantaged kids. I totally understood. We planned and built an orphanage in Brisbane together, with the funding coming from my cash-loaded building developments. Rhonda and I had found a new common ground, and I managed to justify my dealings to myself through my benevolent contributions. At the completion of the orphanage, we handed the reins over to the Catholic Church and, of course, our divine contact Father O'Reilly from down at the Rusty Nail was pleased as punch to come up to Brisbane to organise the setup of the orphanage. Rhonda and I chipped in and bought him a wonderful Studebaker Bullet motor car. Black, of course. He used to stay with us at Holland Park, where he and I would play tennis on my beautifully kept grass court. He was an excellent tennis player.

We had expanded our house to cater for parties, so we agreed that a housekeeper was required to keep order in the house. We interviewed several ladies for the position and settled on Norma. She was everything that we needed—quiet, business savvy, and honest; you just felt relaxed around her. We had a self-contained flatette for Norma at the rear of the house, which gave privacy to us all. I had to have privacy when I was on the telephone with all that was going on. Norma fitted in very well—always had a meal ready for us at six o'clock sharp, and if one of us couldn't make dinner, she would keep our meal warm in the oven for when we eventually got home. She also made sandwiches for my tennis mates when we played every Wednesday afternoon—fresh white bread, leg ham off the bone, hard butter, pepper and salt, cut into four triangles. Those sandwiches became legendary throughout the years.

My tennis club was a great place to relax, and of course attracted many powerful and influential men. We developed a saying: if you were a member here, you died here. That was certainly the case as the players got older and the younger players would compensate for them with extra effort to keep our doubles games competitive. The main rule was that if there was a dispute over a call of in or out, it was my decision to call, whether or not I had seen the shot. In or out, it was my call. The tennis club went on for forty years.

After Norma took control of the running of the house, Rhonda had more time to get involved in the orphanage. Father O'Reilly was now full-on with the Tweed orphanage that Rhonda and I funded at Monastery Hill, so a new priest was appointed to look after the new premises here in Brisbane. Brother Stephen was the right choice. He was a wonderful, caring, and trustworthy priest, and our dormitories were at a maximum capacity with one hundred and twenty orphaned kids—sixty boys and sixty girls. We even started primary school teaching from grade one through to grade five. The teachers were private lay teachers, handpicked by Rhonda for their caring and loving natures. It was a successful model.

Rhonda fell in love with one of our little girls called Tracey, who had cystic fibrosis and needed special care. Rhonda's medical background was of significant benefit not only to Tracey but all the littlies that came her way. She was absolutely devoted to Tracey, and we shared her care with the orphanage—three nights with us, a few nights with the home. Doctors didn't expect Tracey to have a long life, so she got special attention. Her biggest thrill was when I took her to town in my black Fairlane motor car. I was now Tracey's number one fan, and she knew it. Tracey found the strength to walk under her own steam into the shop where we were greeted by the owner of the store whom I'd telephoned the day before. I bought her a pair of brightly polished, red strap over shoes. I still tear up when I think of that day as she beamed with pride.

Unfortunately, she passed three years later, and again Rhonda fell to pieces. It took a super effort to dig herself out of the depression that took control of her. 'The orphanage needs you,' I would insist. She rose above her grief by expanding the orphanage by fifty kids. If the children had not been adopted by the time they turned ten, they were sent to one of several Catholic boarding schools that I had set up a trust fund for. We tried not to separate kids who had grown up together, so they settled better. I took great heart in knowing that up to two hundred children were now under our care.

Christmas was a special time for us and our kids. A Christmas present appeal was launched at City Hall, complete with extravagant decorations, platters of delicious treats and loud Christmas music. Our kids, dressed in their 'best' outfits, were able to meet and thank their loving, generous donors. Those connections often generated new relationships and sometimes kids were taken home for a Christmas stay with the present-giving family. It worked that a large percentage of the stayovers turned out to be permanent ones. Who says that money can't buy happiness? I was so proud to use my position for the welfare of the children. Maybe Saint Peter would have a spot for me down the track.

Rusty extended the monastery down at Tweed Heads as a holiday destination for kids from our children's home in Brisbane. It was a fantastic trip to the coast when we somehow got fifteen kids in the back and front of the black Fairlane to take them down the coast. I always felt safe about leaving the holiday kids with Rusty because he was very aware of kid safety. As part of the expansion, he built an impenetrable barrier around the perimeter of the monastery. Of course, before we built the fence, I made a few minor 'adjustments' to the new title deed to allow for future expansion. We gained about forty percent of land on top of what we already had. Dubious means, justified by good ends. Of course, the trip back to Brisbane was the same deal, except the boot was half full of cash … got to keep the pot boiling and keep the kids safe and secure.

The Rusty Nail was buzzing with excitement as Peta Rosé had fully recovered and was coming back home to resume her rightful place at the Rusty Nail tavern. Sandy Shores and Peta were going to share the lead roles on stage—I couldn't wait to hear them bounce their jokes around. Rhonda had been down to the health resort in Currumbin Valley several times to see Peta during her recovery. Peta laughed when she told Rhonda that she had 'washed that man right out of her life' and was quick to say that she had learned from

Holly, another star in the show, that the young Brazilian boy had dumped Howard who was now seeing his own shrink. Funny how life goes.

CHAPTER FIVE

Moreton Star

Following their disclosure at the blessing of the fleet, Ann and Rusty continued to build their relationship, spending a lot of time together. Ann decided it was time for her to move on with the rest of her life as a wife and mother. So, she and Father O'Reilly completed the documentation for her release from the Sacred Promise, planning the separation to take place on a Sunday morning after Mass. Ann's few belongings were packed and placed near the main gate, then there was a lunch for staff only in the beautiful monastery garden. Ann was very emotional, but she knew this was the right thing to do. Rusty was waiting for her at the monastery gate and quietly swept her into a generous embrace.

Jacob was now eighteen years old and had come to live in an apartment across the road from the Rusty Nail. Jacob was the apple of Rusty's eye, but Rusty was firm with him and his approach to the business. As well as studying kung fu, Jacob surfed and competed in local surfboard riding contests. He was super fit and had a positive outlook. He also knew who he was, the only son of one of the most powerful and wealthy men in the country. He had Rusty's handsome, surfy dude looks, and he also kept a low public profile.

Jacob would soon be heading to the University of Tasmania to study marine biology. With the construction of the state-of-the-art cannery complete, marine science—hands-on knowledge of all things fishy—would be of great benefit to the family business. The cannery just happened to fit perfectly on the additional suspect land grab that Rusty and I dreamed up some ten years previously. The cannery would employ seventy locals, from technical food processing staff to basic on-the-floor processors.

The canned seafood was to be exported to ports all over the world, opening up opportunities for cans of cocaine concealed among the shipments. Rusty's business skills were as sharp as ever, and his power in the northern rivers had grown at an amazing rate during the twenty or so years since I met him at Rainbow Bay. We had both been true to our handshake, and his empire still included his mullet net fishing on the beaches from Ballina to Surfers Paradise. With prawn trawlers, snapper boats, and oyster leases, his fleet of boats was enormous. But it still got back to the old saying: *Don't fuck with Rusty.* You only got one go, and if you stole from him, he would find out. Your punishment was the same—from a kilo of prawns to a box of cans of cocaine, the punishment was terminal. I never got involved in the grizzly bits of Rusty's operation; that was left to Rusty and his dozen-strong bikie drug mules that controlled the east coast of Australia from Coffs Harbour to Tweed Heads.

I had a panicked call from Rusty one night. 'Hecky, one of the prawn trawlers went missing overnight. No radio contact from the trawler for six hours.'

He explained this was very unusual. The fleet used to talk on sea radio all night, sharing information on who was catching the most prawns and where they were catching them.

Sharpie Stevens, Rusty's most trusted skipper, telephoned Rusty saying he was down at the dock having a crisis meeting with the other skippers and deckhands. Rusty raced down to the dock and addressed the group. 'Who's missing?'

'*Moreton Star.*'

'Fuck,' said Rusty. 'Kev Skinner, fuck, fuck, fuck.' Bad news travelled fast, and pretty soon Kev's wife turned up at the dock. She was crying out to us all to get back out to sea and find the *Moreton Star* and its beloved crew. Rusty sent one of the men up to the monastery to inform Father O'Reilly of the situation so he could support the families if our search for the *Moreton Star* was unsuccessful. Sharpie Stevens took over the rescue plans and called for one of the crew to grab his sea map from the wheelhouse of his boat, the *Honeybee*. Sharpie called out to all the skippers, checking if they needed to take on more diesel fuel. All the captains reported they had plenty of fuel and were good to go.

'Okay, gather around skippers and we'll make a plan. The tide's now at full bore running out and the big swell will make it bloody hard to get out over the Tweed bar. Give each other plenty of room going over the bar. I'll test it in the *Honeybee* first so watch where I go and if it works, follow. Use your smarts don't take any unnecessary risks.'

'All good,' a loud call rang back.

'Once we're over the bar, all you deckhands get up on top of your wheelhouses and keep your eyes open; your mates are counting on you. The rest of you skippers, stick to your coordinates, and don't chatter on our radios. I'll need as much airtime as possible to control the situation. All clear?' No answer. '*All clear?*' Sharpie yelled out again.

'All clear!'

'Okay, let's get on with it.'

Father O'Reilly had arrived and was comforting Rusty and Ann. Missing skipper Kev Skinner and Rusty went back a long way. Plus, there were two other deckhands on board, both with young kids.

Rusty excused himself and said he would head back to the Rusty Nail and rally the assistance of Langham's Air School. He said he'd give the pilots Sharpie's radio frequency.

Father O'Reilly let people know that he would hold a special mass up at the monastery to pray for the missing men.

Out at sea, Sharpie had the search in full swing. The two Cessna aeroplanes were now in the air looking for Kev Skinner and his crew of two on the *Moreton Star*. The search had been going for about three hours, but they saw no floating debris, nothing, just a beautiful blue ocean. The gentle swell gave no indication of what was now looking like a recovery, not a rescue. The threat to any surviving crew member was being eaten by tiger sharks that follow the trawlers in the dark, feeding off the by-catch that comes with prawn trawling—anything from stingrays, other small sharks, all sorts of easy prey, that the crew threw over the side between shots. The trawlers would pull the nets behind their boats until the skipper thought it was time to check the net for prawns. That was when all the by-catch was shaken out of the nets and thrown over the side. Each trawler had a bright lighting system over the work area on the stern of the boat, so the sharks were quite visible. Sometimes dozens of sharks gathered behind each boat, a very dangerous place to be. Every trawlerman understood the risks involved in this job. They worked in a very high-risk environment and respected every one of them.

Sharpie pulled back on the throttle and let the *Honeybee* glide to a stop. He called out to his two deckhands to join him in the wheelhouse so they could rethink the situation. The three of them were extremely concerned about not finding any trace of *Moreton Star*. Sharpie swung around in his skipper's chair and studied *Honeybee*'s sonar screen to establish the speed and direction of the ocean current. 'Ah,' he said, 'three knots of current heading southeast.' He quickly called Mickey Fredericks, the skipper of *Tuff Justice*.

'Go ahead, *Honeybee*.'

'Mickey, we have three knots of current to the southeast, and it's now twelve noon. If *Moreton Star* has gone down, she would have gone down at about the same time in the tide as now, over.'

Mickey responded, 'Yes, agree.'

'Well,' said Sharpie, 'we should extend our search out to the thirty-sixes, over.'

'Kev is pretty hard to kill. The water's twenty-three degrees, so their chance of survival is still good, over.'

'Attention all skippers, extend your search out to the thirty-sixes.' The Cessnas heard the message, understood the instruction to move to the deeper water, or thirty-sixes, and moved their search further out to sea. About fifteen minutes later, one of the Cessnas came in on the radio saying he'd spotted a person clinging to one of the large foam floats that the snapper fleet used to mark their large fish traps. A coordinate echoed across the airwaves, and soon all boats were at full throttle to investigate the Cessna's reported sighting. About half an hour or so later, Sharpie was pulling a sobbing and physically exhausted Kev Skinner up and over the gunnel of the *Honeybee*. It was exactly as Sharpie had worked out: Kev Skinner had chosen not to swim twenty miles back to shore, but to swim six miles further out to sea and find one of these fish trap floats. He'd managed to get himself up and on top of the biggest float to get out of harm's way. It was a truly brave move. To swim further out to sea in the dark must have taken a lot of guts and belief in himself. Sharpie put a call out on the radio to let the other boats know Kev was alive, and for them to stand their boats down until Sharpie had time to talk to Kev to see what had gone wrong. The crew onboard *Honeybee* dragged Kev up to the skipper's bed. Kev was still delusional, but a warm cup of tea topped up with a sip of Bundy rum started his recovery. He stopped crying and began to make a bit more sense.

'Now, mate, tell me what happened.'

Kev was still shaking with shock, but it was important that Sharpie got the information that he needed to continue the search for the other two men.

'Well,' he said, 'at around one am my starboard trawl net must have snagged on a piece of the reef. I was asleep at the wheel and didn't hear the change of the throb of the engine. *Moreton Star* kept on going forward but pulled herself under. I swam out of the wheelhouse door and up to the surface, but no one else came. Both of my boys are gone, trapped in their lower bunks so I decided my only option was to swim out to the fish traps hoping to find a float.'

As Sharpie went quiet, the four men onboard *Honeybee* all broke down in tears. Sharpie put out a call on the radio. 'Cancel the search. Kev's the only survivor, two men lost.' Rusty was stunned. Kev was a great friend; to lose him would have been terrible. But two young men chasing their dream of a boat overflowing with prawns had died. Before calling me, Rusty called Jacob to let him know that his surfing mate, Stinger McFadden, had gone down with the trawler. Jacob said he'd catch the next available flight back to Coolangatta Airport.

He arrived early the next morning and Rusty and Ann hugged him tightly before climbing into their car. 'This is such a sad time, Jacob. We hope our news might cheer you up a little.'

'News?'

'Yeah, your mother and I are getting married.'

Jacob again fell to pieces. 'Oh, that's wonderful news!'

Then, in a half-broken sob, he asked his dad to take him down to *Moreton Star*'s vacant spot at the port.

'Are you sure you want to put yourself through that?'

'Yes, Dad. I'm sure.'

Jacob wasn't the only person wanting to show their respects, and a large spread of flowers was laid on the vacant mooring pen.

Ann spent a lot of time with Rhonda who then kept me abreast of the goings-on in the Tweed. Apparently, life back at the Rusty Nail was getting back to normal, as all the entertainment cast supported and inspired Rusty. There was to be a memorial service in a fortnight and Father O'Reilly and his volunteers were busy with final preparations. It was decided that the annual blessing of the fleet would be brought forward in order to give the remaining boats of Rusty's fleet a fresh start. Rusty, of course, made lifetime financial arrangements for the families of both lads who were lost at sea.

Jacob contacted his university to let them know the situation and that he was staying on to work through his grief of the loss of his surfing buddy. The memorial for the two deckhands was a solemn day. An extremely touching part of the sail past was that there was only one boat in the procession: it was an unnamed trawler painted completely white. Rusty, Father O'Reilly and Kev Skinner gave the sail past their salute. Father O'Reilly gave a quick prayer and recited a poem by AJ Holland:

'I am a man, a man of the sea,

And all I ask, Lord, is for a star to remember me.

To those we have left, let them be free,

To continue their life on their journey to Thee.'

It was free drinks and food for the rest of the afternoon, and Kev Skinner, the sole survivor, announced he was never going to sea again. Rusty respected his decision and found a place for him at the cannery with responsibilities to expand the oyster farm's capacity. It was a perfect role as Kev's new job would keep him on the water working on boats where he belonged, not stuck in an office. Rusty had plans to add the canning of smoked oysters into the range of exported seafood products. The list of canned seafood would now include smoked mullet roe, smoked oysters, anchovies, smoked mackerel, and spanner crabs.

Jacob started the ball rolling with spanner crabs which he was researching at uni, perfecting a method he and Rusty had devised of commercially catching the unusual crabs. They would respect the catch restrictions—allowing the crabs to complete their breeding cycle was critical for creating a sustainable species. This venture would provide them with a yearly pattern that the cannery could rely on. People hadn't taken these delicious crabs seriously until recently, but their flesh had a perfect texture for canning. It was a bit tougher to get the flesh out of their shells, but a new technique developed by the cannery staff using low pressure air blowers made short work of the task.

CHAPTER SIX

A life-changing opportunity came when I was invited to a site meeting with two local Brisbane City councillors—Henry Jacobs and Tim Waites—in Bulimba, a Brisbane suburb. The meeting was about a parcel of land where the zoning prevented the land from being built on. I drove my Fairlane to the meeting and as I pulled up, I spotted a makeshift camp. Five men had pulled together some humpies under a flowering jacaranda tree. It was summer and the ground where the men were sleeping rough was festooned with bright purple flowers. When I walked over to the group, one of the men stood up and addressed me. 'Morning, Hecky.' I was staggered; Hendo, my old 'it's not the dog in the fight but the fight in the dog' batting partner from Southside, who had also been a foreman on one of my sub-divisions. This reliable, tireless worker had clearly fallen on hard times.

'Hendo! Why are you sleeping rough?'

'Well,' he said, 'it's quite the story. My house burned down.'

'I'm so sorry, Hendo.'

'But that's not all. My wife and kids were asleep inside when it went up in flames. Something to do with a tea light.'

'Oh, my God. How awful.'

'Yeah. I was out of town visiting Mum and Dad. Dad had been so sick, and we thought he was going to die. And then the fire … We had no insurance coverage and I just drifted for months. I was drinking heavily and then I found these blokes.'

He choked up and started sobbing.

As I wrapped my arms around him, I was overwhelmed by the fact that he'd obviously not showered for some time. It was difficult for me to conceive.

When he regained his composure, he explained that this camp under the jacaranda was the last place of refuge. He and the other homeless men looked out for and supported each other.

The story deeply moved me. Then I remembered Hendo was involved in the rescue of one of his workmates who had been half-buried in a trench collapse. If it hadn't been for Hendo's quick thinking, his workmate would certainly have died.

I sat on the ground with them and promised I would personally do something for not only their group but for many men in the same situation. I could have pulled out cash but decided that would have been an insult and would only make their situation worse. The Bulimba pub was just down the road, and alcohol was the last thing that these men needed. I had found a new mission.

I said goodbye and wished them well, before walking over to my two colleagues to start the meeting. Handshakes all around and some small talk about the weather and Christmas. Henry and Tim were both well-respected councillors in the city's town planning department and trusted my town planning experience.

'Okay, let's get down to business. Now, where are we with the zoning issue on this five-hectare site?'

Henry piped up. 'Bulimba was fast running out of usable land for residential development and the city needs more developed sites to bring in additional revenue from rates and charges.'

'Hmm, yes. Do you know what just happened to me over there?' I pointed to the five men. 'It would appear to me,' I said, 'that a place for our homeless men is also important. Would you both agree, gentlemen? I've been a successful businessman here in Brisbane for many years, and in that time, I've achieved a lot with the help of great forward thinkers like yourselves. Believe me when I say there is no greater feeling than putting your head on your pillow at night, knowing that you have honestly helped other human beings do the same thing. Those men over there have all been hard workers for the city; now their problem is nowhere to live, poor mental health, reliance on grog, loneliness, and hopelessness. They have lost their self-respect.'

'What are you proposing, Hecky?'

'Well, you have the power to change this parcel of land into a special development, and when it's changed, I'll personally make sure that those five individuals out under the jacaranda tree have a roof over their heads and the opportunity to get the care and direction required to return them back into employment.'

The two councillors went very quiet.

'Yes, Hecky, certainly food for thought,' said Tim. 'Let's push like hell to get this rezoning through the next town planning committee meeting.'

We shook hands, and I excused myself. On my way back to the car, I bid the five men under the tree goodbye, assuring them I had heard them.

'Thanks, Hecky,' one of them called out. I enjoyed being called Hecky; it gave me a sense of connection with my fellow man.

It was Wednesday afternoon, and I was running a little late. One of the tennis boys would have the tennis net up and the chalk lines ready for the day's play in my backyard. Being a little late was a small price to pay after the result achieved at the meeting. On my drive home, I wondered what the five homeless men camped up under the jacaranda tree would have for dinner. I vowed to myself to push ahead with creating housing for the men and to also look into the possibility of starting a charity to guarantee basic food for situations like this. Little did I know how much support I would get from my business colleagues.

The tennis was, as always, very competitive with Nick, Bobby, Graham, Steve, John, and a special guest player, Ashley. And of course, Norma's ham sandwiches, topped off with a couple of long neck beers. I got into an extended drinking session with my lifetime friend Bobby, a chief justice in the children's court of Queensland. Bobby had been a great supporter of the orphanages, having put kids in crisis into care on many occasions while their parents' legal fate was determined. Bobby was full of enthusiasm for my plans to build a home for disadvantaged men. 'How will you fund the project, Hecky?'

'Well, that's always the hard bit, but as you know, Bobby,' I said, 'money speaks all languages.'

'Yes,' he agreed. 'There will be a way.'

'Most importantly, the home must be sustainable, not controlled by a Commonwealth department.'

Bobby was very aware of my view on committees. I truly believed in the principle of a committee, as long as I was the only person on it. No infighting. Just like at my tennis club—my decision was final. Bobby also pointed out how important mental health issues were in his field. He explained that most domestic violence was caused by alcohol. 'I'm sure you could get the right politician to support your proposal, especially if you included mental health counselling in the planning.'

'Yes, that is a good point, Bobby. I'll put that point to memory.'

It was late in the evening, and we were both a bit under the weather. Bobby felt that he was a bit too drunk to drive, so I agreed and attempted to drive him home in the black Fairlane. I thought I was going pretty well until we got somehow to Bobby's house where we both got out and walked around the front of the car. We were amazed and neither of us could work out how a large branch of a tree was entangled in the grill of the Fairlane. Grabbing hold of the branch, we both pulled and tugged until it came free. Neither of us was ready for the branch's departure from the front of the car and we both fell back down the driveway, rolling, laughing, and making a hell of a noise. This got dogs barking and neighbours' lights coming on. The worst was still to come as Bobby's wife Janet was standing at the top of the stairs, calling out to us to stop making any more noise. On that, we both started laughing again. This time, Janet came down the stairs and grabbed Bobby by the arm. 'Come on you two, get upstairs and have some coffee.'

At the kitchen table, I said, 'Bobby, how the hell did that tree get tangled up in the front of the car?'

'Shit, I don't know. I was too busy helping you steer the car.'

Again, we both broke down with laughter. Janet asked me if I wanted a cup of coffee, but I said that a nip of scotch usually sorted me out after drinking beer. Bobby was always a great host and poured me a stiff glass of Glenfiddich whisky. Janet was pouring black coffees into Bobby, and I was enjoying my scotch. Janet reminded Bobby that he had a major trial starting in the morning and that we'd both better get to bed.

'Will you be okay to drive, Hecky?'

'Nah, I don't think so.'

'Well, I'm feeling a lot better after the coffee so I'll drive you home in my car.'

Much to Janet's disgust, off we went. We both started laughing again all the way back to Holland Park. As I disembarked Bobby's car, I asked him if he'd like a nightcap. Without a blink, Bobby was out of his car and sitting at my kitchen table enjoying a nightcap of scotch. By this time, we were both back to where we started and I decided to call a cab to take Bobby home.

'Good idea, old mate.'

The next day was interesting as neither of us had a car, so we met halfway. As we exchanged car keys, Bobby said, 'Great times, Hecky, great times!'

'Yes, Bobby, the old tennis club lives on.'

'Oh,' Bobby said, 'just for the record, how did that tree get tangled up in the front of the Fairlane?'

'I still don't know, but before we both talk it up, we should get a copy of the morning newspaper and read the overnight police reports to see if we need to contact our lawyers.'

We pissed ourselves laughing again.

'See you next week.'

CHAPTER SEVEN

Iwas in my office, enjoying an early morning read of the
Sunday Mail when my personal telephone rang. That
was unusual, as few people had that number. I picked up
the phone and was greeted by a 'Good morning, Hecky.'

'Who's this?' I asked.

A dignified voice answered back. 'It's Gough, your
Prime Minister.'

I was startled by the response. I immediately thought
that it was my old mate Bobby having a crack at me.

'Oh yeah.'

'Hecky, this is Gough Whitlam. Can we have a chat?'

Heart pumping, I snapped to attention and responded,
'Yes, of course, Mr Whitlam,' not knowing what was to
come next.

'I'm sorry to bother you on a Sunday morning, Hecky,
but it's urgent that we have a meeting. In fact, it is extremely
important that we get together as soon as possible.'

'Certainly Mr—'

He stopped me short and asked me to call him Gough.

'Where do you want to meet and when?' I asked.

'Well, I'm in Brisbane today and have to be back in Canberra for a sitting of parliament tomorrow morning. I have a favour to ask you. I would prefer to keep our meeting away from the press and Sunday seems to be the day to do it. Can you come into my hotel at around one o'clock today?'

'Yes, of course I can.'

'Great, thank you. Oh Hecky, don't bother with the collar and tie. Let's keep it casual. Canberra Hotel, here in the city, at one.'

'No problems, Gough. See you then.'

I don't remember hanging up the telephone. The *Sunday Mail* took a back seat, and I yelled out to Rhonda, who was still in bed. 'Did you hear that telephone conversation?'

'Yes, I did, love. Gough, as in the PM? What does Gough want you for?'

'He didn't say, but he asked me to keep our meeting under wraps. I'm meeting him at the Canberra Hotel at one.'

I went back into the bedroom where Rhonda was sitting up, all pumped up with pillows and cushions

'Must be big,' she said. 'Sunday and all.'

'Yes, it must be important. Do you want to come into town and have a look around while I have my meeting?'

'No thanks, love. I'm pruning the roses in the garden beds up the driveway because they're starting to get a bit spindly. I'll be happy to stay home and do my thing. Have you noticed that red climbing rose making its way over the tennis shed?'

'Yes, the tennis boys were commenting on the masses of flowers. What's your secret with those roses, love?'

'They know I love 'em, Hecky.'

I sat beside her, leaned over, and kissed her deeply. She responded, and half an hour later, I was on top of the world, back with the love of my life, feeling ten feet tall and brimming with confidence. My community projects were financially independent and now the Prime Minister wanted to have a meeting with me. As I stretched out on the bed, Rhonda organised Norma to prepare toast and coffee for me on a tray.

I showered and, with Rhonda's help, selected an appropriate outfit for my meeting with Gough. We settled on a pair of cream pleated slacks paired with a casual, open-necked, long sleeve business shirt that Norma was kind enough to iron. Rhonda was a great fan of the Prime Minister and when she heard about my meeting with Gough, she gave my shirt a special light starch. A pair of tan slip-on shoes and a matching gold buckle belt and I was ready for my drive into town to meet up with the Prime Minister of Australia. I still could not believe it. *Must be important*, I kept saying to myself, *must be important*. As I pulled up to the front entrance of the Canberra, a valet in full uniform stepped up and opened my car door for me. One of the security men led me through the foyer and into the lift. Gough greeted me at the entry of his presidential suite. 'Thank you for coming on Sunday on such short notice, Hecky.'

'Not at all, Gough. As a matter of fact, I'm excited by the fact that you called me. How can I help?' I asked.

'Well, sit down. Coffee, Hecky?'

'Yes, please. White with two, thank you.'

The security man took my order and went into the kitchen to make my coffee.

'Now go ahead, Gough.'

'Hecky, as you know, there's been an increase in severe weather events in our northern waters lately. Several months ago, a major cyclone just about flattened the city of Port Moresby.'

I nodded, recalling the terrible images on television. 'Yes, dreadful loss of lives and of course massive devastation.'

'Well, you know my passion for Papua New Guinea.'

'Yes, wasn't that one of your first pledges to the Australian parliament? That if you were elected in 1972, you'd ensure their independence by the end of 1975?'

'Indeed. And I know that the transition from this devastation will probably be quite difficult. I've made it clear that we will not abandon our dear neighbour. The Australian Government has committed to rebuilding the city for both humanitarian and strategic reasons. People need help and we don't want to see Port Moresby in the wrong hands. Over the years, I've noticed your town planning and construction activities and I've seen how successful you've become.'

I felt a degree of awe. This man was known for his impressive wit and brilliant speeches: *Men and women of Australia! … It's time for a new government – a Labor Government.* And he spoke just as powerfully in private.

'Thank you, Gough.'

'I've also noticed your commitment to community organisations, and I thank you on behalf of all that you have helped.'

'Thank you again. Rhonda and I have built our lives around what we think is the right thing to do.'

'Hecky, if I offered you the job of rebuilding Port Moresby, would you consider it?'

I was shocked. 'Why me?'

'Well, we have commissioned a lot of Australian construction companies who have set up camp to carry out the reconstruction work for us. Nothing constructive is actually happening and the costs are spiralling out of control. If you took on the job managing the project I think—with your hard-nosed business attitude and engineering skills—maybe we can turn things around.'

I sat back in my lounge chair and contemplated what he had proposed.

'So, what do you think, Hecky? Are you in?'

'Do you know, I think it would work well if you and I were the only people calling the shots. Our decisions are final.'

Gough didn't hesitate. He put out his hand and said that he promised to make that happen, with or without the opposition's approval.

'Okay, Gough. I'll do it. How do we start?'

'Well, as I told you this morning, I'm back in Parliament tomorrow morning and I'll announce you have agreed to take over the reconstruction. There will be a lot of flak coming from the Libs because many of them have an interest in the construction companies over there. Let me handle that; I'm an expert at diversion. I'll make sure they pull their heads in.'

'How will I get around? I'd want to have fortnightly meetings with you to keep you well and truly up to date with finance. There will be a huge volume of money involved.'

'I'll make a government jet available for you to travel back and forth. And, while we're talking money, my finance officer tells me that there is a large number of unpaid invoices from many companies. Tomorrow I'll make a statement to say that we will hold all unpaid invoices in abeyance until you are established with the correct accountancy backup we can muster. That will take the pressure off everybody and at the same time give you instant respect. Money wins every time, Hecky.'

'Yes, it does. I'll ready myself to leave this Thursday. Don't want to miss my weekly tennis game with the boys on Wednesday.'

Gough chuckled. 'You know, Hecky, I'm a handy player on the net. We should have some of our meetings at your home and I could join in with a game or two. That way, we can both have some fun.'

'Good idea, Gough. All the boys would welcome you, I'm sure.'

My time in Papua New Guinea was one of the highlights of my life. I invested a great deal of thought and effort into getting Port Moresby functional again and I relished the challenge. Rhonda joined me and was in her glory as she got totally committed to the welfare of children who had been displaced by the mammoth storm.

We stayed in a modular single level house which was part of a complex for the international community of volunteers from all over the world—doctors, dentists, engineers—all sorts of specialists who gave a few years of their lives to help the people of Port Moresby. One clever engineer from the USA, Austin Gurlinger, designed and built a modular house production plant that was manned by some of the local natives. What a champion of a man he was.

In the early days, as well as authorising the construction of houses, I approved the construction of a bar. Our American friend Austin came up with a magnificent design of post and beam construction, sourcing a lot of the building materials with the help of about a hundred local men. The bar gradually evolved and several weeks later our community members were relaxing on a magnificent deck. Austin had also engineered a good covering to protect us from the nightly torrential downpours of monsoonal rain.

Another of our volunteers was from Durban, South Africa. Raynor Van Gratton was a hydraulic engineer and specialised in anything and everything to do with water such as sewerage and pumping systems for the reestablishment of mains pressure water, the most important issues our team had to deal with.

Unfortunately looting was a big problem. A group had formed, calling themselves 'Rascals'. These young men were dangerous: armed with machetes, spears, and anything they found in amongst the rubble of the destroyed city. They were not to be fucked with. Our team erected a three-metre-high electrified razor wire fence to keep them out. At my request, the local police were backed up by Australian Commonwealth Police who had the power to arrest. This was critical during the rebuilding of the city.

As the days turned into weeks and weeks turned into years, the city started to get back into its original fun-loving way of life. There were several jogging enthusiasts at our headquarters and, with encouragement from Rhonda,

I joined the first international Hash House Harriers running group which was made up of a combination of walkers and serious joggers who met at four o'clock every Wednesday. There was a new hash master each week who would leave the compound on Tuesday afternoon, accompanied by several of our security team, with about two kilos of white flour to mark out a trail for the runners to follow. The hash master deliberately included a few dead-end trails. All the top Harriers and Harriettes would charge out enthusiastically, and when they came to a crossroad, flour trails would be heading off in all directions. The fast runners would often follow the wrong trail, arriving at a dead end. Then they'd have to backtrack to the intersection. By this time, the slower Hashers would have caught up. The object was for us all to finish the run at roughly the same time so that we could meet back at our barracks to enjoy cold ginger beer and delicious food, usually cooked by Raynor. He was a big-time barbecue specialist. If the main ingredient of our feast had either walked, flown, slid, hopped, jumped, or swam, Raynor knew exactly how to cook it. His only stipulation was that nobody was allowed to ask him what the thing on the barbecue spit was; just take a deep breath and dig in. No one ever complained because whatever it was always tasted great.

A funny yet scary thing happened to me and three of my Aussie mates while competing in a hash night run. There was me, Peter, who was a crown prosecutor, Mick, an accountant and Ron, a mechanical engineer. We somehow got lost and became separated from our security team and found ourselves walking along a relatively busy road, theoretically heading back to our compound. We heard a rattling vehicle and along came a rusty, old Toyota trayback Landcruiser, carrying about six rough-looking armed men. They pulled up in front of us and the four of us near shit ourselves. We stood back-to-back, ready to do whatever we could to defend each other. The Rascal boss and his associates stepped out of the cruiser and surrounded us, the boss swaggering towards us, brandishing an AK-47. He seemed to command great respect from his boys. He yelled at us to take off all our clothes, right down to our bare skin, and of course our watches and anything of value. So, there we were, stark naked, huddled together, pondering our future, and feeling pretty humiliated. The boss yelled at his lads to gather up our belongings. After following his orders, they all headed back to the Toyota. After a few paces, he turned and came back, standing directly in front of Peter. They looked each other over, and I could see they recognised each other.

'Ahh, it's you, you fucken prick,' said boss man.

I took a quick look at Peter who was now certainly showing a degree of concern for his own wellbeing. The man went on. 'I bet you wish the judge had listened to your plea for me to do some time in jail, then I wouldn't be standing in front of you. Fortunately, the judge could see my *good character* and let me off with just a fine. How fucken wrong was that dumb-arse judge?'

He laughed, softly at first then louder, until all his men were doing the same, then he said to Peter, 'Hey this is your lucky day. Get on your way. And by the way,' he turned and pointed, 'your compound is that way; you were heading away from your camp.'

Whoops, I thought, *there went all my scout training as a kid.*

By now, Peter had gained a bit of composure and he gave a return grin. 'Mate, I've got a really crook foot. Do you reckon I could have my KT26 runners back to get back to camp?'

The man started to laugh again and yelled out to the lad carrying all our running shoes. He looked carefully and picked out the KT26 joggers. 'Which foot is crook?'

'The left one,' Peter replied. The bloke threw Peter the left shoe and then started to laugh again as he climbed back into the Toyota. With his entourage in the back, they disappeared down the road.

So, there we all were, stark naked with Peter holding his left running shoe! He put his shoe on. 'If we're going to walk, then one side of me may as well be comfortable!'

What a sight we must have looked, hobbling along the road, buck naked, Peter wearing one running shoe. Thank goodness it wasn't long before our security crew found us. Our trip back in the Toyota troopie was full of banter about what had just taken place. As we drove through the main security gate, I felt very relieved. I'm sure things would have been different if Peter had not been with us. He was a high-profile figure in the legal system in Papua and the boss man knew better than to mess with the court system.

As we all got out of the Toyota, a loud roar went up from the deck where our other Hash House teammates were gathered. Smoke was billowing from Raynor's open spit fire, and we were greeted with an ice-cold beer. It looked like there had been a change in the beverage selection: it was beer, beer, beer, and our story of survival became more exaggerated as the party got into top gear.

One of the best investments I ever made in Papua New Guinea was the purchase of a piano. Nothing fancy, just a black Paling upright. We were never short of a person to play, and tonight it was Rhonda's turn. She was hard at it playing *Rocket Man*. I took some time to watch her playing and became very emotional. Maybe the events of the day had a bit to do with it, I don't know. I re-joined the group gathered around Rhonda and finished off the last strains.

What a night that was. Rhonda and I somehow found our way back to our house, and both collapsed naked on our bed. I recall a poor attempt to make love to Rhonda, but we somehow got so tangled up in our mosquito net that we both gave up, pissing ourselves laughing. You should have seen the state of our bed in the morning; the net was almost torn from the ceiling. How we both didn't catch malaria I will never know.

At breakfast I tossed in the idea of us leaving Papua to head back to Australia. The incident the day before had been a warning shot for me, and while we were proud of our contribution, the political climate was unpredictable following independence. Rhonda agreed our job was done and said she wanted to return to her role at the orphanages.

PART THREE

CHAPTER EIGHT

Gang war starts

Four weeks later we were back in Holland Park, me playing tennis with my mates, Rhonda back in her role as governess of the two Brisbane orphanages. The timing of our exit from PNG was great, with Gough Whitlam losing his position in the 1975 Constitutional crisis.

One morning, I got a call from Rusty, who sounded distressed.

'Hecky, do you remember meeting Splinter Woods, my head coke runner? He's gone missing. I'll have to put a hold on the cocaine deliveries.'

I started putting things together. 'Rusty, does that mean what I think it means?' We never mentioned the word *cash*.

'Yes, Hecky. I won't be able to continue with our arrangement until I get the situation under control.'

I was stunned. 'Look, Rusty, I'm okay for about a month. Get your feet on the ground and I'll come down on the weekend. Does that suit?'

'Yes, I really need a sounding board. You couldn't come down tomorrow, could you?'

'Of course, I can. Hey, let's leave Rhonda and Ann out of this for now.'

'Agree.'

'See you around ten. I can stay till Saturday night.'

'Okay, see you tomorrow. And thanks, Hecky.'

I slept poorly that night. I'd had previous experience with lying wide awake at two in the morning—worrying about all the things that were going wrong, and agonising about how I could fix them. But as I got older, I became more confident in my ability to solve problems, reminding myself of one of Father O'Reilly's many maxims, 'It's always darkest before dawn.' We all worry ourselves to death in bed, but just trust yourself and trust your mates. All the worries in the world have a solution and the solution can be found by people talking to each other.

As I walked into the Rusty Nail the next day, I was transported back to my first visit to the Nail with Mum, Dad, and Rhonda. This place had a different feel in daylight, but the funky beer smell and memorabilia pinned on the walls captured its night-time vibe.

I headed towards the boardroom which was strategically positioned so Rusty could monitor his tavern operation, its huge window flanked by heavy curtains that could be drawn if privacy from prying eyes was required. I could see Rusty sitting at the head of his boardroom table. He stood up when he spotted me, and we exchanged handshakes.

'So great you could make it, mate. Take a seat.' and Rusty pointed me to a chair before pulling the curtain completely across.

'Thanks, Rusty,' I said. I looked around the room and recognised the faces. There were the usual suspects, including Senior Sergeant 'Tunner' Meskle. Tunner got his nickname from his massive frame, a hundred and twenty kilos of rippling fat.

'Coffee, Hecky?'

'Yes, thanks.'

Rusty pressed a buzzer, and a waitress was quick to appear with a pot of black coffee.

'Well, Hecky, you know all of us here, so there is no need to hide anything about our missing biker friend, Splinter.'

Tunner spoke up. 'I was called out to an accident at Kempsey. Someone had found a burnt-out motorbike. Looked like Splinter's bike but no sign of Splinter or his cargo.'

He went on to explain that one of his truckie informants had called to tell him he'd heard Splinter had been abducted by an organised truckie gang which had woken up to Splinter's late-night rides when he'd been spotted speeding flat out, overtaking some of the gang members' trucks. There was also chatter that a crooked copper was involved in the abduction, and that was how they caught him. It seemed the crooked copper chased Splinter down, firing gunshots to make Splinter pull over. We think Splinter was tortured until he gave up the entire operation.'

'Shit!'

'We believe that Splinter's dead, Hecky, so we've taken the other couriers off the road for now.'

No one moved. Rusty just sat with his hands under his chin, thinking. Then he thanked Tunner and said it would be best if they took care of the next move. As Tunner left the room, he assured Rusty to call him if needed.

'Thank you, Tunner.'

'No probs.'

Rusty had a large whiteboard at the end of the office, and he started laying out a plan on the board. At that point, I thought it best for me to leave the room and excused myself.

'Good thinking, Hecky. Your room's ready and there is a secure telephone beside the bed. I'll catch up with you for dinner. I've already told Ann I'll be late.'

Rusty later explained to me at dinner that a lot was riding on the success of the cocaine trade in Sydney. 'I swear I'll get my business back on track. We've come too far to let it go. The orphanages, the monastery, the cannery, the major expansion of the oyster farms … about two hundred and fifty men and women rely on me for their weekly wages, and of course you Hecky, with your building activities.'

'Yes, the refuge for homeless folk is halfway through construction.'

'I won't fail them, Hecky. I won't let some unknown bunch of truck drivers destroy what we have all strived to achieve.'

I was convinced that Rusty would stop at nothing to regain his position as kingpin in northern New South Wales. I tried to comfort him. 'The first step is to find out who our enemy is and whether a truce can be arranged to keep that side of the business trading.'

'The problem, Heck, is the coke has all been ordered. Several ships are on their way; they'll drop the coke over the side so my fishing boats can pick it up in the dark and bring it back to the cannery for processing.'

'What do you mean by "processing", Rusty?'

'Well, Heck, the cannery is a legitimate business and is very profitable because the seafood that we process is top-end quality. Jacob has been instrumental in the commercial catching and processing of spanner crabs. We've converted six trawlers to catch tons of spanner crabs, which are very easy to catch. It's nothing for a trawler to catch two tons a day, bring them back to the dock, unload and get ready for the next day's adventure.'

'All sounds wonderful.'

'And we've managed to incorporate some "special" products. Two of the more trustworthy cannery staff hide small, sealed plastic bags of coke in some of the cans. Then the boxes with cans of coke are specially marked and coded for when they get to their foreign destination. I'm paid for each carton of coke prior to it leaving the cannery. That part of the operation will continue, but with the volume of wages and fuel and other overheads, I need the Sydney trade to keep the whole big picture going—all the kids in our orphanages, Father O'Reilly, Rhonda, and now the new project with the Hecky Parker home for men.'

I interrupted him. 'This is what you need to do, Rusty: get our friendly accountant Trevor Jones involved. Explain your position without telling him the reason for it. Ask him to come up with a financial plan to keep the operation going. I also think you need to find the right person to take care of sorting out the Sydney operation. With Christmas on the doorstep, the cash flow generated by the Nail will be huge—lots of money around at Christmas. Also, you must be seen to be doing business as usual.'

'Thanks, Hecky. I knew I needed your level head.'

'Look, Ann and Rhonda are flat out with the Christmas preparations for the orphanages. The Kids in the Community Christmas Tree Appeal is a great success and lots of the kids will be fostered out for the Christmas period. That will keep costs down for six or so weeks.'

'Yes, that's a positive thing.'

'It might surprise you, Rusty, how strong your associated businesses are. Trev will come up with a cash flow for the next three months and by then you will have sorted your enemies out.'

'You're right, Heck. I'll call an urgent meeting with him in the morning. Thanks, mate. And let's you and me have weekly meetings at the Nail to see if you need to make arrangements to secure funds based on your assets.'

'No problems, we will rise through this. Remember this, Rusty: you might be under attack, but you're defending home soil, and in warfare, attackers have a bigger barrow to push. You're defending your home and your family, and that's when you're prepared to do anything to survive. I know you; you're a survivor.'

'Thanks again, mate. More coffee?'

'No thanks. Now I know the situation, I'll come up with my own strategies to ensure my survival.'

'How's home life, Heck?'

'Okay, I guess. Rhonda and I are somehow getting through life together. I regret being unfaithful to her, letting my dick do the thinking instead of my brain.'

He looked down and nodded. 'I know from my own experiences that a standing dick has no conscience, if you know what I mean.'

'Hmm. Double lives are not easy. Now, back to the Sydney problem. We need a man that understands the pressure we are under and is also totally committed to our cause.'

Rusty interrupted, 'I know, Geoffrey!'

'Who?'

'Yes, Geoffrey is the man.'

I knew Geoffrey was adaptable. He really enjoyed his stint at the Gabba; all that friction about the wicket was just a front. But Geoffrey had retreated back to Nimbin, and I wondered if he'd be keen to work with us again. 'Are you sure, Rusty? He's been settled back into sleepy Nimbin for a few years now. And we're not dealing with maintenance or turf.'

'Yes, Geoffrey is the man. You forget Geoffrey's capabilities. For instance, did you know he was a special forces commando in the Vietnam war?'

'Yes, I did, but I thought he was pretty gun shy after his time in 'Nam.'

'Look, you can only ask him. He thinks the world of you, Hecky, and he'll do whatever it takes to get the orphanages back on track financially. Plus, I reckon his experience and low profile are the key ingredients to taking back control of Sydney.'

We agreed I would leave in the morning to start the ball rolling with contacting Geoffrey and reviewing my business processes while Rusty would get Trevor to prepare a spreadsheet of the Tweed operation.

'Okay, let's sleep on that plan—we'll talk soon. Hecky, can you set up a separate safe phone line to give us more flexibility with our discussions?'

'I will. Sleep tight.'

I had a renewed vigour for survival. For most of my business life, I had been reliant on Rusty for his never-ending flow of cash, and the way I did business was complicated. All the builders working on my land developments had their methods of dealing partly in cash. Rusty was right when he said that hundreds of people were going to be affected, so when I got back to Brisbane, I invited them to individually come to my home office, have a cup of tea and go through the transition of no more cash. They all took it surprisingly well, trusting my judgement. The land developments were in high demand and my preferred builders were engaged on a handshake block-for-block arrangement. They would find the buyer for a particular house. Then, as soon as we finished one house and settled the deal with the purchaser, I would have another block waiting for them. The only difference now would be that all money was accounted for. If we had problems with the transition, I would send them to my accountant to guide them through the process, so it was all done in an orderly fashion with no real problems. Rusty's situation was a lot more complicated, but with my support and direction, and the permanent employment of my accountant, life went on.

I was truly surprised when Geoffrey jumped at the opportunity to get involved with Rusty's outfit and a couple of weeks later, I got reports back on his progress. Geoffrey was proving to be the man for the job. I heard he started with the crooked cop down in central New South Wales, Dickenson, whose reputation as a prize prick was well known. Dickenson drove a Mini Cooper S that looked just like any other private vehicle. He'd hide behind trees and low signage to catch unsuspecting drivers he thought were going faster than the speed limit. He particularly targeted truckies. Because he was so relentless with his speeding ticket handouts, it didn't take long for a group of truckies to strike up a deal with him. This deal gave them an enormous advantage over their competitors in the transport business. Not being pulled over and given a total going over by Dickenson was a huge saving to the rogue truckies.

We confirmed that Dickenson had been responsible for Splinter Woods' demise, tracking down Splinter's number plate and passing it on to Rob 'Big Mack' McDermott. McDermott ran a fleet of trucks and was feared as a ruthless leader whose main interest was shifting cocaine behind the legitimacy of his trucking business. Our great friend Splinter would have suffered badly at Big Mack's hands and Big Mack was going to pay dearly for his actions.

Once Geoffrey had been given all this information by Tunner's informant, Rusty did not get involved in any of the day-to-day planning of the future negotiations with or action against Big Mack. After what had been done to Splinter, the level of violence was set. Whatever Geoffrey planned to do to that person had to be so shockingly violent that it would scare off any opposition. Geoffrey was protecting what was Rusty's, and all the people who depended on him. Rusty's only stipulation was that the target truckie had no kids; that was stepping over a line.

CHAPTER NINE

Finding my faith

At the end of each year, Rhonda and I brought a carload of kids down to visit the nuns at the monastery. This year, Father O'Reilly had put together a Christmas lunch in the monastery's garden. Over the years, the garden had grown into a paradise, full of beautiful water features and lotus lily flowers. Father O'Reilly still practised kung fu, his students coming and going as they grew up. Father O'Reilly was a most beloved priest and to date had given his parish all that he had sworn to do some thirty years ago. The Christmas lunch was magnificent. There was incense burning, and the sound of tinkling water on the cloudless summer's day. The four children we brought down for a holiday, who had not been fostered this year, brought along their musical instruments to perform as a string quartet during lunch.

I looked around the garden while all of this was going on and felt wistful. As a couple, Rhonda and I had achieved so much, and I knew she had deserved better. I had lowered the standards that my parents—wonderful, honest, caring people—had set when they were around. I wondered how I could have sold myself so short and cheap for a woman whose only intent was to seek personal gain from getting pregnant and have a son that I could not even claim as my own.

I decided to speak to Father O'Reilly about repenting. I wanted to know if I could become a Catholic. My request surprised the priest, and he asked why I wanted to follow the faith.

'Well, I've done some stupid things in my life that I deeply regret and, as time has gone on, I've wanted to come clean.'

'I understand,' he said. 'You know, Hecky, I can take confession from you if you want, but not as your priest. I'll do it as your friend. I'll treat what you tell me in confidence of course. If you get what you need out of the confession, then maybe you can speak to me, and I'll make arrangements for you to join the church. How does that sound?'

We agreed to get together the following morning. I really just wanted to find peace with myself. After all, Rhonda was Catholic and maybe this move would help mend some of the hurt that I had caused her.

We were still staying at the small flat that Rusty had renovated for us years ago and had found our way back to sleeping in the same bed. But that was it. We were not sharing each other physically, but somehow, we still had a connection. One morning, I felt my past was weighing heavily on my mind. I confessed to Rhonda how much I loved her, and I was totally committed to our relationship. She turned to me in the half-light, looked me in the eye and whispered that I was the love of her life and as a true and committed Catholic, she never wanted to lose what we had and what we would further achieve in the years ahead. Overwhelmed by her sincerity, I paused and thought that this was the appropriate moment to tell her of my desire to join the Catholic faith.

'Rhonda, what I'm about to tell you is something that I have thought long and hard about for a long time. It is something that I believe is necessary for both of us to find common ground.'

'What is it, Hector?'

'I looked around us today and saw the joy that has come from our relationship with Father O'Reilly.'

'Yes, go on.'

'I want to be part of all this.'

'Yes?'

'I asked Father O'Reilly to take my confession tomorrow, and if I still feel the same, I'll ask to be confirmed as soon as possible by Father O'Reilly.'

All went quiet between us as we looked deeper into each other and realised that this move would make all the difference. I didn't attempt to pressure Rhonda into any spur-of-the-moment decision. We just held each other and fell asleep. My last memory of that night was a deep sigh.

When morning came around, I left Rhonda in bed and walked up the road to Monastery Hill where Father O'Reilly was hard at it with several of his students in a mass kung fu routine of complex katas. He acknowledged my arrival with a quick wave. I walked over and sat on a beautifully carved bench seat, a water feature trickling behind me with large golden carp that swam happily among this year's crop of lotus lilies that were magnificent at this time of summer. Plenty of sun and no wind are the key to lotus lilies. I noticed some of them were heavy in flower with extraordinary, unforgettable pink flowers. A short time later, Father O'Reilly came over and sat down.

'Good morning, Heck. Have you slept on it?'

'Yes. Can you take my confession, Father?'

'Yes, of course, Hector.'

He led me to a private corner of the church, away from prying eyes. He looked down at his feet and quietly asked, 'Have you sinned, my son?'

'Yes,' I replied. 'Yes, Father, I have.'

'And what is your sin, my son?'

'Father, I have been unfaithful to my wife, Rhonda.'

'Go on, my son.'

'I have no excuse, and I have carried the guilt for many years. The woman that I had an affair with bore a son, but we have agreed that the secret will be kept.'

'Go on, my son.'

'I deeply regret my actions and seek redemption.'

'My son, as well as I know you, this sin is a serious break in trust, but it is the first step for forgiveness, from both Rhonda and God. Hecky, I look forward to welcoming you into our church.'

I burst into tears, stood up and found my way back to the Rusty Nail where Rhonda was sitting up in bed looking out of the window at the fishing boats coming back into port. I went over to her side of the bed and whispered, 'I love you.' She wept softly. I vowed never to take Rhonda for granted again.

The rest of our Christmas holiday was taken up with giving the children from the Brisbane orphanage the best possible opportunities to enjoy themselves. When we bought ice cream, we bought lots so some of the other monastery children could join us. Our orphanage was our life, and the kids were our life. Whenever the chance arrived, Rhonda and I would push for one of our kids to have the opportunity to go forward. Music had a big influence in our community, and we held charity concerts whenever we needed extra funds. The standard of classical music was exceptional. My position as a wealthy and successful land developer had brought me great advantages, and I had a huge list of contacts. My commitment to the newly completed Hector Parker Home for Men was now paying off and it required more and more of my time. I had also purchased a hundred-acre site of flood plain land which I intended to break up into ten sporting venues for sports from swimming to basketball. I hoped each sport would eventually be self-sufficient and go on well into the future.

Life was full-on; my achievements were all bearing fruit for the benefit of my community. Although Rhonda and I spent less time at the Rusty Nail, Rusty kept me up to date with Geoffrey's progress with regaining control of his Sydney activities.

PART FOUR

CHAPTER TEN

Geoffrey and five of his most trusted associates—Stevo, Christiano, Nick, Peter, and Billy—set up camp in a farmhouse near the town of Brunswick Heads, about thirty minutes' drive south of Tweed Heads. The farmhouse, leased under a false name, had easy access to the Pacific Highway running between Sydney and the Tweed. Rusty organised for a trusted local to live at the farmhouse to cook and keep house. Drugs and alcohol were both banned. Geoffrey's men were all highly trained former SAS mates who had killed before. This was a military-style operation, and if they were to be successful, his men all had to be at their best to help them win back Rusty's position as the man in charge in the northern rivers of New South Wales. The house had a training room with weights and a boxing ring. A cache of weapons was well-hidden. They knew Big Mack would be expecting a reprisal after Splinter's death and they had a plan to kidnap as many truckie members as possible, one at a time. They would attack the target truckies some distance down the road away from their headquarters, so as not to give up the covert operation.

Their first unlucky victim would be dealt with cruelly to put the fear of God into the minds of fellow truckie gang members; have them start wondering who would be next.

Geoffrey's second target would be the crooked cop, Dickenson, but he would be killed on the side of the road and put on display. Geoffrey figured these actions should get Big Mack's attention, and maybe push him to the negotiating table. The entire group knew that violence was the only response.

Geoffrey and his associates waited patiently for Tunner Meskell's truckie informant to feed them information. They didn't have to wait long. Five days later, the call came through from Tunner—rego number, driver's name, and truck type, and also the time he was expected to pass through Brunswick Heads on his way to Sydney. Geoffrey could calculate the time that the truck would arrive at the hit spot which was at the top of a steep hill about a hundred and twenty kilometres south of Brunswick Heads. They knew the truck would be in low gear nearing the top of the hill, a perfect time to strike.

The morning before the planned attack, the men checked their weapons. They were equipped with a mix of Remington 11-48 semi-automatic pump action shotguns and SLR M-16s backed up with hand grenades for major impact. Geoffrey recapped the steps with his men. 'Stevo, you're in charge of the chainsaw. On my signal, you'll drop the tree onto the road in front of the truck. Christiano, you're going to do some body sculpture on the driver. The rest of you know your roles.'

The truck would travel through Brunswick Heads on its way south to Sydney around one in the morning, so the team had to be in position at two-thirty, ready to swing into action. On their way down the highway, the mood was quiet. No talking, just focus. They had two vans, Geoffrey in the lead van, and they had two-way radios to keep in touch with each other. This was going to be a quick and precise action and these men were all up to the task.

They arrived at the selected spot and set themselves up as drilled, Stevo checking that the chainsaw was working. The highway traffic was very quiet. One of the vans went up the highway to wait for the unsuspecting truckie to come past. They would beep a signal over the two-way.

Half an hour later, the two-way radio beeped six times signalling the tree drop. There was no other traffic, and they could hear the grunting and groaning of the truck slowly crawling its way to the crest of the hill. The chainsaw roared into action and a minute later the tree crashed across the bitumen road. The truck heaved to a stop, air brakes screaming. Suddenly, the passenger door swung open and a man wielding a semi-automatic weapon dropped to the ground and started firing in their direction. It looked like they may have been expecting some trouble. The truck driver joined his mate on the road and was firing wildly when a minute or so later, the second van pulled up behind him, Peter and Billy leaping out to return fire. Moments later, when his mate went to ground screaming, the truck driver surrendered. The team stopped firing and moved to disarm the injured co-driver. He was dead; the two shots to the head had done the job. The driver was sobbing and begging for mercy.

Geoffrey knew they had to move fast as there would be more traffic along sooner than later. 'Hey truckie, we're gonna give you a message to take back to that boss of yours. Grab him, boys, and blindfold him. Now pin his arms against the truck.' As Billy and Peter restrained the struggling man, Christiano shot a single round through each of his hands, at the base of his fingers, blowing a couple of fingers off each hand. 'Now, you fucking prick,' Geoffrey screamed at him, 'you tell that piece of shit of a boss that he has poked the wrong bear, and that this is just the beginning. Got it?'

The driver fell to his knees, blubbering and screaming. He struggled to pull off the blindfold, then his shirt, frantically ripping it in two with his teeth to awkwardly bandage each hand.

'Okay, lads, let's get out of here.'

'But what about the tree, boss?'

'Fuck the tree. That's his problem.'

The team left the scene, keeping to the speed limit and driving about a hundred metres or so apart. No one said a word, and they kept their M-16s ready just in case there were any surprises, but the trip back to their farmhouse was uneventful. Geoffrey insisted on the team taking turns at two-hour watches at the house so the others could rest comfortably. They now had to lie low for a week or so and plan the capture and death of the rogue copper. Tunner was going to give them the word on the copper's shifts, so they could carry out the necessary murder. Geoffrey also arranged for security to be stepped up at the Rusty Nail and at Rusty's house. They had to be careful now that war had been declared—and war it was.

With all that was going on with the Sydney truckies, it was impossible for Rusty to keep it hidden from Jacob who had graduated and was now increasingly involved in Rusty's cannery business. Rusty was so proud of his son's measured and mature reaction. 'Dad, I probably know more than you realise. I'll always stand by you.' Rusty knew that Jacob's martial arts training gave him great confidence.

Rusty also had to fill in Father O'Reilly as the monastery orphanage was potentially vulnerable. Father O'Reilly said he would commence training in some 'group manoeuvres' at the dojo with a few of his past and present students. The students wouldn't be told the full story, just that there was a potential threat, and they may need their skills to keep the premises secure. The response was fantastic, with twenty students responding to the opportunity.

It was now hanging on the determination of the ex-SAS boys down at Brunswick Heads. Rusty sent a message to Big Mack through Tunner and his informant, requesting a meeting in Sydney asking if he was interested in getting together to strike a deal. Mack responded with, 'Go fuck yourself.' Obviously, Mack had not thought things through. He would pay and pay hard he did.

Next stop was the crooked cop back at Kempsey. The rest of the week was put into the team going down to Kempsey, sussing out the area, talking to locals, getting the word on where the cop hung out when he was on the prowl for innocent truckies and regular drivers going through town, and establishing the pattern of the copper's movements. When the tip-off came, the team knew his work program for the coming week. Time to show Big Mack that Rusty meant business. Dickenson was rostered on evening shift the following week, which suited their program perfectly. Geoffrey moved his team and the two vans with false rego plates the day before. Kempsey was a large town, so they spread themselves across a couple of motels for the Tuesday night before the hit on Wednesday night.

The cop's shift ended at midnight, so they aimed for eleven pm. Geoffrey knew the place where the cop would be hiding in his Mini Cooper S. Two of his team had already placed themselves in the bushes behind the copper's hiding spot. They decided that shooting and killing the cop in his car was the best option.

'Okay, we're on,' said Geoffrey. With the two hit men in position, it was a simple matter of one of the vans doing a drive-by to see if the cop was in his hiding place which they'd confirm with six beeps on the two-way.

Six beeps, no traffic. The two men moved through the bushes towards the Mini, as the second van drove in quickly, slewing it to block the cop from escaping. Two shots through the driver's side window and it was over. Time to put the icing on the cake.

Geoffrey and Stevo threw a rope over a large tree branch above the cop car. Stevo opened the car door, dragged the dead man from his car, and put the noose around his neck. 'Okay, let's do this.'

The cop was pretty solid, but with two strong, determined hangmen on the job, it didn't take long to get his body suspended to a height that all the locals could see. Hopefully, the local newspaper would take a few shots. Geoffrey picked up the copper's highway patrol hat and put it on top of his car. Then using a spray can of white paint, he wrote on the windscreen, 'Hey Big Mack here we come!' Geoffrey knew Big Mack's reputation within the trucking industry would draw attention.

Both vans turned around and headed back to Brunswick Heads. Again, no speeding, but they kept radio contact just in case one of the vans got into any sort of trouble. The next day, the radio news was alive with reports of the cop killing. It was a stroke of genius that really made an impact. It got the attention of government officials in Sydney who stood up and declared that an immediate enquiry would commence into the interstate trucking industry.

Geoffrey had another trick up his sleeve. Before they'd removed Dickenson from his car, Geoffrey had taken a photograph of him slouched over his steering wheel, dead. He mailed a copy of the photo to Big Mack in Sydney with the words 'Hey, you prick, leave us alone!' across the bottom. He knew this would give Mack something to lose sleep over. The question was, would Mack hand it over to the police, or would he just pull his head in and let Rusty get on with his life back at the Tweed?

Geoffrey's gut told him they should all batten down the hatches and expect the worst. Even though Jacob had put additional security measures into place, a drive-by shooting happened at the front entrance of the Rusty Nail the following day. Geoffrey was right; Mack wasn't going to stop without a fight to the death. When the drive-by happened, Jacob was standing close to the front door. Shaken and furious, he immediately jumped on his high-powered motorbike and followed the shooters back to their stronghold on the outskirts of Kingscliff, staying far enough back as to not be seen. Once Jacob was sure of their whereabouts, he rode back to the Rusty Nail to report back to Rusty about his remarkable chase.

'Are you sure you weren't detected, Jacob?'

'Yes, Dad. I know that area well, so yes, I'm positive they don't know I followed them.'

Rusty called Geoffrey and gave him the Kingscliff address.

'I'll bring the team up immediately. What were they driving?'

'Jacob said it was a gold-coloured Valiant station wagon.'

'Hopefully, they're still there. We'll deal with them if they are and Rusty, if we catch them, they'll be kept alive, okay?'

'What do you mean, Geoffrey?'

'Well, I was thinking they might enjoy a little fishing trip, if you get my drift. Our response has to be brutal. Do you think Kev Skinner is up for another trip?'

Rusty was quick to respond. 'Geoffrey, Kev will do anything necessary to keep our ship afloat.'

'Okay. Don't do anything yet. Just ask Kev to fuel up our best trawler. Be ready just in case.'

'Should I get Tunner involved at this point?'

'No, not yet. Let's keep some powder dry with Tunner. He doesn't need to get involved in this. It's going to be messy.'

'Are you sure about this, Geoffrey?'

'Yes. Let's send that fucking fat piece of shit another message that this is our area, not his.'

When Geoffrey got back to Brunswick Heads his troops were pissed off to hear the news of the drive-by shooting. Geoffrey assured them no one was injured and told them about Jacob's great presence of mind. They knew they'd have to move fast to capture these bastards. 'Remember,' Geoffrey stressed, 'we want them alive.'

Fifteen minutes later, the six vigilantes were in the vans and heading north towards Kingscliff. They'd be there by nightfall.

As they cruised through the area, Peter asked, 'What car are we looking for, Geoffrey?'

'A gold Valiant station wagon.'

'Good, shouldn't be hard to identify.'

'No, hopefully, they're still there.'

The idiots made it easy for them and they soon spotted the Valiant parked in the driveway of a low-set house. There were lights on inside and, with the van window down, Geoffrey could hear loud rock music blaring. He signalled the other van to keep moving down the road.

'Now that we know that we have the right arseholes, we need a plan. We know there were three shooters in the drive-by, so we have to assume three is the number. We know they're armed, so the only way forward is to hit the house with tear gas. We need to avoid a massive gun fight so's to keep them alive. How many gas cannisters do we have in stock?'

'Twenty, boss.'

'Christiano, Stevo, you're in charge of the cannisters. Nick, you go round the back. We'll fire some high shots to keep them inside until the gas gets the better of them. They won't try to come out the front for fear of being shot.'

'We'll hit a window each while you stand guard on the back door, Nick, and as we throw the gas cans through the windows, you let go with a big blast of heavy fire.'

'Have we got ropes?'

'Yes, heaps

'All good?'

'All good.'

No pep talks needed for these men. They drove slowly back to the house and stealthily left their vans, Soon, they had the house surrounded on three sides. As the first gas canisters smashed their way through the windows, a deafening roar of about thirty rounds blasted from Nick's M-16. The music was still going, but a blast of gunfire came from inside the house. With all the tear gas deployed, the six men stood back and fired repeatedly into the top part of the house. The roar of six M-16s unloading was enough to scare the shit out of anyone. The roof and walls of the house were being torn apart by the volley of lead. The front door opened, and Geoffrey called out, 'Police, put down your weapons!'

The three men staggered out onto the front lawn, gasping for air, and begging for mercy. They loaded the culprits into the two vans to transport them back into the hands of Kev Skinner. It wasn't going to end well for these three.

CHAPTER ELEVEN

Geoffrey pulled over at a telephone box and called Kev, who was happy to come out of retirement as a skipper for this special fishing trip. The *Belfast Dreamer* was ready to go, three fish traps set up, and the tide was good to carry out the bar crossing. Docked at the southern end of the marina, the *Dreaming* was a fifty-foot sharpie design that had been part of Rusty's fleet for about ten years. Rusty bought her after Stiffy Murphy passed away of lung cancer. She was beautifully built and maintained, just like all the other vessels under Rusty's charge. She got her name because Stiffy had been from Belfast.

"So, the three men are gagged and tied, Kev. My crew will carry one man at a time onboard. Give me a torch flash when everything's okay.

'No problems, Geoffrey.'

The two vans got to the marina around eight pm. The trawlers were all tied up in their individual pens, just below the monastery. Geoffrey hoped that Father O'Reilly was having an early night, as he was the last person they wanted involved in this operation. They turned off the headlights as they approached the *Belfast Dreaming* to unload their reluctant passengers, kicking and thrashing. It was now very obvious that they knew it was going to be a one-way trip for the three of them.

As they got underway, the mood was sombre, and Kev was very quiet. He had not been to sea since the sinking of the *Moreton Star*. Geoffrey grabbed him by the arm and nodded reassuringly.

If you were part of Rusty's family, you knew you had an automatic place in his kingdom. These three pricks were part of a threat to destroy it. Some of the Rusty family had given their lives, including Kev's two deck hands who had gone down serving their place in the family. Rusty always looked after the immediate relatives of any man hurt in the line of duty, putting the families to the top of weekly outgoings. In return for their loyalty, every employee knew their partners would be cared for and their children given the best possible education, and at the completion of their education, be offered a position in one of Rusty's businesses. This is part of what made Rusty so powerful.

It was a perfectly calm night so the *Belfast Dreaming* had no trouble negotiating the Tweed bar. There were three large steel-framed fish traps, two metres square, on the back deck of the boat near to where the three men waited, still blindfolded. God knows what was going through their minds; no one cared.

It took almost two hours to get to the edge of the continental shelf where the bottom drops to around a thousand feet of water. As the trawler glided to a stop, the six vigilantes swung into action.

This was no place for the faint-hearted.

It took about ten minutes to prepare the fish traps for the grisly extermination of the three condemned men. Before being loaded into the traps, the men would need to be made more 'attractive' to the snapper below. As a young man, Kev had worked in a sheep abattoir, so he was an expert with a sharp filleting knife, and accustomed to handling kicking, thrashing victims.

Three of the team grabbed the first man and held him flat on his back while Kev cut away the front of his jeans. Kev grabbed a handful and then, with a quick flick of the knife, off came the truckie's cock and balls. The salt air filled with the tang of blood as the poor devil thrashed and screamed. He was loaded and sealed into his wire coffin as the next victim was prepared for castration. And the next.

Now drenched in blood, Kev ordered the men to winch the fish traps over the side of the trawler above the water. The three men were unconscious as Kev went to the wheelhouse to switch on the spotlights at the rear of the trawler and find his Polaroid camera. He captured the grisly scene, being careful not to include any identifying features of *Belfast Dreaming*.

Fish traps are a perfect way to get rid of a body. The snapper entering the traps would completely strip these poor devils of their flesh. Then the pig fish would grind down what remained of their bones. When Kev returned to retrieve the traps, there would be nothing of the men's bodies left in the traps, not even shreds of clothing. In their place would eventually be hundreds of snapper and pig fish that Kev intended to process into fillets, which would then be snap frozen in twenty-kilo boxes. These *particular* boxes would be marked as coral trout fillets coming from Cairns before being shipped to Big Mack's headquarters in Sydney. A lover of reef fish, Big Mack was sure to devour the twenty kilograms of fillets.

After the traps had been released over the side, there was complete silence onboard, other than the sound of the water pump used for hosing down the deck and rails. Everybody on board understood the gravity of what had just happened. Rusty wanted Mack to know that he would stop at nothing.

Kev was quite calm as he noted the coordinates of their location and restarted the engine to head back to the Tweed.

It had been a long day and most of the crew went below deck and found either a bunk or a corner to fall asleep in, leaving Geoffrey and Kev to get the *Dreaming* back to port. She was a great old boat and Kev was completely at home behind the wheel. Geoffrey went down to the icebox below and brought back two stubbies of beer, popping the tops, and toasting the success of the night. 'Quite a night, hey?'

They reached the dock around midnight. It would have been easy to let the team sleep on, but it was better to disperse the crew before the rest of the fishing fleet returned back to port early in the morning. Before disembarking,

Geoffrey addressed his team and told them they'd be having seven days off to let the dust settle—with full pay, of course.

Geoffrey slept the rest of the night at the apartment in the Rusty Nail so he could have breakfast with Rusty and bring him up to speed. Kev stayed the rest of the night on board to answer any questions from the incoming skippers about why he was back in port early. He would simply tell them that he'd had a gear failure in his trawl nets. That was a regular problem. As Geoffrey found his way back to the Nail, the two vans disappeared into the darkness.

CHAPTER TWELVE

Next stop Sydney

Rusty and Ann had moved from Bilambil valley into a new home that Rusty built for them on a magnificent one-acre block on the banks of Terranora Lakes. The home looked north over his fifty acres of oyster racks, the life-blood of the oyster side of the cannery export business. This business was a truly magnificent display of what money can achieve in the right hands. As Rusty was increasingly pre-occupied with finding a way to regain control of his coke business, he started to hand over the reins of the day-to-day running of both the cannery and the Rusty Nail to Jacob. Both businesses were booming, and he wanted to distance Jacob from the coke trade.

Rusty put all his energy into planning their next move, preparing for another assault from Mack. If Mack had been smart enough to realise the combined strength of Geoffrey and Rusty, he would have pulled his head in and placed the Tweed coke business into the too-hard basket.

Two mornings after the one-way fishing trip for Big Mack's men on the *Dreaming*, Kev was motoring his way around the oyster leases trying to get his head together. Kev loved his dinghy, the *Lady Lee*. She had a wooden clinker hull built by local Kingscliff boat builder, Chooky Fowler and a primitive, wooden, handmade tiller, very much a part of that style of boat. Her engine was a single-pot Yanmar six-HP diesel that made a pom-pom-pom sound.

Rusty could see Kev's boat from his verandah and waved Kev to come over. The pom-pom-pom went quiet as Kev glided up to Rusty's jetty, throwing Rusty a bow line.

'Hello, mate. Got time for breakfast?'

Ann was standing on the top deck of their home, waiting to see if Kev would stay.

'Yes, mate. That'd be great.'

Rusty called out to Ann, 'Yes, love. Breakfast for three.'

'Coming up!' she called back.

'Well, Kev, are you okay?'

'This business of defending can be a bit challenging.'

'Yes, mate, I know.'

The two friends made their way to the upper deck.

'Well, Kev, tell me about the trio the other night.'

Kev went into great detail about the trip, not holding anything back about the grisly execution. Rusty went very quiet, sat back in his chair, and said, 'Kev, do you think Geoffrey's going too far with his violence?'

Kev also sat back. 'No. I'm not condoning it, but these pricks in Sydney are bad news. I'm afraid that if we don't attack these fucken arseholes, then they'll get on top of us, and we'll lose everything.'

'Yes, but castrating three men and putting them in fish traps and photographing them—God, that's extreme.'

'It's just the unknown direction of the future, Rusty. Let Geoffrey and his men sort things out. This is war.'

Ann arrived with breakfast for three and settled into her seat.

Kev picked up his fork. 'Looks delish, Ann. Thanks. Rusty, after breakfast, can we have another private word?'

'Yes, of course.'

Breakfast was special, and Kev had a chance to bring the two of them up to speed with the progress of his twin sons who were both in their final year at university. Norman was following Jacob's lead and was studying marine biology, and Peter was in his final year studying geology. Ann commented that it seemed like only yesterday that she had assisted Father Bourke, God bless his soul, in baptising both of the boys. 'They both screamed their lungs out if I remember.'

Kev smiled.

'Okay, you two. I'll clear up this mess and give you two worry warts a chance to finish your chat.'

'Thanks for breakfast, Ann.'

'It's always a pleasure, Kev.'

'Okay, Kev, what's on your mind?'

'Well, yesterday was my first time behind the wheel of a seagoing boat since the sinking of the *Star*.'

'Yes, I know. How'd it feel to be on the waves again?'

'Mate, I felt so at home, even though the trip wasn't a normal day at sea.' Kev cleared his throat and moved on.

'You know I've been training three young local kids over at the oyster farm for many years. Those three kids are now all specialists in your oyster farming business. Michael Robertson, Albert's eldest, is skilful with his hands. His building skills come naturally. Seems he takes after his dad. If there's a shed to build or some new oyster racks to be built, Michael is the man. Tom Barclay grew up on Wallis Lakes just north of Newcastle. His dad was a third-generation oyster farmer—not much he doesn't know about growing oysters. And the third lad is not a lad; she is a young lady. Lisa is the youngest daughter of Gladys McNab, the cannery's production manager. So, I was thinking I'd like to withdraw as manager of your oyster farms and hand the reins over to these three young forward thinkers—put them equally in charge of their responsibilities and I take a back seat. I suggest you put the three new board members on a profit share just to give them that little extra to make them feel part of the oyster business.'

'Can you still come along to the monthly board meetings?'

'Oh yes, and I'd be grateful, Rusty, if you could find the time to come along and chair the board meetings because now you're living on the lake, you can also keep an eye out.'

'And what's next for you, Kev?'

'Well, I want to go back to sea and chase those bloody king prawns. I miss it badly. *Belfast Dreaming* felt good and I'm sure that I could draw two capable deck hands from our pool of young folk.'

'When are you thinking of mate?'

'I was thinking the end of the financial year, about four weeks away.'

'Okay. You go ahead and speak to everybody concerned. I'll chair the next board meeting and congratulate them on their appointment.'

'I think it would be appropriate for Jacob to attend the board meetings, too.'

'Yeah, great idea. I'll speak to Jacob about it. I'm sure he'd love that. You go ahead and set up the *Belfast Dreaming*.'

'Oh, before I go, Rusty, I had another thought. Wouldn't it be a good idea to set up the spanner crab, snapper boats and prawn trawlers into a similar structure as the oyster farm?'

'Terrific idea.'

'This'll take the pressure off you a bit and put the responsibilities back onto your employees to hold their monthly budgets.'

'I'll make the arrangements before the end of the financial year. You, Kev, are worth more money. I just can't make myself say it,' said Rusty with a laugh.

'Don't worry, Rusty. I do all right.'

'I know you do, mate.'

Nothing happened during the week as Geoffrey and his men took a break. This gave him time to think about taking the fight up to the enemy. He knew Rusty had a backlog of cocaine in his bunker back at the Tweed and was keen for Geoffrey to find a market. Geoffrey assured Rusty he was on to it, but they couldn't just barge in and start negotiating the sale of a ton and a half of cocaine without raising eyebrows. He knew there would be suppliers in place in Sydney, so this first step was critical to their success.

Rusty had asked Geoffrey to make contact with an old trading partner called Roberto. Roberto Garcia was Colombian and up to his neck in the coke business. They also needed to check out local transport competitors. An established trucking business would be a smart asset for Rusty's operation. They already used the services of several local freight companies, and interstate would mean easier access to the rest of Australia, meaning Rusty's coke movements would be more controllable. Rusty told Geoffrey to establish where Big Mack fitted into the Sydney commercial jigsaw puzzle—whether he was a major player or just a small punter wanting to climb the pyramid and make his cash fortune. The question was, how would they get their hands on Big Mack's interstate transport business? Transport companies were very lucrative and offered other opportunities for government contracts.

Big Mack's freight company operated out of Alexandria, an inner-city suburb of Brisbane. He owned and operated about one hundred trucks, a fleet of local delivery trucks, and some small and some large refrigerated semi-trailers. Most of the prime movers were the 'Mack' brand which was originally built in the USA by the Mack brothers, but only recently were being assembled in Brisbane. The chrome bulldog on the top of the front of their cabin was a sort of mine-is-bigger-than-yours status symbol. Geoffrey had a bit of a chuckle from a mental vision of Big Mack's balls and cock hanging from one of his pride and joys.

So, Geoffrey had to get his crew set up in Sydney, preferably somewhere near the Sydney waterfront. He decided to go ahead on his own and let the others go back to Brunswick

Heads, pack up and then continue to Sydney with the two vans. Geoffrey would have a base for them to move into when they arrived.

It only took him a couple of days to find a suitable block of apartments in Bourke Street, down near the Woolloomooloo Hotel and very close to the shipping action of Sydney harbour. He took a lease on two apartments to give his men more room to move. Geoffrey didn't have a telephone connected to either of the apartments, as security was important. Who knew who got to look at applications for new phone connections in that neighbourhood?

About one hundred metres down the road was a night-club called The Astor. It didn't look much from the outside, but it played a major role in the activities of the local crime scene. The Astor was also a motel of about sixty rooms and prostitutes were the main source of income for whoever was running the joint. Geoffrey thought of moving into one of the rooms, and using it as his base, leaving the crew in the apartments, but he decided against it.

When his crew arrived the next day, it would be business as usual, sorting out the armoury, making a list of anything that they needed. Operating in a city would require different tactics—silencers, grenades, more tear gas, Glock pistols, M-16s, ammo, the list went on. He had the contact details of a gun dealer who was an illegal importer of the latest armoury from all over the world.

He would warn his group not to socialise when out having a beer or out for dinner as this part of Sydney was a heavy scene, with Kings Cross on the doorstep and drugs, prostitution, and money laundering on every street corner. He wanted them to blend in with the locals and never disclose any personal names. Security was the key as these heavyweights only played dirty. Local intel suggested a gang from the Republic of Kazakhstan controlled Kings Cross. These Kazakh criminals had no boundaries when it came to violence. Their leader, a man known as Sergei, had the support of the local Cross police.

Geoffrey teed up a meeting in three days with Roberto. Rusty wanted him to get the number one buyer of their coke back on board. Roberto would want to know four things: quality, quantity, price, and how often. It was a supply and demand business; the customers didn't give a flying fuck about their problems.

Geoffrey started stewing about Mack again: *That short, fat prick thinks owning a hundred fucken trucks makes him important … I get pissed off when I think about what he's attempting to do. Big fucken Mack, I'm coming for you.*

He had to steady himself when he got this way because his anger sometimes let him down. A woman's touch might help. Since his breakup with the love of his life some years earlier, he hadn't been able to completely get his head in the right place. He knew what he needed, and that was a night in the cot with a young, caring prostitute that he could find through the personal column of the *Kings Cross Whisperer*. He was feeling under the pump about the meeting with the Colombian customer and needed some loving.

He took himself off to a local café at Circular Quay. The coffee and cake in Sydney were very different to the Tweed. Many of the Sydney bakeries were owned by Vietnamese refugees who had been given political refugee status in Australia.

Way back, Vietnam had been a French colony, bringing with it the art of pastry baking and the pastries reminded him of his earlier days in Vietnam. Geoffrey adored the pastries, and he was conscious he'd need to keep up his jogging around Farm Cove on the harbour to avoid the awful feeling of the weight piling on.

So, it was coffee, cake, and a trawl through the personal column. He had to read carefully into each advert. You just didn't know who had placed the ad—male, female, maybe both.

He found a likely prospect:

Hello. I'm a Japanese student seeking casual, professional sex. I speak English and I'm very private. I have my own apartment and you can leave me a message in PO Box 127 Kings Cross.

Sounded promising. Asking the waitress for a pen and pad, he wrote a short note, suggesting that if she was interested, the student could meet him at the bakery in Riley Street the following Saturday morning. With a quick summary about himself he mused that she probably wouldn't be hard to identify if she was really Japanese. He went up to the post office and pushed the letter into box 127, thinking, *Fortune favours the brave.* He felt he was now starting to show his age and unsure about her reaction.

He felt good about his quick action. Sometimes in his life, he'd made quick decisions that turned out well; on the other hand, some of those decisions had turned out badly. He figured he'd learned that it was the quality of the people you get involved with. If you didn't get a good gut feeling within the first ten minutes of meeting someone, just get the hell out of there as quickly as you can.

Deciding there wasn't anything more he could do, he put all of his personal life aside to concentrate on his meeting with the Colombian at Lady Macquarie's Chair at noon in three days' time.

Friday came around soon enough. Geoffrey dressed in a new sports jacket, matching dark blue trousers and a striking pair of Karandonis dark tan boots. Feeling strong and confident about his meeting with the Japanese student the next day, he had a spring in his step. Walking from Bourke Street, he passed the pub and Boy Charlton Swimming Pool. He enjoyed swimming, combining swimming with running to keep him supple and fit for his age. He had to be, in this life and death business.

There were three naval vessels in port at the Gardens Shipyard on the right, one of them called the *Port Moresby*. It made him think of Hecky, whom he hadn't heard of for years. *What a good man,* he reflected. *Wonder how he's going.* At the end of the path, he looked up and spotted a guy sitting on the piece of carved sandstone designed and built by Governor Macquarie for his wife's comfort during her morning walks back in the early 1800s. There was no mistaking Roberto—well-dressed in a hound's tooth jacket, light brown trousers and dark tan slip-on shoes, his gold-rimmed sunglasses accentuating his tanned skin. As Geoffrey approached, Roberto put up both of his hands to stop him in his tracks.

'Geoffrey? Hello. This is only a precaution.' And on that, a big burly bloke came seemingly from nowhere. 'Geoffrey, please forgive my mistrust, but I must insist on a pat down. You must understand.'

'Yes, of course.'

Geoffrey was really taken aback but summoned Roberto's man to come forward and pat him down. It seemed he was looking for a gun or wires. He nodded the okay to Roberto.

'I'm sorry for that, Geoffrey. You can never be too careful.'

Geoffrey nodded and took up a seat beside Roberto.

The heavy seemed to disappear as quickly as he'd appeared, although Geoffrey knew that he and Roberto were not alone.

'Good to meet you, Geoffrey. Although you and I have not done business before, Rusty has given you great praise and has explained the reason you're in Sydney.'

'You know I'm here to eliminate a man?'

Roberto stopped him. 'Geoffrey, what you don't know is that your person of interest is one of my major suppliers.'

Geoffrey wasn't ready for that bombshell, so he resolved to shut up and let Roberto have his say, hoping he'd have an idea about how to move forward. Geoffrey realised Roberto had commitments and if he got rid of Big Mack, all sorts of recriminations could result.

'Geoffrey, you must not put me in any danger. My life is quite simple—I buy cocaine from reliable sources. Personalities don't come into it. Do you understand?'

'Yes, I do.'

'I do understand Rusty's problem, and I hear he's not been able to get rid of the volume of coke that he was selling before the "hiccup". What I'm prepared to do is take seventy percent of the coke he is holding and pay in the usual manner with a discount of fifteen per cent.'

Again, Geoffrey was shaken.

'Geoffrey, I want you to understand that I'll have to take some risks in taking on this transaction. I don't need an answer now. You go back and put my offer to Rusty.'

A silence came over them as they both stood. Feeling the need to fill it, Geoffrey remarked on what a beautiful place the harbour was. The Manly ferry was punching her way to the northern suburbs, and to their left were the Harbour Bridge and the latest masterpiece, the Sydney Opera House.

'Amazing, just amazing.' Roberto reached out to shake Geoffrey's hand. 'It's been a pleasure, Geoffrey. We'll talk again, I hope.'

'I'm sure we will, and I'll bring the sandwiches,' Geoffrey said, as a show of friendship.

'I'll hold you to that, Geoffrey. I'll bring an appropriate bottle.'

As they shook hands, Roberto gave the eye contact that Geoffrey was looking for.

When they parted, Roberto and his man headed towards the Opera House. Geoffrey's walk back to the apartment was full of mixed feelings. *How will Rusty take the pay cut?* Other than that, he felt the meeting had gone well. The sandwiches offer was a good touch, although it wasn't a bullshit thing. Having a sandwich and a special glass together symbolised trust, the foundation premise of Rusty's business.

Geoffrey knew he did not need to worry about mistrust. There was a saying about Rusty that the only reason that you would not make old age was if you had either had a serious health issue or you had betrayed him; then you deserved everything you got. His justice was fatal, and they all knew it and lived by it.

Back at the apartment, he wrote down some important points for his telephone conversation with Rusty later in the afternoon.

Geoffrey knew that Rusty would have finished golf by five.

'Hey, Rusty. How did you play?'

'Thirty-three Stapleford points.'

'Not bad.'

'Yeah, it's blowing hard up here, and the swell is up so none of the boats can go to sea. Gives the crabs a chance to get bigger.'

Geoffrey let out a laugh.

'Did Roberto turn up?'

'Yes, he did, and it went well, or at least I think it did.'

'What did he say?'

'Well, although he is sympathetic to your situation …'

'Yes?'

'Well, he's been doing business with that fucking arsehole, Big Mack.'

'Fuck, I knew it!'

'Rusty, calm down. It gets better.'

'Sorry mate, go on.'

'Well, Roberto knows that you probably have a stockpile.'

'A fucking stockpile? I have about one and a half tons of the fucking stuff!'

'Rusty, calm down.'

'Go on,' he half-yelled.

'The bottom line is that he will take seventy percent of the coke that you have stockpiled at a reduced price of fifteen percent.'

'Fuck. How did I know that this was coming?'

'Rusty, Rusty, settle down. I can only deliver the messages.'

'Sorry, mate. I know.' He paused. 'Mate, can you ring me at eight tonight? I'll speak to Trevor Jones to get an accountant's point of view.'

The chat ended. No small talk, just a click from Rusty hanging up. Geoffrey went back to the apartments to see how his team had settled in. He had a nervous wait for his watch to finally climb its way up to eight o'clock and went out to the local phone box. Rusty answered the call on the second ring. 'Hello mate, I apologise for today's performance.'

'That's okay. I'm with you, Rusty.'

'I know that mate. Ed's done the numbers, and I'll go ahead with Roberto's offer; it makes a lot of sense. This way I can keep the shipments coming and keep the coke business flowing.'

'Good call, Rusty. What do you want me to do?'

'Well, first, I need you to keep planning the elimination of that fat piece of shit, and two, think about how you're going to handle getting the one and a half tons of coke to Roberto's preferred delivery spot and then how you're going to get almost three million dollars back here to Tweed. We've got ten days, so think through your plan, then we'll go through it together, okay?'

As he hung up, Geoffrey had a careful look around, just in case someone was listening. All was clear. *Fuck, almost three million dollars, how big is a pile of money to that amount, fuck, fuck, fuck, this is going to be big.*

He planned to brief his crew the following night. Across the road, the Woolloomooloo pub was going off. Geoffrey had a couple of double rum and cokes, then found his way back to the apartments where two of the lads were watching Manly playing South Sydney. Manly were in front by twelve points, with ten minutes to go. A grumble came from both of them, obviously Souths supporters!

He was feeling wound up after the hectic activities of the day and the thoughts of his rendezvous tomorrow. A bit of a pang in his groin was too much to resist, so he did what he had to, then had a shower and hit the sack.

CHAPTER THIRTEEN

Welcome to the Cross

Saturday morning, eight thirty.

Geoffrey skipped his morning coffee, as he hoped he'd be having breakfast in an hour or so. He was excited. He started ruminating: *If she's a student, she's too young to get involved with. It'll all depend on her outlook on life. I guess being Japanese might make a difference if their culture is too different to ours. Stop overthinking things!*

He tried to dress young—blue jeans, crew necked white tee shirt with an unbuttoned casual long-sleeved overshirt, navy blue sliders. It was autumn and quite warm, and he was feeling a bit sweaty.

He walked up Riley Street towards the bakery opposite the police headquarters. ASIO headquarters were on the other side. If she knew this, she would have a reasonable sense of security that he was on the up and up, rather than some devious prick trying to get a free fuck. It was three minutes past ten. There were only three people in the bakery, and one of them was a Japanese woman.

Okay, here goes.

He walked confidently over and greeted her with, 'Good morning, can I get you a cup of coffee?'

She looked up at him and he felt an instant pang in his prick. She smiled back and said that a cup of green tea would suit her better. Her English was excellent, and she spoke softly, but confidently; there was no submission in her voice. After ordering their drinks, Geoffrey sat opposite her and introduced himself. She immediately put her hand on top of his and responded with, 'Thank you for answering my newspaper ad.'

'It is my pleasure.'

She still had her hand on top of his and had a look that he had never felt. He actually *felt* her look; it was beautiful. He thought that if this did not go any further, he would have experienced something that he'd never had before—a calm came over him. He wasn't trying to find anything to say; he was just spellbound by her mystery.

'Can we share breakfast, please?'

'Yes, that would be great.'

He got the waiter's attention, asking for a menu. 'Can I ask you your name?'

She responded, 'Issey.'

He commented that it was a beautiful name. 'What does it mean in Japanese?'

'It means first-born. I have a brother and one sister all living in Osaka with my mother and father. We all earn money to help pay for our parents' care. That is why I am seeking a supplementary income. Hopefully, I'll find a man that cares about me and my family.'

At this stage, he was ready to give her the deeds to his house, but common sense took over, and he started to regain some control.

'And where and what are you studying?'

'I'm studying at the University of New South Wales. I'm in my third year of medicine and will major in paediatrics.'

'Do you plan to go back to Osaka after you graduate?'

'No, I have applied to become an Australian citizen.'

'Let's order, shall we?'

While they waited for their eggs benedict, she again held his hand and asked him what he did. He told her he worked in the seafood business and that he travelled around the country as a project manager.

'Any family?'

'No family. The company I work for is my family, and I'm very happy with the arrangement.'

'Well,' she said, 'what are you looking for?'

'I'm looking for casual sex. I'll treat you well, not ask anything about your private life, and always be respectful. We could start a professional part-time life together. On some nights, we might go to the theatre, or to the Opera House for dinner and a performance. I'm not in a relation-ship and nor will I be looking. If our arrangement works, then that will be enough.'

She hadn't taken her hand away, which he thought was a positive thing. She went on to explain that her studies were of prime importance to her. He appreciated her sincerity.

Their order arrived, and they both enjoyed a great breakfast, chatting for about two hours. He didn't want breakfast to finish but thought that he'd better broach the business side of their proposed arrangement before they left the table. She wasn't backward in coming forward.

'For our successful relationship to work, my rent is sixty-five dollars a week. Can you think about that?'

Think about it? No problems.

'If I know that my rent is covered, then I can concentrate on my studies and, of course, our time together. What do you think? Do you want to have a month's trial? I think we'll get on fine.'

He was in a bit of a spin, but he felt buoyed about having a relationship with a beautiful, young, intelligent woman that knew exactly what she wanted.

'Oh,' she said, 'any social activities we have will be at your cost.'

He expected that, so he agreed.

'And the bonus is that I can cook us a Japanese dinner, of course.'

He put his hand on top of hers and agreed. He would start with a month's rent and if things were working, then he would continue on with the financial arrangements.

'These are my real estate agent's bank details. I'll tell them of my new arrangement and that you will be in on the first of each month to pay the rent.'

'Agreed. Oh, there is one problem.'

'What is that, Geoffrey?'

'Well, if I had to go away on business, could a credit arrangement be agreed to? Although, if there are more days away, that will be my loss.'

'Mine too,' she replied.

'Okay, what night next week?'

'Wednesday is good for me.'

'It's good for me as well.'

He leaned forward and kissed her on the cheek. She accepted the kiss and handed him her address.

'Ah, Rushcutters Bay, just a walk over the hill. See you at six on Wednesday.'

'Don't forget to pack your pyjamas,' she said with a grin. He had a chuckle and decided to head down to Paddy's Market to do a bit of clothes shopping. He wondered if she was the real deal—med student and all.

I hope I'm not going to be a soft touch. I won't let that happen at my stage of life.

He needed to keep his business totally private and also his address, as it was a lot easier just to vanish, and of course, he had no idea how long this mission in Sydney was going to take. But what he did know was that he needed the warmth of an honest woman's touch. He could only turn up on Wednesday with an open mind and give it a try.

The weather was starting to get cold, so a winter clothing shop was one way to make him feel good, not that he needed much more to feel good after his breakfast with Issey. She had dragged him out of the dark underworld and woken him up to the real world, reminding him that what he did was just a job. Who knew what was around the corner?

He'd arranged to call Rusty every night at six o'clock, except Saturdays, so that day-to-day planning could flow. His first question to Rusty on his call the next night was, 'How big is two point seven five million dollars?'

Rusty laughed. 'Do you mean in weight?'

'Yeah. I'm still sorting out the transport details for the pick-up and deliveries.'

'At a guess, in one-hundred-dollar notes, it'd weigh almost three tons. Too much for your wallet to hold so you'll need a couple of sturdy bags. Of course, the one point five tons of coke will take less space.'

'Anything else?'

Geoffrey hesitated.

'Geoffrey?'

'Well, Rusty, you pay me to think and to cover all bases.'

'Yes, I do.'

'Well, how fucking much do we trust Roberto?'

Silence.

'I get you, mate. When you think of it, if Roberto was to double-cross us it will probably cripple us, correct?'

'Sadly mate, it would.'

'Have you given Roberto any details of the coke delivery?'

'No.'

'Well, we have time to carefully think things through, and if our gut tells us that the risk is too great, then we'll come up with a diversionary plan to protect the goose that lays our golden eggs.'

'Okay, yes mate, you're right. Let's both keep thinking it through before we make a call on our next move,' he agreed.

'Rusty, remember Christiano? One of my lads? He's brought me a lead I want to follow up.'

'Yeah?'

'Christiano seems to have some sort of links with a Kazakh here called Sergei. We know that here in Sydney, the Kazakhs are the kingpins.'

'Okay, go ahead and get Christiano to make contact. See if you can set it up asap.'

'When is the next half-ton going to arrive, Rusty?'

'The ship's early. It'll do the drop sometime tomorrow night. Kev is all set to go. There's a big swell running, so Kev's going to use the new centre console fast boat to do the pickup.'

'That's good timing.'

'What do you mean?'

'Well, maybe we can have a backup plan, Rusty.'

'Keep going, mate.'

'Well, Roberto would have no idea of our capabilities with firepower, correct?'

'Yep.'

'Rusty, where did you usually to do the coke and money exchange?'

'It's usually done in a small parking area on the southern side of the art gallery, just up from the Opera House where there are no parking signs. It means we can have side-by-side car bays and it has three access points, just in case.'

'Can you recall? Are there any large trees there?'

Rusty paused. 'Yes, I think there's a huge garden area.'

'Good, I'll take a couple of my boys to that spot tomorrow and suss out if we can set up some hidden sniper cover in those gardens. The boys all have silenced Remington sniper rifles that would eliminate Roberto and his minders in ten seconds flat if things turn to shit. I'll be doing the exchange with the one existing member of my crew. We'll only take offensive action if Roberto and his boys decide to take the coke without paying for it. If Roberto does become a dick and turns on us and we take him out, then that will fuck up our old fucking arsehole truckie mate Big Mack. His biggest coke market will have gone up in flames.'

'Good thinking, Geoffrey. Good fucking thinking.'

'Rusty, tomorrow I'll take care of assessing the art gallery carpark and ask Christiano to try to get an audience with the Kazakhs, whoever they are. I see three benefits: one, if Roberto is straight up, we cash up again. Two, if Roberto is a fucking arsehole, then we gain a shitload of money and keep the coke. Three, if we set up the sale of the half a ton being picked up tomorrow, that will be another million, and we get to sell Roberto's one and a half ton in our own time for full price, no fifteen percent reduction in our price.'

'Well done, mate. I won't forget this if it all comes off.'

'Rusty, please don't take me wrong with my next request. My fee for those three achievements being successful is that you continue to pay all the bills here in Sydney. I'm going to take the Big Mack thing to the next level; I'm going to take him down. I'm not going to kill him, but I'm going to take his trucking business and turn it into the largest freight business in Australia. By the time I'm finished with that piece of shit, he's going to beg me to buy his business for a dollar.'

Rusty replied with a chuckle. 'You're really going to do this?'

'Yes, I am, and to repay you for keeping my men on the job, I'll run your freight at a reduced rate to pay you back. I'll also be able to clean plenty of cash.'

'Geoffrey, you make all of our targets happen, and you will have my full support.'

'Thanks, mate. You know, Rusty, they say you can't have mates in business, but we've proved them wrong. We are mates and I treasure that.'

'So do I, Geoffrey.'

'These coming months will be tough and, who knows, with all the danger involved, I may get killed. If I do, I'll have gone down believing in you, mate, and that will be enough.'

'Fuck, Geoffrey, good luck tomorrow.'

'Relax, Rusty, I'm on it.'

'Let's talk tomorrow night.'

'Yeah, good night, Rusty.'

Geoffrey slept a lot better after that telephone conversation with Rusty. Their agreement for him to pursue Big Mack gave him real direction for his future. If successful, he'd stay in Sydney. He really felt comfortable there, and only two days to go until he and Issey started their 'business' relationship.

CHAPTER FOURTEEN

Geoffrey woke early on Monday morning and went for a run around Farm Cove to the Opera House stairs. They were a perfect height to run up and down, and running was good therapy for thinking things through before the day ahead. He thought he'd take Christiano for breakfast to his favourite café in Crown Street. Christiano was one of his most loyal team members, and Geoffrey needed to have a chat with him about his links to the Kazakhs.

Christiano was just coming out of the shower as Geoffrey came back to the apartment. 'Hi, boss, what's happening today?'

'Well mate, how about breakfast?'

'Yeah, great. I could eat a horse.'

'Let me shower and we can walk up to Crown Street.'

At breakfast, Geoffrey deliberately didn't jump straight into the reason for their meeting, instead asking Christiano about his family background and where his parents both came from. The young man explained that both his parents were refugees from Almaty in Kazakhstan and that his father had passed away two years ago. His mother was living in north Queensland with his only brother, who'd taken over the family sugar cane farm and was doing a great job.

'My dad worked his arse off for thirty years on the farm until he contracted lung cancer from smoking.'

He said that he had several relatives in Sydney and had not had any contact with them since they moved their drug operation to Woolloomooloo.

'Do you speak the language?'

'Yes, of course. The family only speak Russian at home.'

'How would you feel about concentrating your time to try to set up a meeting with your contact? Our intel suggests those guys are the people to do business with here in Sydney.'

'Well, that will be easy. Sergei is the boss of the Sydney coke operation.'

'Could you set up a meeting asap? Of course, you'd be paid well for your efforts.'

'Okay, I'll start today.'

'A meeting on Thursday would be good.'

'Mm, I'll see what I can do.'

'Thank you, mate. My shout for breakfast.'

They engaged in some more small talk while enjoying breakfast. Geoffrey told Christiano he was taking three of the other lads up to check out the grounds of the art gallery later that day because he and Rusty smelled a rat with a possible double-cross by Roberto. 'Can never be too careful.'

Christiano nodded and continued eating his breakfast. On their way back to the house, Christiano said that he would speed things up a bit and take a detour up through Potts Point so he could have a walk through the Cross to find Sergei.

'Well done, mate. I'll catch you later. Good luck.'

'Luck won't have anything to do with it,' Christiano said. 'We'll be dealing with hardened criminals. Our word will always be our bond. Working for Rusty McCloud gives me the confidence to arrange this meeting. I know Rusty won't jeopardise our arrangement here in Sydney.'

'Okay, talk this arvo.'

'Yes, we will.'

Geoffrey's reconnoitre of the gardens at the art gallery on Tuesday went well. The lads had a good look around and drew a mud map of the proposed site. Plenty of cover, and a distance of about one hundred and fifty metres, far enough away to take cover and also close enough to keep good visual contact.

After catching up with Christiano again, Geoffrey called Rusty to tell him that a meeting with the Kazakhs was scheduled for Thursday at a pub in the Rocks precinct at two o'clock—a one-on-one meeting, probably with the usual pat-down procedure. Rusty was excited about the prospect of opening up a new market. He said the latest coke shipment had arrived and was ready to go to Sydney if an agreement was struck with Sergei.

That afternoon, they chatted on the phone and Rusty asked, 'Geoffrey, have you got a plan yet for the pickup of the coke stockpile from up here in Tweed?'

'Yes, I'm bringing all the team up, leaving around eight pm this Friday. We'll be using both the vans, and as usual, we will be heavily armed. We'll split the coke into two halves for our return trip. I'll also bring back the latest half-ton delivery, hoping that our Kazakh friends will take a quick early drop. I take it you have your storage bases covered for storing the two ton of coke at the Tweed?'

'Yes, I do. I won't go into that over the phone. Just know that it is safe, Geoffrey.'

'What day do you want me to set up the delivery with Roberto?'

'Sunday night, midnight,' Rusty replied.

'Okay, mate. Just keep me informed.'

'I'll see you Saturday morning at the Rusty Nail. The boys will load up the coke, drop me off and then go back to Brunswick Heads for some sleep. They would have been awake all night just in case of an incident and will have to be awake on Saturday night on our way back to Sydney with our precious payload.'

'Okay, see you Saturday morning.'

'Thanks, Rusty.'

On Wednesday morning, Geoffrey's first call was to Roberto. The call was taken by one of his minders. After a few security questions, Roberto finally took the call.

'Hello Geoffrey, I was hoping to hear from you. I'm still keen for us to go forward.'

'That's why I'm calling, Roberto. Rusty is all go as well.'

Geoffrey threw Roberto a dummy by telling him that their delivery was already in Sydney and that this coming Sunday night was the exchange meeting time, at midnight in the usual place. He also informed him that he'd be in charge of Rusty's side of the operation with one man with him to help unload the coke and asked if he could have one man with him to assist in the unloading.

'Yes, that'll be perfect. I'll also send a substitute for myself, 'cause I have family business to attend to.'

Geoffrey didn't push him any further and agreed to the Sunday night arrangement, but as he hung up, he was worried. The fact that Roberto wasn't going to attend the exchange on Sunday night was a dead giveaway that he was going to double-cross them.

Geoffrey rang Rusty with the news. He was really pissed off and kept cursing Big Mack. 'That fucking prick!'

'Yes, mate. I know. If he hadn't put his fucking big nose into our business, then we wouldn't be in this situation.'

'Well, Rusty, if it wasn't Big Mack, it would have been some other cunt trying to climb an easy ladder.'

'Yes, I suppose you're right.'

'Rusty I'm not around tonight. I have some personal things to take care of. We have all our ducks in a row; let's just stick to our plan.'

'Okay, all good mate, and I hope all goes well with the Kazakhs meeting at the Rocks tomorrow.'

'Yes, mate. Things are hotting up.'

'They certainly are.'

CHAPTER FIFTEEN

Geoffrey was gearing up for his first meeting with Issey. He walked to her place in Rushcutters Bay, which only took about thirty minutes. He dressed young again; it gave him confidence as he didn't feel his age. Her apartment was on the fifth floor, a modest two-bedroom, typical layout. Her view was magnificent, looking directly north towards Manly. She greeted him and asked him to take off his shoes and all of his clothes. He wasn't embarrassed, as this was a business deal. *It's just business.* She helped him put on a silk Japanese dressing gown and a light pair of slip-on scuffs. He noticed she had candles burning in various parts of the living room. Neither of them had said a word at this point. He attempted to say something, but she put her fingers over his lips and stopped him, then she took his hand and led him to the bathroom. More candles and a round spa bath shimmered in the corner of the bathroom. By this time, he was completely erect; he could not help it. The scene in the apartment was amazing. He did not know what to expect next. Then she untied his gown and ushered him into the steaming hot tub. The heat took his breath away as he lowered himself into the water. He lay back and, through half-closed eyes, watched Issey undress and then slide into the hot tub. *My God!* She had a great body, medium, firm breasts, shaved pussy, and her legs were fit and beautifully shaped. At that point, he was in a completely different world. As she settled into the tub, she leaned over him and whispered, 'Welcome.' He almost blew his load but had to contain himself.

The next hour was all about him. She washed his hair, sponged his entire body, and gave his cock a suck that he would never forget. After the hot tub, she dried him off with a hot towel and redressed him in his gown.

Their conversation then started, about her day, then his day. Of course, he didn't go into the finer details of his day; just small talk to get things going. He found himself trying to make more conversation. She sensed that and joined in. She was obviously quite worldly and started talking about her parents and where they lived in Osaka. Her father was a retired fisherman, and the family owned a small tuna boat. Her brother took over the family tradition and continued on from where her father left off. Geoffrey told her that he was a keen fisherman, and it wasn't long before they were chatting easily about tuna fishing. Issey was also a very experienced sea person, so they had plenty of things to talk about. As she was preparing seared tuna steaks with seaweed salad for dinner, she explained that she was pescatarian and only ate from the garden and the sea. Her quiet manner was refreshing, and he was beginning to settle. She seared the tuna in a large stainless steel flat frying pan on high heat, explaining that the tuna would be seared for about one minute on each side. Issey knew exactly what she was doing, and the seaweed salad was set ready to be served. Geoffrey was seated at her dining room table in the gown she had given him in a state of 'this is too good to be true.' He watched her standing at the stove and could not help but bar up again. He was at this stage, ready to hand over the keys to his house.

As she placed his tuna steak in front of him, she kissed him softly on the back of the neck. He was intensely aroused and rose to kiss her. Issey put her hand on his shoulder and whispered, 'Enjoy your dinner.' She had two candles burning, and the soft light was beautiful on her half-naked upper body. He could tell that this wasn't a one-way street; Issey was also enjoying the experience. They shared a cup of warm sake that went straight to his head. How his life had changed. He had not had one thought about his life outside the walls of Issey's apartment. He was totally focused on the moment and very grateful to whoever was responsible for bringing Issey into his life. He also knew that Issey would play a major part in his life.

After dinner, she cleared the table and led Geoffrey to her couch to enjoy another sake. Again, the candlelight was setting the scene for a trip to her bedroom. Their first night together in her bed was the greatest sexual experience of his life. After a quiet, passion-filled hour or so of fantastic, simultaneous orgasms, Issey went to the bathroom and returned with a small warm damp towel. She gave him a sponge bath, and he was so relaxed that he was half asleep as she slid in beside him. They spooned, and he could feel her incredible body wrapping around his. He did not stir through the night, and they awoke in the same position that they went to sleep in. He looked at his watch on the bedside table. Seven o'clock. As he moved, Issey slid out of bed, standing naked in front of him, and before she turned to go to the bathroom, she gave him a smile that said it all. On her return to bed, Issey again whispered, 'You stay there, Geoffrey. I'll bring you toast and coffee. How do you have it?'

He responded with, 'short, black, and strong'. She smiled again and said that was her preference as well. The sun was up and shining through the large bedroom window, revealing a spectacular view of the harbour. While Issey was preparing breakfast, he started thinking about his day and his first meeting with the Kazakh coke boss. He was a bit apprehensive about the meeting, acutely aware that these men represented crime at the top level, and he couldn't afford to promise them anything that he could not back up. He felt sure Christiano would have given Sergei a rundown on their operation and also their reliability.

Issey delivered his breakfast on a tray, and they both sat up in bed and enjoyed it. She explained that she was working at Saint Vincent's Hospital that day. She had to do several weeks of hands-on experience in the children's ward, learning about children's health problems. She went on to explain that she treasured her days there.

Geoffrey thought it opportune to ask Issey her age.

'Thirty-three.'

'Oh, that's very young.'

She said she wasn't concerned about their age gap, as this was a business arrangement and that was all. Geoffrey didn't know how to handle this reply. After the night of his life, he'd forgotten the reason for them getting together. He looked at her and tried his best to agree. She smiled back and reassured him that he was her only client and that she too had enjoyed their night together. He walked over to her and, putting his arms around her, he gave her a slow, soft kiss. She responded, and then he was given a fresh towel. He had a shower, shaved, and dressed.

His walk back to the apartment was filled with all sorts of wonderful thoughts, and as he got closer, he began to focus on the day in front of him. Noon at the Rocks with Sergei. He considered what he would wear: casual, long trousers, sliders, and an open-neck shirt—no jacket, as it was a warm day.

CHAPTER SIXTEEN

There was no one home in the apartment. He knew the lads had a lot on with picking up the armoury, planning the meeting with Roberto's men on Sunday night, and ensuring the vans had a service before their trip back to Tweed Heads to pick up the coke. They would pack additional fuel in both vans to eliminate stops at service stations. Their road fuel stops would be done off to the side of the road out of highway view, with a fully armed member of the crew on guard.

He had another cup of coffee and reviewed the whiteboard, which showed a full program of what was on the go right up to Sunday night with Roberto's boys.

He walked to his meeting with Sergei. Sydney Rocks is situated on the opposite side of Circular Quay on the western side. There were several old pubs in the Rocks precinct, the Ox on the Rocks being the most famous, legendary for its steaks. He was hoping to have lunch with Sergei today.

On his walk around Farm Cove, just before the entrance gates, an old Italian fisherman was hard at it fishing off the low sandstone handrail. Just as Geoffrey was approaching him, the old man swung into action. His rod was bending over, straining. Whatever he had on was certainly big. Geoffrey stopped and gave him some encouragement. The fish was swimming powerfully from left to right, and Geoffrey was about to tell him to give the fish a bit of slack, but just as he opened his mouth to say the words, the fish jumped out of the water and shook its head violently. Unfortunately, the fish shook the gang hooks. Well, did the old Italian spit the dummy? He threw his rod onto on the ground, cursing himself for his stupidity.

Geoffrey was careful not to get involved, and continued on his walk, leaving the fisherman to his misery. Geoffrey hated losing fish, especially when he had not identified the species of fish. When the fish jumped, he saw that it was a large greenback tailor, probably about one kilo. Even when he was about thirty metres from the fisherman, Geoffrey could still hear the old bloke cursing and swearing. He knew that fishing was not a matter of life and death; it was far more serious than that! He had a bit of a chuckle and picked up the pace.

He hoped to get to know Issey a lot better. Maybe with her background, she would like to give fishing in the harbour a go. He could get a couple of suitable fishing rods and some blue pilchards for bait. This time of the year was tailor season. He'd mention it to see her reaction.

It was a longer walk than he'd anticipated, but he walked into the Ox right on noon. Geoffrey spotted a big bloke sitting at the side of the room with a full view of the door. He strode over and thrust out a confident hand, looking Sergei straight in the eyes, Rusty-style. 'Sergei? Thanks for making yourself available at such short notice.'

'That's not a problem, Geoffrey. Can you please head out the back and see my guys?'

'Okay.' He headed past the kitchen to a back alley where a mountain of a man was waiting and, after a thorough pat down, he was given the okay to join Sergei. When he got back to Sergei, he asked, 'How do you know I'm clean?'

Sergei said jokingly, 'Mate, how I know you're clean is that you returned to me in one piece!'

That's when Geoffrey knew these guys were the real fucking deal. You don't get to the top of the coke trade in Sydney by being a softy. Sergei chose a table, and they sat and made small talk, Geoffrey sharing what had just happened with the Italian fisherman. When Sergei seemed genuinely interested, asking about the size and type of fish, Geoffrey marked him for a fisherman. It was certainly a good meeting opener.

Geoffrey then went on to tell him about Rusty's operation up at Tweed Heads.

'Yes, I've heard a lot about him. Word is that he is a good and trustworthy man.'

'Definitely,' he agreed. Geoffrey went on to tell him of their problems with Big Mack. Sergei shook his head when he mentioned Mack's name. 'Geoffrey, that fucking arsehole deserves a fucking bullet.'

'Well, we think the same. He killed and tortured one of our best men and then sprayed the front of our tavern with lead. We've retaliated, and retaliated hard, but Rusty—like you—is the sort of person that can't let bygones be bygones. He has to stay in control of his little patch.'

'I understand, yes. There's no place for people that think that they can just come in and fucking shake somebody else's tree that they have spent a lifetime growing.'

Geoffrey nodded.

'You got time for lunch?'

'Yes, of course, Sergei. Of course.'

'What'll you have?'

'Well, I'd like a rump steak, medium-rare, thank you.'

A waiter seemed to sprint to take Sergei's order, and when the waiter left, Sergei asked him to continue. Geoffrey continued with Rusty's story, mentioning his financial commitment to the local Catholic Church monastery in Tweed and several orphanages in Brisbane, two of which were well-managed by a powerful entrepreneurial businessman, Hecky Parker, Rusty's long-time friend.

Sergei was very touched by Rusty's story. 'If we are to agree on doing business, I'd like to meet him.'

'I'm sure Rusty would also want to meet you. In this game, there's a lot of trust. Relationships are the key.'

Sergei went on to say he understood that sometimes timeframes were disrupted. 'We all know that. I'd rather get a phone call to explain why there is going to be a timeframe issue rather than having to pick up the phone and ask the fucking hard questions.'

'You and Rusty share similar thinking. I think you'll get on well and may become good friends.'

'We'll see.'

Sergei asked how much coke Rusty handled monthly.

'Half a ton.'

'Well, that's significant,' he remarked.

'Yes, half a ton. He can get more if required.'

'Where is it from?'

'Colombia.'

'That would work well with me,' Sergei replied.

'Sergei, if we get to the next level, could you work out the financial arrangements with Rusty? He never discloses those details to me for several reasons.'

'No problems,' he replied.

The steaks arrived and looked fantastic. Between mouthfuls, Geoffrey brought up the possibility of a spare half-ton that had become available and could be delivered early next week if Sergei was interested.

'How do I go about buying it?'

'Call Rusty on his safe line.' Geoffrey removed a piece of paper from his wallet and wrote down Rusty's private number. 'When you call him and he picks up the call, say the words: "are the oysters plump?" That will give you clearance to continue the conversation. If you want me to get you a sample of the product, let Rusty know, and I'll arrange it.'

'Okay.'

'Keep the conversation as short as possible and trust him.'

They completely demolished their steaks, had another cold draught of Guinness, and both shook hands.

'Thank you.'

'Geoffrey. Here's my card; don't hesitate to call if you need me, okay?'

'Okay, and thank you for lunch, Sergei.'

'Oh, I don't remember saying that it was my shout.'

Geoffrey was startled by his comment and went for his wallet.

'Just kidding,' he said with a laugh. 'I own the pub. What sort of a bloke would I be if I didn't shout a potential client lunch in my own pub?'

'You got me, you got me,' Geoffrey replied. 'My shout next time, or maybe we could wet a fishing line together.'

'Now you're talking. Let's get things rolling a bit and see how we go.'

'Agreed.'

'Geoffrey, may I ask who is buying your coke at the moment?'

Geoffrey hesitated and said that Rusty had been selling to Roberto for many years, but since the attack on their operation, they had been stockpiling their product.

'How much are you holding?'

Geoffrey paused and said, 'Considerable, Sergei. I'll let Rusty talk to you about that.'

'What is the main reason you want to supply me and not continue with Roberto the Colombian?'

'Roberto has started buying his coke from that fat bastard Big Mack, our mutual enemy, and Roberto is trying to stitch us up for fifteen per cent off our normal price.'

'Oh, now I understand.'

'Sergei, can I ask you if you deal with Big Mack?'

'No, I don't and never will. He's developing a bad name for himself. He'll need to pull his head in, or he will eventually get it blown off.'

'Yes, I agree. We have a saying back home: "Don't fuck with Rusty." Unfortunately, Roberto has gone too far with that piece of shit, Mack.'

'I hear you, Geoffrey. Let's talk soon.'

Geoffrey agreed and bid him goodbye. The walk back to his apartment was a worried three-quarters of an hour as he started going over some of the information he'd disclosed to Sergei. He kept reassuring himself that Rusty would have also laid his cards on the table. Geoffrey thought he'd give Rusty a call early before he left the Rusty Nail.

He picked up the pace a bit, and on his return to the apartment, he was greeted by his entire team, who were excitedly unpacking the shipment of new armoury that Christiano had picked up. They also asked how the meeting went with the Kazakh. He just gave them the thumbs up and moved on to another subject. The new weaponry looked the part.

Geoffrey excused himself and said they'd all meet at six that night to finalise the plan for the rendezvous. 'I'll order pizza.'

Nick, their youngest man, said they only ate Arthur's Pizza from up in Oxford Street.

'Yes, I know what you mean; they're the business.'

He thought he'd probably have to order five large pizzas. These boys would certainly make short work of a large pizza.

He took some phone money from the jam jar on top of the refrigerator and headed off to call Rusty, who picked up the phone at the end of the second ring.

'Hello, mate. How did it go with our new best friend, Sergei?'

'Well, I think he's keen to start a business relationship with you, and I've given him your number to talk out the finer points about your latest half-ton delivery.'

'Did you give any indication of price to him?'

'No, I left it up to you, although I did explain you've been dealing with Roberto for many years and that he was trying to stitch you up for fifteen per cent. He didn't blame you for being a bit pissed off. I told him that Roberto has started buying from that fatso, Big Mack. Sergei hates Big Mack too and believes he needs a good twelve gauge to the side of his head.'

'Wow, that's handy to know.'

'Happy to leave the door open for someone to carry out this fitting end to fatso after I've finalised *acquiring* his trucking business.'

Rusty gave his stamp of approval with a big chuckle. 'Okay, mate, I'll wait for Sergei's call. Are you ready for Roberto?'

'We will be. I have a briefing with my crew tonight to go through the finer details, and of course we're travelling tomorrow night back to you to do our coke pick up.'

'Yes, Kev Skinner is expecting you at the cannery. Any hiccups, I'll call you.'

'All good, Rusty. I'll see you Saturday morning.'

Geoffrey bought the pizzas and raced back to the lair as quickly as he could, so they were hot. Nothing worse than five little boys whingeing about cold pizza.

'How's the new weaponry?'

Nick was first to respond and, with a mouthful of pizza, gave Geoffrey the thumbs up. The boys had drawn a mud map of the art gallery carpark, and Christiano said they were good to go. Geoffrey nodded and took another piece of pizza.

'Great pizza, Geoffrey.'

'We're leaving in both vans tomorrow night. Are we all prepped?'

'Yes,' was the call from everybody.

'Leaving at eight o'clock tomorrow night, okay? Both vans about ten minutes apart.'

'Yes, okay.'

'Good night, you bunch of pizza pigs.'

Geoffrey didn't remember anything but a vision of Issey sitting at her table half-naked in the candlelight. He could hardly wait till next Wednesday night. *She's exactly what I need.* Their arrangement was perfect. It eliminated the hassle of dating, dinners, and the 'You didn't call me' explanations, and all the issues that came with a full-on relationship, and of course, it worked both ways. She was free to enjoy her life and had the comfort of an honest sexual relationship. Geoffrey made a mental note to ask her for her birth date so he could do something with her when it came around. He was too wound up so he put on his joggers and headed off to do some stair training. He was becoming very fit from running the sets of the Opera House forecourt stairs. Having Issey in his life motivated him to stay fit. It was a beautiful evening, and on his run, he reviewed the plans for their trip. On his return to the apartment, there was a hive of activity with the lads taking the gear down to the vans before turning in. Geoffrey asked Nick if he'd double-checked the two-way radios for tomorrow night.

'Working perfectly, Geoffrey.'

He went up to the phone box to call Rusty and ask if he had received a call from Sergei. Rusty was upbeat and confirmed that he and the Kazakh had struck a deal. He'd be taking the half-ton shipment.

'You did well, Geoffrey.'

'Thanks, mate. That's why you pay me the big bucks, mate.'

'Everything on track for tomorrow night?'

'Yep. I'll be at the cannery by eight on Saturday morning.'

'Great. I'll confirm that with Kev Skinner. We'll have breakfast together while the boys load the two vans then head down to the house at Brunswick Heads to get some sleep and get ready for the trip back to Sydney Saturday night.'

'Do you mind if I use the flat at the Rusty Nail to have some sleep after we get our meeting done?'

'Yes, of course you can. I'll make sure it's ready for you.'

'Thanks, mate. Oh, and can you drop me down to the Brunswick house to the lads to save them travelling back here with all that coke on board?'

'No problems. See you at the Nail for breakfast, mate.'

Geoffrey went back and reviewed the plan. Now that he knew that Sergei was on board with the half-ton, the finer details of Sergei's delivery would unfold at his breakfast meeting with Rusty.

CHAPTER SEVENTEEN

They were all aboard, the two vans travelling about two kilometres apart and in full radio contact. They weren't expecting any trouble on the way up to Tweed with empty vans, but with each van carrying a ton of coke on the way back, it would be a totally different situation. Geoffrey's team was fully aware of the weight of responsibility they all carried. The vans rotated drivers every three hours to keep fresh drivers at the wheel. Going through Kempsey was a bit chilling. They drove slowly past the spot where they'd taken out the crooked copper. The tree had a dead bunch of flowers tied to it. *Fuck you, copper, fuck you.* His involvement in killing their beloved mate Splinter Woods still made Geoffrey angry. Splinter was a great bloke, and Geoffrey often reminisced about their times together.

The team drove through the night, and Geoffrey spotted the crimson sun just poking its head up above the horizon. It made him think of his dad. 'Red sky in the morning sailor's warning; red sky at night shepherd's delight.' His dad had passed about six years ago when he was ninety years old, his mother passing six years earlier. They were a great couple and when his mum died, his dad never got over it and was heartbroken. He'd decided it was time to join her rather than go to an old people's home. Geoffrey didn't understand it at the time, but he did now. It was a brave act at ninety.

A gust of wind buffeted the van, interrupting Geoffrey's reverie. Rusty would be disappointed with the wind being up. It stopped his fishing fleet from going out. Fishing was a feast or a famine, a bit like farming … floods and drought. It was hard to find a happy medium.

They were passing through Murwillumbah at seven o'clock, and the town was starting to stir. Geoffrey calculated they'd be half an hour early getting to the Rusty Nail, better early than late. His lads would soon be loading each van with a ton of coke while he caught up with Rusty over breakfast.

They'd rest at Brunswick Heads, taking turns to watch their booty which was worth nearly three million dollars now that Sergei was on board. This was big business, and sometimes, when he thought about it, it scared the shit out of him. He kept telling himself, *It's just a job.*

It would be a totally different scene when he took over Big Mack's trucking business. He hoped it would be possible to transcend from all of this violence to some sort of normality. Another vision of Issey flashed through his mind. *Fuck she's beautiful. Hope we continue with our arrangement.* He knew that only his silence about what he did for a living would keep any wolves from the door in their arrangement. With the new business with the Kazakhs starting, he needed to think about moving away from Woolloomooloo and possibly finding a small apartment in Balmain to protect Issey from being involved in his risky business. If he disappeared into the Balmain area, the chances of him being followed to Issey's place in Rushcutters Bay would be far more remote. He thought his crew would prefer that too—better than living with the boss.

Finally, they were driving up and over Sexton's Hill as Tweed Heads was just waking. Five minutes to go. He was looking forward to his catch-up with Rusty. He missed being around this area; it was in his blood.

As they drove up into the carpark of the Rusty Nail, he could see Rusty standing in the front entry of the middle building. He still looked very sharp and strong, but Geoffrey noticed he had put on a little weight. *Must be in a good paddock with Ann's cooking at home.*

Both vans pulled up to a stop and as the men gathered around Rusty, Geoffrey took a long look, noting that the five of them were in top condition. None had lost their hard, all round, good-to-go appearance.

Rusty greeted them with a warm welcome, handshakes all round.

'Rusty, can the lads have breakfast here before they start to load?'

Rusty replied that he had already organised the kitchen just in case they were early.

'Thanks, mate. Okay, you boys, follow Rusty to the dining room.'

The dining room was empty except for several cleaners that were busy wiping and sweeping the massive main room of the tavern after another full house last night. The place reeked of cigarettes and stale booze. Rusty led the lads to the dining room where they attacked the hot breakfast buffet.

Geoffrey had decided to send Jack, the cook, back from Sydney because the lads were not eating at the apartments as often as he expected. And who was serving out the food? Yes, it was old Jack. He was excited to see the team again. 'You look well Jack,' Geoffrey remarked.

'Thanks, Geoffrey, and your boys seem to have lost a bit of weight since I left.'

'Yes, they have. That was the main reason that I sent you back here.'

'Good move,' said Jack. 'I was missing the Tweed.'

'And our customers were missing you,' Rusty piped up. 'I have always said that if the food is good, then it doesn't matter what the show was or if the roof had blown off the pub. If the food is great, they will turn up in droves, and if the tables had blown away with the roof, they would probably eat off the floor.'

The men hooked into the delicious spread.

'Geoffrey, now that the lads are set up, let's you and I go and have our breakfast out on the deck.'

'Great, mate, lead the way.'

The western end of the deck had an area that canti-levered well out over the crystal-clear water of the Tweed River, a spectacular spot. The locals would sometimes come to blows over who grabbed the outermost table.

Geoffrey luxuriated in the warmth of the winter sun as their eggs benedict was placed in front of them. He started the conversation, opening with their new best friend, Sergei the Kazakh.

'Oh yes.' Rusty paused as he broke off a piece of toast dipping it into his Hollandaise and egg yolk mixture.

'Yes. Sergei. I've made a few enquiries about him, and he checks out okay. All he wants is good quality coke at the right price on a regular basis. We just have to get rid of fucking Big Mack, and the guaranteed supply can happen. How are you going with uncovering Big Mack's business activities?'

'Well, we've had a lot on. If we can pull off the ton and a half to Roberto and the other half-ton to Sergei, then we are back in business. Then we can concentrate on that fucking cunt.'

'Yes, mate. I agree.'

Geoffrey had a second coffee and sat back in his chair, while Rusty excused himself and went off to take a call from Kev Skinner. On his return, he said that Kev was at the cannery, ready to start loading whenever the lads were done with breakfast.

'Now let's go through Roberto's delivery tomorrow night. What's your plan, mate?'

'Well, as you know, Roberto has told us that he has a "family matter" on tomorrow night,' he air-quoted, 'and that two of his men will be at the carpark beside the art gallery at midnight.'

'Hmm, what do you think, Geoffrey?'

'I think the whole thing stinks. I think he'll have the money there just in case, but if he thinks that he can get on top of us, he will shoot me and Nick through the head and disappear with your one and a half ton of coke.'

'I hoped you weren't going to say that.'

'Rusty, I'll not let one and a half ton of your coke slip through my fingers and into the hands of some fucking Colombian import that has no qualms about who he deals with. I vote that if all goes okay tomorrow night and the Roberto deal goes ahead as planned, we stop dealing with Roberto. His connection to Big Mack can only be bad for us. That's why I'm doubtful that all is going to go well tomorrow night.'

'Yes, you're right.'

'Well, the lads and I have devised a plan. If I put both of my hands in the air and step back, that is the signal for the four lads hiding up in the trees above the car park to shoot Roberto's two men in the head. If there's a third man in the car with the bags of cash, Nick will step forward and shoot the driver of the car. All going well, we will secure the coke, take control of the three million, and hopefully disappear with the lot.'

'Sounds like a good plan, Geoffrey,'

'Yes, it all sounds okay, but the downside to the plan is Roberto might plant more of his men in other positions around the area. My lads are going to do a recon of the area fifteen minutes before the scheduled meeting for any threats that Roberto has set up. At that point, and before Roberto's money men turn up, the lads will be back into their original planned positions, ready to shoot on my signal.'

'Sounds good, mate.'

'How are you going financially, Rusty?'

'Why'd you ask?'

'Do you need a loan of some money?'

We looked at each other and laughed.

'No mate, I mean can you survive if we don't get the money tomorrow night?'

'Yes, I can, providing that you do the half-ton deal with Sergei next Thursday night at his pub at the Rocks.'

'Is that the arrangement that you made with him?'

'Yes, he is all go. He just wants a quality check before the handover.'

That will be no problem. I would have expected that anyway,'

'Okay, sounds like you have it sussed, mate.'

'Big bucks, remember.'

'Yes, mate I do, and I also remember our arrangement with Big Mack's trucking business.'

'Thanks, mate. That is my transition to a less stressful life.'

'I get you mate, keep it going. I'm right behind you.'

As they made their way towards the Rusty Nail's massive front doors, Geoffrey could see Jacob and Father O'Reilly coming in from outside, both dressed in their karate suits, black belts tied appropriately across their waists.

'Geoffrey! How are you?'

'Ah, good morning, Jacob. Good morning, Father.'

'What brings you back to the Tweed?'

Geoffrey was stuck for words and muttered something about the winter down south starting to become very cold, and he had just come up to get some sunshine. He tried to shift the topic, saying how fit they all looked and asked Father O'Reilly how the monastery was going.

'So good. It's now a combination of a primary school and an orphanage. Thanks to Rusty and Hecky, the Brisbane orphanages have expanded as well as the accommodation for elderly homeless men. Those two men are certainly leaving their mark on the world.'

Geoffrey turned to Jacob. 'How's your mother?'

'Oh, she'll be here shortly. She's holding a Tai Chi class up at the garden with some of the teachers and nuns.'

'Geoffrey, have you got time to look around the monastery garden? '

'Sorry, not this time. I'm only here for a while and I've got a few things on my plate.'

'How's the fishing fleet going, Jacob?'

'The cannery, spanner crab and oyster businesses are absolutely booming. Kev and I are currently working on developing a new fleet of spanner crab boats—twin hull catamarans with enormous outboard motors. They're the brainchild of a clever man called Bruce Harris up at Labrador near Southport. These boats handle the Tweed bar a lot better, so we're converting the rest of the trawlers.'

'Impressive stuff! Keep up the good work. Good to see you both.'

'You too, mate.'

After an exchange of handshakes, Geoffrey was on his way to the cannery where he was greeted by Kev, who had unlocked the main gate to let him in. Kev leaned forward and gave Geoffrey a warm man hug and a pat on the back. Geoffrey wasn't much of a hugger, but with a person like Kev, you sort of made a half-hearted response.

'Welcome, my friend. How was breakfast?'

'It was great. Old Jack has certainly got the right touch with eggs benny.'

'Yes, he's a keeper! How's the loading going?'

'Almost done.'

Geoffrey could see the two vans were sitting a bit lower, each loaded with a ton of coke. Slamming the doors shut, he called all the lads to gather round to go through the plan for the day.

'So, I'm staying here to go through some business. You lads are going to take the vans back down to Brunswick Heads and wait there until I get driven down to join you. Take it in turns at sleeping today with two men guarding the vans. Make sure you don't box the vans in, just in case of an attack. We want to be able to drive away if the shit hits the fan.'

'What time will we head for Sydney?'

'About eight. Traffic should be light. Now, lads, we are all aware of the value of our cargo. We need to be absolutely ready to respond to any situation, and if we are attacked, use whatever force necessary to save the coke—hand grenades, tear gas, automatic firepower, whatever is necessary. There's a lot riding on our success.'

As Geoffrey finished his pep talk Rusty came over and gave handshakes to the lads. 'Geoffrey, a quick word?' They stepped outside.

'Problem?'

'No problem, mate. I'm just thinking you shouldn't stay here today. We've discussed everything we need to, and I'd feel better if you stayed with the vans, just in case.'

'Sure. No worries.'

CHAPTER EIGHTEEN

The drive back to Brunswick was uneventful and Geoffrey was hoping the house was still okay. They hadn't been anywhere near it in months. But as his van pulled into the driveway, something felt wrong. The front driveway gate, usually locked up tightly, was off its hinges. He yelled into the two-way to the second van.

'Don't turn into the driveway!'

The trailing van stayed on the highway. 'Stop here, Stevo.' Geoffrey grabbed his automatic weapon and got out of the van. 'Nick, cover me. Stevo, reverse back up the drive-way and turn the van to face south. Stay with the van.

Crouching low, Geoffrey and Nick made their way back to the smashed gate. There were no cars in the driveway and no sound coming from the house as they crept up the path.

Geoffrey thumped on the front door which swung open lazily. 'Anybody here?' No response. 'Anybody home?' he called louder. He pushed the door right open and heard Nick cock his gun behind him. As they both carefully entered the front of the house, it was obvious that the entire house had been ransacked. They moved cautiously from room to room. It was a fucking mess. Any clothes and small bits and pieces they hadn't taken to Sydney were totally ruined. 'We won't be coming back here, Nick.'

'No way, boss.'

They carefully made their way back to the van to give Stevo the all-clear.

Then, 'Fuck!' Geoffrey called. 'Fuck Nick, that's not Stevo!'

Geoffrey dropped to the ground and rolled into the nearby bushes. Nick did a half-roll up to the base of a large paper bark tree and let go the full thirty rounds from his weapon. Then he reloaded his M-16 for the next volley. Their unknown opponent was scrambling for cover. Thirty rounds of an AK-47 would scare the shit out of anybody.

Then Geoffrey spotted Stevo lying face down in the dirt beside the van. 'Oh no, no, no.'

He had no time to think as two other gunmen ran up the driveway towards them. Nick was quick to respond. 'Geoffrey, cover me!' Geoffrey jumped to his feet, releasing a full clip of thirty rounds. The intruders dropped to the ground as Nick disappeared into the heavy scrub. Geoffrey kept them occupied with plenty of spurts from his M-16.

Suddenly, he heard gunfire coming from behind the driveway, and then a scream. He wondered if they had got Nick. There was another major blast then a boom, and in a flash, the two gunmen were thrown into the air by a grenade blast. Geoffrey quickly got to his feet and blasted the fuck out of what was left of them.

'Fuck, *fuck*!' Geoffrey called out.

'All clear, boss,' Nick called.

Geoffrey carefully made his way up to the van and rolled Stevo over. He was dead, shot in the side of the head, poor bastard.

'Fuck! The coke!' Geoffrey called out. He threw the van door open and gave a sigh of relief. The coke was safe.

'Come on, Nick, give me a hand with Stevo. No, wait. Let me call the guys in the other van and let them know what happened. They may as well keep driving.' Geoffrey called the other van and told them to get as far away from Brunswick Heads as possible. 'Be careful not to speed. Stay under the speed limit.' His men had missed out on precious sleep, and he was concerned for them.

As they were struggling with Stevo's body, Geoffrey saw that Nick had blood coming from under his left arm. 'Fuck, mate. You're hit. You okay?'

'Yep, I took a shot early in the exchange. I'll live.'

They covered Stevo's body and got back into the van, both on high alert.

'Fuck, that was close,' Nick said.

'Yes, mate. We're not out of trouble yet. Let's get out of here. The noise from the grenade explosion is bound to get the neighbours ringing the cops.'

Travelling during the daylight was a real risk because there were far more cops on the road. Plus, the cops on night shift were not as diligent and would spend most of their night shift asleep.

Geoffrey was still shaking from the attack, reflecting that poor Stevo would not have known what happened. His life was over in a blink. 'Nick, that was fucking brave of you to go around and outflank them, mate.'

'Yes, they weren't expecting that. And the grenade up the arse—that fucked 'em.'

'Yeah, they were definitely not military trained.'

'Yeah, but that doesn't help our mate Stevo.'

'No mate, it doesn't.'

They kept driving for three hours. Geoffrey was still reeling from the attack. *Fuck, this is heavy shit; who the fuck were those pricks back at Brunswick, and more importantly, who did they work for?* He'd bet his house on their employer being Big fucking Mack.

He knew he had to get his shit together and come up with a plan. Their safest place was on the road. But if a nosey cop pulled them over, they'd either have to kill him or take him hostage, put his car off the road into the bush and take him on a trip to Sydney.

'How's our fuel going, Nick?'

'About two hours left in the tank. That should easily get us to Nambucca Heads.'

Geoffrey got on the two-way and told Christiano the situation and that they would fill up the vans at Nambucca. 'Nick and I will stay back a bit while you fill up with fuel, have a piss and get some food. Let us know when you're back on the road and we'll stop and refuel. We should probably get to Sydney around eight, all going well. Once Geoffrey knew that Christiano was back on the road and he gave him the all-clear, he'd also stop and refuel.

After the Nambucca stop, Geoffrey took over the driving so Nick could rest. They'd patched up the bullet graze.

Four centimetres to the left and it would've been curtains for Nick. Geoffrey said he'd practise his needlework once they got to the apartment. He was an expert at stitching cuts and wounds in the hellhole of Vietnam.

Geoffrey was churning things over in his head during the drive to Sydney. Who the fuck had anything to gain from their elimination? Roberto? Was he trying to skim off some of Rusty's profit margin? He had nothing to gain by destroying them. He needed them. And Sergei the Kazakh, he wanted them to supply coke. He knew their coke was Colombian grade one, uncut. Sergei had the opportunity to cut the coke a second time, making his profit margin far greater. It could only be that fat bastard, Mack. Geoffrey was sure that with Roberto taking Rusty's one and a half ton, he would have cut back his orders from Big Mack, fucking up Mack's cash flow and his dreams of buying more trucks to expand his empire. With all that had happened up at Tweed, Splinter, and the raid on the Rusty Nail, it had to be him. If Mack was doing all of this shit without Roberto's knowledge, then there was a better chance of Roberto's deal of one and a half-ton being legit. He hoped so; there'd been enough gunfire for one day.

He checked in again with Christiano's van. It was about five kilometres in front of Nick and Geoffrey, and they were travelling okay. It was tough to settle down with Stevo's body in the back of the van. Geoffrey didn't know what Rusty was going to say. He knew Rusty would make the necessary arrangements to have his body picked up by an undertaker who wouldn't ask too many questions.

Their arrival at Woolloomooloo was a solemn affair. Christiano parked the van carrying Stevo's body under the building while Peter took the other van down the street. Meanwhile, Geoffrey went to the phone box and made the call.

'Rusty.'

'I was worried about you.'

'I'm okay.'

'All hell has broken out up here at Tweed with the local press—they're buzzing; something about three gunmen found blown to pieces after a gunfight in Brunswick. I'm putting two and two together …Thank God we put the lease of the house in a false name.'

'Yes, mate. But there is some bad news.'

'What?'

'Well, the front gate was hanging off and, well I smelled a fat rat, so I left Stevo in charge of the van to guard the coke while Nick and I checked out the house. It had been turned over, not a thing salvageable. Then on our way back, we were attacked by three heavily armed gunmen.'

'Go on, mate.'

'Well, we both took cover and returned fire.'

'Where was Stevo?'

'Unfortunately, he'd been shot through the head, instantly dead.'

'Fuck, mate. How about the coke? Is it intact?'

'Yes, it's in our garage downstairs, and both vans are safe.'

'Thank God, mate. What do you need?'

'I need you to engage that friendly undertaker of yours to pick up Stevo's body asap. You know where we are, sixteen Bourke Street. I can ring you back, say in two hours, and you can then give me the body pickup details.'

'Okay, yes, mate. Do you think we should abort tonight's exchange?'

'No, we need to get the coke out of our hands and into Roberto's hands or somebody's hands asap.'

'How are the lads?'

'A bit shaken but all go for tonight. We know that the coke deal has got to happen. Rusty, who do you think is behind the attacks on us?'

'Has to be Big Mack. The only hiccup with tonight's exchange is that if Roberto is working with that prick, then there could be a shootout tonight.'

'Fuck, you could be overrun in sheer numbers by a combination of Mack and Roberto's forces and lose one and a half tons of high-grade coke. You need more good gunmen.'

Geoffrey went quiet for a moment and then suggested that he give Sergei a call for an urgent chat.

'What for?' asked Rusty.

'Well, let's put our cards on the table and tell him our concerns about the situation. He told me to contact him if I needed anything. Maybe he will organise some backup.'

'What have we got to lose?'

'Yeah, nothing. Sergei is really keen to get his hands on the other half ton of coke. What do you think, mate?'

'Yes, I'll call him and see what he says.'

'I'll aim for him to be collected before eleven, before you get underway for the Roberto exchange, okay?'

'Yes, I'll keep things under control down here.'

CHAPTER NINETEEN

When Geoffrey called Rusty back later for an update about the midnight exchange, he said he'd spoken to Sergei. 'Looks like we're getting into bed with the cops.'

'What?'

'They are friends of Sergei's, on his payroll. They are all detectives and will back us up if Roberto becomes a cunt. I have done a deal with Sergei for the cops to guard us for the Roberto exchange tonight. In fact, they're already onto it.'

Geoffrey looked out at the two black Fords.

'I know it sounds insane, working with the cops. But tonight's exchange is big, fucking big, and we don't want more blood on our hands in losing any of our boys there in Sydney. By the way, Rusty, you should double up on security at the Nail.'

'I already have, and Ann and I have moved into the apartment at the Nail.'

'I'm cabbing it over to the Ox pub to meet Sergei for a quick meeting, devise a last-minute plan.'

At nine o'clock, Geoffrey rang for a cab. He hoped Sergei was being straight with them. If he was going to double-cross them, they'd most certainly all be killed at Roberto's midnight exchange. This was going down to the nitty-gritty for him. There was no way he'd risk his life and the lives of his four remaining young mercenaries for money. He felt certain Rusty wanted them to survive, not die for his cause.

Geoffrey's taxi dropped him off at the Ox on the Rocks ten minutes early. He walked on past the pub till he was under the Harbour Bridge. This bridge never ceased to amaze him—so many pieces of steel to form such a magnificent structure. Centring himself, he took a couple of deep breaths then found his way back to the meeting. Same greeting, same minder, before he was taken through the bar and out the back to Sergei's beautifully furnished office.

'Welcome, Geoffrey. Interesting times.'

'Yes, Sergei. Fucking interesting times. Thanks for agreeing to help us tonight.'

There were two other men in the room, introduced only as Todd and Jim. He suspected they were Sergei's 'friendly cops'. Geoffrey and Sergei went over the night's exchange, and how Geoffrey intended to handle matters if Roberto turned bad on them. He explained that he'd already lost one of his men in a gun battle up at Brunswick Heads.

'Yes,' Todd said. 'Quite a show, apparently. I heard the gunmen defending themselves threw a grenade and blew the fuck out of Big Mack's men.'

He went on to say that he had a mate that went to the scene. He didn't give up his mate's name, but smiled when

Geoffrey said, 'Tunner?' The fact that Tunner knew these cops gave Geoffrey a lot of confidence to speak more freely.

Sergei spoke up. 'Rusty is the sort of person I want to do business with. I'm a man of my word and Rusty's character is hard to find in this business.'

Geoffrey was reassured by Sergei's words. Could it be that with his help and connections, they might come through this night alive?

'Okay, tell me and Todd more about the plan,' said Jim. 'What time is the deal going to happen?'

Geoffrey replied, 'Midnight, at the art gallery carpark. I'll have my men up in those trees, ready to shoot whoever is doing the handover for Roberto.'

Jim went on. 'We've received intelligence to say that Roberto's going to be doing the handover and that he's intending to kill you and your men. So, the plan is for the snipers to kill Roberto and his men on your signal.'

Geoffrey nodded.

'At exactly three minutes past twelve, I'll do a slow drive by and so will two other unmarked patrol cars. This activity will either spook them or convince them to hand over the cash. How much money is involved?'

'Two point seven five mill,' replied Geoffrey.

'Fuck,' said one of the cops. 'If they decide to go on with the exchange, make sure you do the usual sample test. This will give them confidence that the deal is on. Then you step back out of the line of fire. What are your men armed with?'

'M4-A1 sniper rifles and silencers.'

'Perfect. I've organised two of my cop mates to drive your vans up to the art gallery. They'll stay behind the wheel as back up just in case.'

'Fuck,' Geoffrey said. 'Should I be armed?'

'Fuck, yes,' was the answer. 'You and your offsider double up. This whole operation will be all over in about four minutes. Once they're all dead, you and your mate grab the cash.'

'Got it.'

Sergei added, 'Roberto wasn't backward in coming forward in demanding fifteen percent off.'

'No, he wasn't, and he is dealing with Big Mack. I hate that fucking cunt. He's next on the list.'

'What is going to happen to the coke?' Geoffrey asked.

Sergei took a deep breath. 'We'll look after that. I've been in touch with Rusty, and we've struck a deal. You grab Rusty's money and drag it to the closest van and my drivers will take you down to the Astor Motel in Plunkett Street.'

He paused, handing over a motel room key before continuing.

'You and your mate get the bags of money up into the room and keep your heads low. There is plenty of food and two beds. If you need anything out of the ordinary, there is a Chinese gardener called Ricky on my team. He looks after the ornamental garden, the motel's feature attraction. Stay there until I make contact. There are phones in the room, and when I call you, we only talk generally, nothing specific, okay?'

'What about my snipers?' Geoffrey asked.

'Get them to wear some casual clothes under their work gear. Make sure that one of them has a small shovel to dig a hole to bury their guns and clothing. They know how to disappear, I'm sure?'

'Yes,' Geoffrey replied. 'Do they go back to the apartments?'

'Yes, tell them to break up into singles. I'll organise some security to make sure they are safe. What I suggest is that they disappear one at a time. Don't go back to Tweed Heads; just disband and disappear. Any further questions?'

'No,' Geoffrey replied.

'Oh,' Sergei said, 'no more contact with anyone. We all have our plans, so let's just do this.'

The meeting over, Geoffrey almost ran back to the apartments to give his lads the heads-up. They were still guarding the coke in the two vans parked under the apartments, rotating their guard. They seemed okay and Nick had settled down a bit since the shootout. Leaving Peter to guard the vans, Geoffrey gathered the rest in the lounge room of the apartment and went through every detail of the operation. The briefing went well, just a few logistical questions. By the end of the meeting, each man knew exactly what his part in the heist was.

They changed into their work clothes and checked their equipment. They had been into battle many times and knew that tonight would be a life-and-death situation. Having the support of the cops was comforting, but it was still going to be full-on.

Geoffrey, on the other hand, was feeling confident. Having Tunner Meskell on board was a big surprise. It was another testament to Rusty and the respect he had earned by being firm but fair in all his business dealings. He always left something on the table for the next person he did business with. He never skinned a deal so close that the person doing the deal wasn't going to make money, and that was why he was never short of support in the Tweed Heads area, and it seemed Jacob would continue with the same principles—always look after the little fellows; it keeps them loyal.

Geoffrey was pumped. Roberto had gotten in bed with the wrong people, and Big Mack was bad news. He was the opposite of Rusty, a greedy fat bastard. After tonight, Geoffrey would have only one more mountain to climb, and that was his personal goal of owning Big Mack's trucking business. Issey was also on his mind. Having no contact when they were apart was a bit tough, but they were just business partners at this stage.

Eleven pm and a knock on the door startled Geoffrey, but it was Nick letting him know that Stevo's body had been picked up and the two undercover cop van drivers had arrived. Geoffrey picked up his kitbag, tucked his two pistols into the back of his belt, and zipped up his flak jacket. He had a second thought as he went for the door, and turning around he went back to the third bedroom, picking up two grenades and tucking them into his inside pockets. Just in case. He didn't say anything to Nick.

Downstairs, the two drivers had already taken their seats behind the wheel. Nothing was said; they all knew their jobs. Geoffrey sat in the passenger seat of one of the vans, and the lads scrambled aboard the two vehicles. They were dressed to kill, right down to camouflage and black beanies.

The vans travelled together up Bourke Street, right into Crown, then up past St Mary's Cathedral. Geoffrey said a quiet Hail Mary and thought of Father O'Reilly. Then he focused. The vans pulled up about half a kilometre short of the art gallery so the lads could scale the fence and make their way through the gardens, setting up in position among the trees. They waited in the vans until the three of them were safely over the fence then checked their watches: 11:35 pm. Geoffrey aimed to get the vans into position at five minutes to midnight, ready for the exchange.

When they arrived, the carpark was empty. Geoffrey's heart was beating so hard that he could hear it thumping. No one said a word. Then a black F250 twin cab cruised slowly into the parking lot, flicked its headlights, and parked on the Opera House side of the two vans.

Geoffrey got out and walked over to it as Roberto climbed down. 'Hello, Geoffrey.'

'Oh, Roberto, I thought you weren't coming tonight.'

As three dark Commodore sedans filed slowly past the back of the parked vehicles and came to a stop, Roberto went to get back into his vehicle. 'It's all good, mate,' Geoffrey said. 'They're just gonna make sure everyone keeps their side of the bargain.'

'Geoffrey, I underestimated you.'

'It's just a precaution, Roberto.'

Geoffrey walked forward with three bags of coke. 'I have the test samples for you to inspect.'

'Have you got the money?'

'Yes, I have.' Roberto's bodyguard came forward. He was a giant of a man. He tasted the coke with a wet finger and gave Roberto the okay.

'Where's Rusty's money?' Geoffrey asked.

'It's in the back.' He nodded to the giant who reached into the vehicle and pulled out two large carry bags, dropping them on the bitumen. Geoffrey kneeled down, unzipped one bag, and pulled out a bundle of cash. As he stood up and stepped back from the cash bags, he pretended to scratch the back of his head, then raised both hands above his head. In a heartbeat, there was a volley of bullets and Roberto and his three heavies were dead on the ground. Roberto's driver attempted to start his vehicle but to no avail as Nick was already at the driver's side window. Two muffled shots ended the driver's escape. The three cop cars quietly made their way from the scene.

Nick dragged the cash bags across to one of the vans. There was no sign of his three snipers, who made them-selves scarce as per the plan. Heaving the heavy bags into the back, Geoffrey slammed the van door and hoisted himself into the passenger seat. His driver calmly started the van and moved off as if he was going home from work. Nothing was said. Geoffrey checked his watch: quarter to one. All over in three-quarters of an hour.

As the van pulled up outside the Astor, Geoffrey opened the sliding door and grabbed the money bags. In a quiet, determined voice, the driver said, 'Don't forget to leave us a bundle.' Geoffrey didn't flinch. He unzipped the bag and pulled out a bundle. 'Here, catch.' He threw a large wad of notes to the driver. He had no idea how much cash was in a bundle, maybe twenty or thirty grand? It was worth it.

He used the room key to open the front entry door of the motel. No signs of life. Mimicking late-arriving tourists, they carried their 'luggage' up to room thirty-seven. As he and Nick closed the door, they were deathly quiet, like they were expecting someone to come blasting their way into the room. Geoffrey checked the two bags of cash. It all looked okay, so they slid the bags under their beds and chaired the room door, just in case. The bar fridge was full, so Geoffrey pulled out a tall bottle of Toohey's beer and poured two glasses. It was too early to celebrate their victory. Never crow early. They just sat and recovered some composure.

CHAPTER TWENTY

Sergei

Nick and Geoffrey had been cooped up for two days when finally, the room phone rang. Geoffrey answered it. 'Is that you, mate? Yes, Sergei, we're all good. A meeting? What about?' Geoffrey was thinking the worst.

'Oh, there's no problem. I know how keen you and Rusty are to finish off what you came to Sydney for.'

Geoffrey gave a nod to Nick to give him some privacy.

'Yes, I know what, I mean who, you're talking about.'

'Geoffrey, I want you to know I'm as keen as ever to continue with removing him from my competitors' list. So how about a dinner tomorrow night at the Ox?'

Geoffrey explained he was booked up Wednesday but could make lunch or dinner Thursday.

'Okay. Let's do a nice steak for lunch at the Ox on Thursday.'

'Sounds good. Were there any problems after the hit on Sunday night?'

'Well, Geoffrey, of course there was the usual jumping up and down from all the supposed do-gooders, but with my extensive contacts, everything is starting to settle. Let's talk about that on Thursday. By the way, I hear you're keen to take over Mack's trucking empire.'

Geoffrey was a bit taken aback by this.

'Look, Rusty's shared with me. You know, mate,' Sergei went on, 'I'm a hundred per cent behind you with your plan to take the business. Having a legitimate interstate, or even an international freight business, would open up all sorts of business opportunities for Rusty.'

Geoffrey was relieved. 'Okay, lunch, Thursday.'

'Oh,' Sergei finished his call with a tongue-in-cheek comment, 'now that you're cashed up, it's your shout for lunch!'

Geoffrey laughed for the first time in a week and hung up with a more relaxed feeling.

He grabbed a glass of water from the kitchen, checked Nick was okay, then returned to the bedroom. Now that he had the all-clear from Sergei, Geoffrey called Rusty. 'The oysters are exquisitely plump.' An instant laugh came back to him.

'Well done, mate, well done.'

'Yes, mate, it was fucking nerve-racking, but the lads and our new best friend Sergei were certainly a handy combination.'

'Yes, I heard. Just had a quick chat with Sergei. We don't have to get into the nitty-gritty on the phone. I'm flying to Sydney for a threesome lunch with you and Sergei on Thursday at the Ox.'

Geoffrey was excited about that news. Rusty heading for Sydney would take some pressure off him. When

Geoffrey asked Rusty if he'd thought any more about getting the golden eggs back to the Tweed, Rusty said, 'What are our lads doing?'

'Just lying low. We'll be catching up at the Woolloomooloo pub on Friday night to go through things—not a formal meeting. Just to play some pool, have a few beers and catch up.'

'Okay, perfect,' said Rusty. 'I'll be there as well. I want to thank all of them personally and make arrangements for some cash bonuses as promised. We'll do some more planning for those golden eggs then.'

'Okay. I can't wait to see them disappear out of my life.'

'I understand, mate, and I'm forever grateful.'

'That's okay, Rusty. I'm here for the long haul, and I'm looking forward to the next phase of my life in the transport business.'

'You've earned it.'

'Oh, by the way Rusty, I'm going to move my personal address to another apartment in Balmain that I'm looking at this morning. It is still close enough to be in contact with the goings-on in the Cross, but I need some space.'

'Good plan. It'll be good to see you settled.'

'I'll book into a hotel in the city for now, and we can spend whatever time is necessary to plan our next moves. I'm keen to get back to our old way of doing business.'

'Yes, mate, bring it on.'

'By the way, Geoffrey, where are the golden eggs?'

Geoffrey chuckled. 'I'm sitting on them, trying to keep them warm.'

'Well done again, mate. See you at lunch.'

'Yeah, looking forward to it.'

When he finished the call, he found Nick gobbling down both their room service breakfasts. Geoffrey shook his head. *I'd rather keep Nick for a week than a fortnight!* The morning winter sun was streaming through a small, east-facing window in the small living area of their hideout at the motel. Geoffrey had the same view from the shower window, and he could see that several naval ships were in port. He was still trying to come to grips with the remarkable impact that he and Rusty had made on this tangled-up part of Australia in such a short time. Then it hit him—it was Wednesday morning; he'd see Issey tonight. He felt a burst of enthusiasm for his day.

Geoffrey was meeting a real estate agent at 10:30 to look at an apartment in Balmain; hopefully, it would suit him. As his taxi cruised through Balmain, he mused that it was a beautiful part of Sydney, with a good neighbourly feel. When he arrived at the building, he was struck by the beauty of the front entry door, which was beautifully polished and set off with opaque glass blocks. The real estate agent greeted Geoffrey and introduced himself as Ross. From the moment he walked through the front entry, Geoffrey felt comfortable. It made him feel like he had arrived home. The entrance floor had highly polished parquet timber tiles, and the rest of the apartment followed the same theme. The kitchen and bathroom had Carrara marble bench tops that were showing their age but looked and felt beautiful after years of loving care. There were only two bedrooms, but a reasonable-sized study was attached to the main bedroom and ensuite. The light fittings were all art déco and set the architectural tone of the space. He was bursting with excitement and asked how much a month.

Ross responded, 'Two thousand, four hundred, plus water, power and gas.'

Geoffrey was comfortable with that amount. Then he asked who owned the apartment and Ross explained that an old, retired architect had lived there for many years. He had gone into care, unfortunately, when he developed dementia. He assured Geoffrey that the family would not sell it until the owner passed.

'If I paid three monthly in advance, can I get a year plus a year lease?'

Ross nodded and explained that he was close to a family member who he'd call today. Geoffrey offered to wait outside and a couple of minutes later, Ross came out and, putting out his hand, said, 'Welcome home.'

Geoffrey had not heard those words for many years. The torrid breakup between him and the love of his life a few years ago had not left him until now. He felt a new beginning was unfolding—Issey, the transport business, and now his new home in Thomas Street, Balmain. He imagined that Issey would also like it, then mentally chastised himself. *Stupid dickhead, stop that shit. You've only just met her; don't fuck it up by trying to push her into a way of life that may not suit her.*

Nick made his way back to the motel. He told Nick about Rusty's proposed visit and the promise of a cash bonus. There was a lot of incentive for Nick to continue with his loyalty, not that Geoffrey ever doubted his character. Nick had agreed to join him in his quest to take over Mack's transport company. He was a good man to have around and didn't take no for an answer.

On Thursday, Geoffrey was spot on with timing the meeting with Sergei and Rusty. He walked straight over to Rusty, who stood up to hug Geoffrey. 'Good to see you, mate.'

'You too, Rusty.'

Sergei didn't get involved in any man hugging, although Geoffrey saw that a half-smile quickly crossed his face. *There must be some humanity behind Sergei's web of steel.*

Rusty had arrived early to chat to Sergei about the deal they were striking for future business coming out of the Tweed. It seemed all was going well with their agreement.

Sergei spoke to Geoffrey and Rusty. 'I understand that you don't want to kill Big Mack because you want to negotiate the sale of his business to you.'

'Well, that was the plan. But what if the deal can be done in a different way?'

Sergei said he was aware that Big Mack employed off-duty police officers to deliver newly built trucks all over Australia. He went on to explain that the cops were paid well for their services and were an essential element in Mack's operation because their involvement gave additional security to Big Mack and a guarantee that each truck would arrive on time and in pristine condition.

So, Sergei felt that before any move was made on Mack, a deal should be struck with the guy who coordinated the drivers to support a successful takeover.

'Fuck,' Geoffrey said, 'I didn't see that one coming.' The last thing they wanted was to upset their police buddies.

Sergei suggested they sit on their hands, let the dust settle. While Rusty and Geoffrey got their booty back out of Sydney to Tweed Heads, Sergei would speak to the copper in charge of the truck delivery business to get his view about a takeover of Mack's business.

Geoffrey was shifting uncomfortably in his seat. He wondered if Rusty and Sergei were positioning themselves as board members; not quite what he had in mind for shifting away from drug running. Geoffrey cleared his throat and was about to speak up, but Rusty had picked up on his unease.

'Sergei and I are in no way interested in being a part of the transport business. We're just offering support, whether it's financial support or business advice. It will be enough that we have access to reliable freight.'

Sergei added, 'My network is not just coke; I'm looking to move cars and all kinds of other bits and pieces. You will have lots of added business, with reliable compensation.'

That made sense to Geoffrey, who nodded, relaxing back into his chair. They were given the nod that lunch was about to hit the table. No business chatter at lunch, just family, and of course the rugby league, with some banter about who was going to win this year's premiership.

Geoffrey was only half-tuned in to their conversation, reflecting on his sleepover with Issey last night. He had never felt this deeply about another human being. He could still smell her beautiful fresh woman fragrance on him. She'd told him the name of her perfume, but he couldn't remember it. Little did he know that her perfume would be forever in his life.

He became aware of a lull in the conversation. The two men were looking at him.

'Welcome back, mate.'

'Thanks, Rusty.'

'She must be special.'

'She is. Early days, early days.'

'So, Geoffrey, are we okay to freight the golden eggs back to Tweed on Saturday night?'

'Yes, we can rally the lads at our meeting at the pub tomorrow night.'

'Of course. We'll go through the details tonight at your motel room if it suits.'

'Yes, we can get in pizza. Nick will be glad to get a break from the boredom of his room.'

'About six then?'

'Yep, at the Astor.'

'Rusty, you and Sergei enjoy the rest of your lunch. I'm going to go and get my new house keys and take my clothes over to the apartment to start setting up. If we're going to the Tweed on Saturday night, we'll need the vans back. Sergei, do you know where they're stored?'

'Yes, they're in a safe place, Geoffrey. Let me know where and when you want them, and I'll get the boys to bring them around.'

'Let's say outside the Astor at six on Saturday.'

'Okay, Rusty?'

'Yes mate, all good. We'll all travel up in convoy.'

'Okay, yes, good plan. See you at the Astor this arvo. We're on golden egg duty.'

'Will Nick be around tonight?'

'Yes, he'll be in room thirty-eight next door, just in case.'

'Great,' Rusty said.

'We're armed to the teeth, so all should be okay.' Geoffrey bid them farewell with a handshake and excused himself.

'Oh Geoffrey, do you need a hand with your gear? My driver's not busy and can give you a hand if you like.'

'Thanks for the offer, Sergei, but I have a few other things to take care of.'

'Okay.'

As Geoffrey walked out of the meeting, he felt relieved that he didn't take Sergei up with his offer to help him move. His privacy in Balmain was vital if he was going to have a fresh start. He had put the apartment in a false name, another precaution. If the shit hit the fan, he could just walk away. The other good thing about a first-floor apartment is that you can always jump if you had to. He planned to find a way to have a quiet life and keep a low profile, just as Sergei did. He was not a social go-getter; he understood the game: if you keep your head down, you have a better chance of keeping it on your shoulders.

CHAPTER TWENTY-ONE

Ricky

Nick and Geoffrey were chatting about getting to Tweed with over three million dollars, including the money that Rusty had collected from the additional sale of the last half-ton shipment to Sergei that arrived while they were in Sydney.

They pulled the bags of cash out from under the bed and started counting, placing the counted bundles into hundred-thousand piles. They had $3,656,000. They'd underestimated the value of Sergei's coke. He must have paid full price for his half-ton. The demand here in Sydney must be huge for Sergei to take on that late half-ton. Anyway, Geoffrey still had to account for the bundle that he threw at the van driver last Sunday night. It seemed like a lifetime ago.

Suddenly, there was a knock at the door.

Geoffrey called out, 'Who's there?' as he stepped to the side of the entry door.

Geoffrey threw a blanket over the money while Nick positioned himself for a forceful entry.

'The oysters are plump.'

'It's okay; it's Rusty.' Geoffrey let go a sigh of relief, and Nick uncocked his weapon.

'Hello, boys.' Rusty put his suitcase on the luggage rack and asked if they had a cold beer. He had cancelled his reservation at a posh hotel in the city to join Nick and Geoffrey at the Astor—added security for the money. Nick jumped up and returned with three cold beers. They toasted their mission. 'Success!' The glasses clinked agreement. With a flourish, Geoffrey grabbed the end of the blanket and, like a magician performing a clever trick, off came the blanket.

'FUCK!' was the reaction from Rusty. 'How much is there?' he asked enthusiastically.

'Just over three point six,' Geoffrey said.

'My calculations were $3,686,000,' Rusty said. 'Why is it short?

'You're right, but we hadn't allowed for paying the driver and his mate.'

'How much was it?'

'Well, I just reached in and grabbed a bundle. Must have been thirty grand.'

'Fuck, thirty grand? But without them, we'd have been fucked.'

'Yep.'

'Got any more beer?'

'Of course.'

Geoffrey turned to Nick. 'We'll be right here now. How about you go and get yourself set up in the room next door?'

'Okay, got it, boss.'

'Don't call me boss in front of our real boss!'

'Okay, sorry, Rusty.'

'That's okay, Nick. Keep your eyes and ears open.'

'Okay, got it.'

After Nick had gone, Geoffrey jokingly said, 'Well mate, you've made your bed; now you'll just have to lie in it.'

'Fuck, mate. If you think I'm going to sleep on top of that pile, you better think again!' Loud laughs from both of them.

They counted the eggs once more. Spot on, less the thirty grand.

'All good, mate. Let's pack it properly, so we're ready to go on Saturday.'

'Only one problem, mate.'

'What is that, Geoffrey?'

'Well, now that I've officially handed over the money, you have to put it under your bed, not mine.' Again, a couple of chuckles.

They struggled to get the money back into the bags, then stood back.

Rusty shrugged. 'You know, mate, those bags could be full of anything, really.'

'You're right. Just like trucks, nobody really knows what's in 'em.

'I always told you that life around me would never be dull.'

'You did, mate, and so far, you have not let me down, Rusty.'

'Let's eat in, shall we?' Another giggle.

Geoffrey got room service going with some Italian seafood ravioli and a good bottle of red. After a great feed, Rusty fell asleep with a fortune under his bed. Geoffrey rolled his eyes at the snoring. He'd have to just put up with it. He propped himself up in his bed, his weapon pointed at the door. He could hear Nick's television through the paper-thin walls. Given the motel was part brothel, he reckoned some mum and dad travellers would walk away from the Astor with a whole new outlook on life.

The night was uneventful except for Rusty's din. When Rusty woke, he got up, went for a pee, came back. 'Morning, mate, sleep well, did you?'

'Oh, like a log.'

'Liar!'

'What do you mean?'

'Well, I have been told by several mates, while we were on camping trips or on an overnighter on one of the trawlers, that I snore like a wounded beast.'

'Yes, mate. That's a good description, a wounded beast.'

'I'm sorry. Let me pay for breakfast to make it up to you.' He turned on the television.

'Well thanks for your generosity, but breaky comes with the room.'

'At least you'll have some cash to tip Ricky the Chinese meal deliverer. He refuses to leave the room without a twenty for his efforts.'

'Twenty dollars for carrying a breakfast tray up one flight of stairs?'

'Yep.'

'I'll offer him ten.'

'Good luck with that, mate. Ricky is *the* man around here. He has all the bases covered, can get you anything from a prostitute to a joint.'

There was a knock on the door. 'Breakfast!' Geoffrey recognised the Chinese accent but kept his weapon trained on the door from under his blanket while Rusty cleared a spot at the end of the table. 'Thank you, Ricky.'

Ricky immediately spun around, put out his hand, and just stood there. Geoffrey tried to look intrigued with the morning TV show and Rusty did everything he could to avoid eye contact with Ricky, but it was impossible to shake him. After he had waited for several minutes with his hand out, Ricky pegged the door back, went outside, returned with a vacuum cleaner, plugged it in and proceeded to vacuum the floor.

'Fuck,' said Rusty. 'Who is this bloke?'

'I did warn you.'

Rusty went to his wallet, and reluctantly handed a twenty over.

'Oh, thank you, kind sir.' And on that note, Ricky and his vacuum cleaner left the room.

They both pissed themselves laughing. Geoffrey suspected he'd hear this story about Ricky many times over a few drinks for years to come. But for now, it was down to business and the planning of getting three point six odd million dollars out of this place.

The breakfasts were great, another good reason that Ricky was worth looking after. 'I'm sure, mate, that if you hadn't paid that twenty just then, the quality of the breakfasts would deteriorate at an alarming rate until the tipping improved.'

'Fuck him; he's red hot! He must be making more money than the poor bastard that owns the place. I mean that, with all the other bits and pieces he supplies. You're right; Ricky *is* the man.' Rusty nearly fell off his chair laughing. 'Now, mate, let's get a plan together for Saturday night.'

'So, here's my plan,' Geoffrey said. 'We travel about two kilometres apart, with a money bag in each van. We split the security, three men in each van, heavily armed.

'You've got some grenades? They're a great deterrent once a couple go off in the general direction of any opposition. That's been proven at Brunswick Heads.'

'Yes, mate. I was stunned to hear you used grenades in the ambush.'

'Well, they started it, and once Nick had spotted Stevo's body, there were no rules. The gunman I shot was so startled by the blast he forgot what he was doing and stepped away from the tree he was hiding behind. Bad mistake as I took him out before he could collect his bearings.'

'Fuck them and fuck their employer!'

'Just thinking, Rusty, I wonder how much it would cost to hire two of Sergei's cop mates. Maybe even the two that they used on Sunday night?'

'Not the two that asked for thirty grand!'

'Yes, mate. Thirty grand split between them was a fair price when you consider the risk they took. They would have also paid something to the other cops that turned up to give us some threatening support against Roberto.'

'I suppose you're right.'

Geoffrey said, 'I wonder how Roberto is going in his new place of abode?'

'He's probably still trying to convince Saint Peter to let him through the pearly gates but having a lot of trouble convincing Saint Peter that it wasn't his fault. Some of those Colombians have a bad reputation in that neck of the woods.'

'Fuck, it's good to have you around, Rusty. We're getting our sense of humour back.'

'Won't be for long, mate. We still have to pull off the trip back to Tweed. As for your suggestion, I think the best plan would be not to travel up the Pacific highway. Maybe we switch our travel route and go the inland road.'

'Now that is a fucking good idea.'

'That'll fox anyone that knows we 're carrying this huge stash.'

'Yes. The trip'll take an hour or so longer, but it'll hopefully be worth it.'

'Ah, Friday. What have you got planned, Rusty?'

'Nothing, mate. I'm going to stay here and make some calls back home and keep in touch. I'll call Ann and Jacob to let them know I'm okay.'

'Looks like Jacob has become an impressive individual, stepping up to the plate and just quietly delivering on all fronts.'

'Yes, mate, I'm very proud of his efforts. Did you know he's taken over the responsibilities of the Rusty Nail?'

'Yes, I'd heard.'

'Yeah, he's currently working with an architect to build another level on top of the Nail.'

'Fuck, what is the new level for?'

'Well, he and Sandy Shores have been negotiating with the managers of some international acts.'

'Like who?'

'Well, like Frank Sinatra, Bob Hope, Pat Boone.'

'Fuck,' Geoffrey replied. 'Why would Frank Sinatra come to Australia? '

'Well, he's being paid a huge amount of money to come and do a concert at World Expo 88 in Brisbane and they've also booked him to appear on the Gold Coast at a new place he's launching on the night—Sanctuary Cove.'

'Really?'

'Yeah. This new place has the backing of Premier Joe and another heavyweight, Big Russ Hinze. Apparently, it's a huge development of saltwater canals where hundreds of waterfront houses are going to be built for the rich and famous.'

'Rusty, how do you know all this?'

'Well, our old good mate—'

'Don't tell me, let me guess, Hecky Parker?'

'Yes, Hecky. He's in the know because he does business with both of them.'

'Ah, good ol' Hecky. How is he?'

'He's good. Still operating out of his office in Holland Park.'

'And Rhonda, how is she?'

'Not well, unfortunately. Serious health issues, apparently. D'you know, Hecky never forgave himself for his stupid, selfish act with that piece of caravan park trash, Leonie. Did you ever meet her when you were on your mission to take over cricket wicket preparation at the Gabba?'

'No, I didn't. You know, Rusty, when I started there, I thought it was going to be a bit of a bore. But it was the opposite. I had a great time. For me to become a world authority on cricket pitches was unbelievable.'

'Yes, mate, they were good times.'

'Is Nick going to stay in here so we can get some sun on our faces?'

'Yes, he is taking over at nine.'

'Well, I'm going to have a shower and make some calls.'

'I'll go and do a little shopping for Ann's birthday on Sunday. I'll be back before lunch.'

'I'm looking forward to her party at home.'

'Only one more sleep, mate, and we are on our way back to paradise.'

'Yes, Saturday night can't come quick enough, Rusty.'

'Any plans for this afternoon, mate?'

'Uh, yup.'

'What are you up to?'

'Well, I thought I might just stay in this fucking room, lie in this fucking bed and think of a plan of how the fuck I'm going to get out of paying that fucking little Chinaman twenty dollars for breakfast in the morning!'

Well, that was it. They were both out of control, laughing their heads off.

Geoffrey called out from the shower, 'Hey Rusty, you haven't heard Ricky the Chinaman's surname.'

'What is it?'

Geoffrey called out in a Chinese sort of broken English, 'Won Hong Lo.' Geoffrey could hear Rusty trying to say it. 'Won Hong Lo.' After about Rusty's fifth attempt, he finally got it: 'One-hung-low! Hilarious mate, very funny. Does he know his nickname?'

'Why don't you try it out on him in the morning and find out? Make sure that we have our breakfasts before you try it.'

Rusty replied, 'I'll have to think about that. He's probably got some sneaky trick up his sleeve for smart arses like us.'

'Hmm. Don't poke the bear.'

CHAPTER TWENTY-TWO

Rusty greeted Nick's knock on the door and his password. 'Good morning, Nick. Did you get a good night's sleep?'

'Good night's sleep?' he whinged. 'There was some deep, heavy snoring going on through my wall all fucking night. Was that Geoffrey?'

'No, mate, it was me. Geoffrey has already told me that I sound like a wounded animal.'

'Fuck mate, there wasn't just one wounded animal; there was a whole fucking herd of them!'

Rusty started his laughing fit again.

Geoffrey was still in the bathroom and could hear the two of them bantering with each other. It was great to see Rusty in this environment, enjoying himself. Before all of this carnage and big money began, Nick and Rusty had just been a couple of young surfers hanging around the Coolangatta area, drinking, smoking dope, surfing, and having a great time at parties. Neither of them had any money. They drank cheap bottles of Stones' green ginger wine and were the life of the party, cracking jokes, and telling lies to young tourist girls to get into their pants. Life was just one big party until Rusty's uncle died and left him the mullet netting business where they'd both had casual jobs. Gradually things changed as Rusty got a taste for money. He slowly bought and sold various fishing-related businesses in the Tweed area until his big move in the purchase of the old rundown pile of rusty roof sheeting and weather-beaten building materials. That's when the Rusty Nail was born. They still loved the sting of saltwater on their skin but right now that all seemed far behind them.

Geoffrey's humble background in Nimbin also seemed far away. He resolved to make an effort to remember those days and be a little more light-hearted in the day-to-day ups and downs of his life. For the moment anyway. He caught a taxi over to Thomas Street and made a mental to-do list for his new home. Geoffrey hoped that when life caught up with Horace Martin, the elderly owner of the apartment, he'd be able to afford to purchase the property. Horace was now living in a nursing home, and it was just down to timing.

When he'd inspected the apartment, the agent had told him that the other apartments in the building were owner-occupied by people of the same vintage as the old architect. So he hoped the building was always going to be very quiet and private. He didn't want to feel like he was under surveillance. He entered the foyer with its lemony timber polish smell and his shoulders instantly relaxed. The apartment was still furnished with Horace's belongings. When Geoffrey quizzed the agent about it, he said the family wanted the furniture to stay at home where it belonged. Their father had selected the furniture piece by piece, and any moves to take them anywhere else were unthinkable. Geoffrey started to understand it after he took the time to sit in the old fellow's chair and take his efforts on board: the leadlight windows complemented the ornate plaster cornices; the art déco paint colours and matching light fittings all began to make sense. *Yes*, he said to himself, *I'll take great care of this property.*

He was so comfortable in the armchair that he fell asleep. The week had caught up with him, and with Rusty and Nick back at the motel, he could relax and take his foot off the accelerator for a couple of hours.

It was two pm by the time Geoffrey had another shower and was freshly dressed for the night out at the Woolloomooloo pub with the lads. He hoped it would be a fun night.

He planned to sleep at the motel again that night, providing Rusty and Nick with additional firepower if required. He packed a small travel bag for his road trip to Tweed Heads. Only one more sleep until they were on their way up north.

He and Rusty still had to decide the fate of Big Mack. Whichever way it went for Mack, Geoffrey was going to need security backup to gain control of Mack's freight business. He didn't envisage just walking into Big Mack's office and saying to him, 'Hey dickhead, hand over the keys to your business, you cunt.' He knew it was going to be a lot more complex than that. He'd make an appointment with Sergei when he got back to get the ball rolling. He hoped

Sergei had talked with his friendly band of cops about the proposed takeover of Mack's business. His gut feeling about Sergei was still up in the air. He'd treat him with care and cross-check any decisions he made. *Early days, Sergei boy, early days* he whispered. One thing about Sergei, he now knew how much stamina, willpower and determination Rusty had, and some place at the back of his mind would be saying, *Don't fuck with Rusty*. Rusty was king, and Sergei was just a well-connected coke dealer in Sydney.

When he returned to the Astor, Nick was reading, and Rusty was on the telephone talking casually to Kev Skinner. He confirmed that they'd be arriving at the Nail around eight am. 'See you then.'

'How's Kev, mate?'

'He's good and healthy. He's like you, made of steel.'

'Fuck off, mate. I'm not made of steel. I'm made of kryptonite!'

'What's that?' Nick said.

'Mate, don't you watch the movies?'

'No, not really.'

'Well, it doesn't matter then. Let's get cracking.'

Nick jumped up and headed for his room to shower and freshen up. He would come back to stay in their room while Rusty and Geoffrey went to the pub with the lads. Then Rusty would take over the watch while Nick went and had dinner.

Rusty and Geoffrey were wearing jeans and surf shirts to blend into the local scene. On the walk to the pub to meet up with the lads, Rusty went over the plans with Geoffrey. 'Tell the lads that the only fuel and piss stop would be at Nambucca Heads. Better to be safe.'

Rusty and Geoffrey were the only ones that knew they were taking the inland route to the Tweed.

The pub was all happening. As Geoffrey stepped up to one of the side entrances, he bumped into someone's shoulder. When he turned around to excuse himself, he saw Won Hong Lo loaded up with bottles of wine and a couple of bottles of spirits. They locked eyes, but he didn't apologise. He was on a mission as he powered back towards his honey pot.

'Well fuck me, Geoffrey, did you see who that was?'

'Yeah. Doesn't he ever fucken sleep?'

'I don't know, mate, he certainly puts in some hours.'

'You didn't upset him, did you, mate?'

'No, I didn't get a chance. He was gone before I could react.'

'Good, that means we're going to get a good breakfast.'

'Oh, that's a relief.'

At the pub, Geoffrey could see the lads all sitting at a long table that was well-positioned to give them a good look at what was happening outside the pub. They seemed to be okay, but Geoffrey and Rusty were on high alert. Handshakes all around and soon they were engaged in small talk about girlfriends, football, and their lives in general. They all ordered steaks to keep it simple—medium-rare for everyone. While they were waiting for their meals, Rusty addressed them in a quiet tone, thanking them for their efforts so far. Then he moved on to the trip back to the Tweed the following night—two vans, three men and half of the cargo per van. They'd be leaving from outside the Astor at eight, when both vans would go around to the old apartment and pick up their weapons, including a box of grenades, just in case. As usual, they'd share the drive at three-hour intervals with each man.

'Okay, I have the bonuses that I promised you.'

Christiano quietly asked how much it was. When Rusty responded, 'Thirty each,' a smile came over their faces. That was a good sign. Thirty thousand was a lot of money; thirty thousand could buy a nice house in a good suburb.

Rusty explained that their money would be handed over to them at breakfast at the Rusty Nail on Sunday morning. Then he asked the table if there were any questions. Peter softly asked if they still had jobs after this delivery. Rusty was quick to say that if they wanted to come back to Sydney for another tour, they'd be welcome. If they decided tonight to continue as a group, he would arrange for stayers to have a seven-day holiday on him up at Surfers Paradise, all expenses paid. As Rusty finished his address, one by one around the table, 'I'm staying.' Five affirmations later, they had the firepower to start building a plan after their holiday. Geoffrey was relieved because now he knew that with the backup of the five lads, he'd have a great chance of pulling off his mission of attaining Big Mack's transport business.

The meals arrived and all the talking stopped. Rusty ate his steak as quickly as he could and then excused himself. 'I'm going to go back to relieve Nick from his watch back at the Astor. I'll explain the details of what I have just told you guys and give him the same opportunity. Good night, boys.'

All the lads stood as a group and raised their glasses to Rusty. Geoffrey thought, *Fuck, the man has some strength; he doesn't have to say much; he just commands respect with his no-frills, no false promises, no bullshit approach to life and business.*

'Good night, men.' On that, Rusty offered his outstretched fist, and they all touched knuckles.

Nick arrived at the pub soon after and Christiano bought him a welcome mate beer, and an hour or so later, one by one, they left the pub and disappeared into the cold Sydney winter's night.

CHAPTER TWENTY-THREE

Geoffrey decided to take a walk along the path up to the Boy Charlton Pool. He was dearly tempted to walk over to Issey's building at Rushcutters Bay. *Not yet*, he thought. What if she had another love life away from him? If she did, she was entitled to it. They were just in a business relationship.

But Issey had captured his heart. Never had he been so totally emotionally entranced by a female. Whether it was the way she spoke, the way she looked into his eyes when he was pushing himself into her wonderful body, or just lying in bed, not saying anything, they were connected.

Before he knew it, he found himself jogging up Potts Point Hill through the Cross and walking up to the keypad at the entrance to Issey's building. He pressed the apartment number and waited, not knowing what to expect. A 'go away, and I'll see you Wednesday', or 'sorry I'm busy'. That answer would be devastating. But he just did not care. Three rings later, her voice answered. 'Hello?'

'Issey?'

'Geoffrey, is that you?' He was trembling with emotion.

'Yes, it is, Issey.'

'Thank God,' she said. He didn't know what to say next. Then she asked if he would like to come up. He took a deep breath and replied that he was going away tomorrow and that he had some freight business to take care of tonight, so no. 'I just wanted you to know I miss you, and I—' Don't fucking say it, don't fucking say it! That *L* word kept tearing away at him.

'Geoffrey—'

'Yes?'

'I love you,' she whispered.

He went weak at the knees, then blurted, 'I love you too!'

They were still talking through a speaker phone. It would have been easy for him to say, 'Issey, press that button and let me in', but this was enough for now.

'Good night, darling,' he said.

'Good night.'

On his way back to the Astor, he didn't run or jog. He just reverberated with happiness. Now that he knew Issey was the real deal, he'd be able to relax and enjoy being in love. He knew he had to get himself as legitimate as possible as soon as possible, so he could offer Issey security and the commitment that is required in a loving relationship. His resolve to get hold of Mack's business would be an Issey-based priority, not that she would ever know the circumstances of how it all came together.

Back at the Astor, all was well. Rusty and Nick were watching the last of the Friday night football. As the whistle blasted for full time, Nick went off to clean his teeth. 'Fuck,' he said to Rusty. 'Paramatta are on the rise.'

'Yes, mate, I thought Souths were going to beat them before half time. I don't know what the Paramatta coach said to his team in the sheds, but it must have been good 'cause they all appeared to grow an extra pair of legs!'

'Well, that's footy.'

'That's right.'

Geoffrey wanted to try to get to sleep as soon as possible in an effort to get in front of the wounded animal struggling its way through the night. He also had a bit of a giggle with a vision of Rusty and Ricky One Hong Lo in his delivery of breakfast in the morning. A clash of the titans.

Unfortunately, it was another long, hard night, and Rusty was relentless with his snoring. Somehow, Geoffrey got through it and got off to sleep with loving thoughts of Issey.

Saturday morning.

'Fuck, ten to eight!' They had both slept in. Breakfast was due in ten minutes. They got out of bed and double-checked their treasure was still there. All was good. Rusty had a piss and got back into bed with his weapon under his blanket. Sure enough, on the dot of eight, breakfast. Geoffrey got out of bed and opened the door.

'Ahh, good morning, Ricky.'

'Good morning, kind sir.'

'Sleep well, did we?'

'Yes, we did, kind sir.'

'You had two visitors come to see you last night,' Ricky said.

'Two visitors?'

'Yes.'

'What time?'

'About two-thirty.'

By this time, he had their attention.

'What happened?' Geoffrey asked.

'These men looked very bad, very bad.'

'Yes, go on. What happened to them?'

'We had a big problem. Two police cars arrived and took the two bad men away.'

'Fuck, thanks Sergei,' Geoffrey whispered. They must have been under surveillance, and they didn't even know it.

'Well,' Rusty replied. 'This is certainly a surprising revelation to wake up to. Thank you, Ricky.'

'No problems. I watched them on camera until cops came and took them.'

They were now out of bed. Ricky was about to put his hand out for his usual twenty, but Rusty beat him to it and tipped him forty.

'Thank you, Ricky, for our stay this time. We thank you for your service.'

'No problems, kind sir. You will stay again?'

'Yes, Ricky. We will, soon.'

'Oh, very good, very good.'

Geoffrey closed and locked the room door. Both men had a 'what the fuck' and 'who the fuck' look on their faces.

'What are you thinking, mate?'

Rusty replied, 'It can only be Big Mack's men attempting to rob us, and Sergei's cop mates stopping them.'

'Fuck, and we were both asleep.'

'Yes, mate.'

CHAPTER TWENTY-FOUR

By now, Geoffrey started to then realise the value of Sergei and how powerful a figure he really was here in Sydney. Rusty was stone quiet, then he said, 'Mate, we have to get out of here, and we need to make it fast. We're not getting our vans back until tonight, so you go up to the Cross at nine and hire another vehicle. Bring it down here and we'll load our stuff into it and you and I are going to just drive as far away as possible from here as we can.'

'Okay. I'll get going now.'

Geoffrey called to Nick through the dividing wall to come into their room for an update. Then he was on the hop to the hire company to get a vehicle to bring back to the Astor. This time, his trip up to the Cross had a different urgency. This situation was fucking serious. If Big Mack decided to have a go in broad daylight, they would be caught with their pants down. It was five to nine, and Geoffrey hoped the hire car mob were punctual with their opening times.

Meantime, Nick and Rusty were packing up all of their gear, nerves buzzing. As soon as they had everything packed and ready to go, Nick left the room and went and stood at the window beside the lift, where he had a full view of Plunkett Street.

The hire car company was a couple of minutes late opening, but the vehicle hire only took fifteen minutes to finalise. By nine-thirty, Geoffrey was parked in the basement of the Astor beside the lift entrance doors. Nick had seen him enter the driveway, and the men were on their way in the lift to the carpark.

'Well done, mate,' Rusty called out. A few minutes later, they were out of the carpark and onto Plunkett Street, going to who-knows-where. Geoffrey drove and his passengers kept watch for any sign of trouble from behind. He noticed something alarming as they turned into Bourke Street—a black cop car with men in the front seat. They gave a wave as they passed, but the cops didn't follow them. They stuck to the speed limit until they got onto the Cahill Expressway, then thought they would drive over the Harbour Bridge to Manly to see if they were being followed, parking on the beachfront. Manly was very busy on Saturday mornings—bike riders, joggers, surfers—and they had no trouble blending into the usual crowd of Sydney-siders enjoying one of the best beachside suburbs in the world. Once they were confident they were not being followed, Rusty said that they'd stay there for the day, moving around a bit from carpark to carpark until the time came for them to return to the Astor to hook up with the lads. Then they could hopefully be on their way back to Tweed.

Then Rusty had a rethink and told Geoffrey to catch the ferry back to Woolloomooloo. 'Nick and I'll stay in Manly with the money while you get our original plan back on track. The vans are being dropped off by Sergei's men at six o'clock and I've told the lads to be ready. Drive both our vans back to us in Manly and we'll transfer the money across. We'll leave this hire car in Manly and head back to Tweed in convoy.'

The day at Manly went quickly and Rusty dropped Geoffrey off at the ferry terminal at four-fifteen, in plenty of time to catch the ferry back to Woolloomooloo.

It was a rough trip back to Circular Quay. The waves coming through the gap at Sydney Heads were huge, but the old Collaroy ferry handled the swell without any trouble. The trip took an hour and Geoffrey still had to walk up past the Opera House, around Farm Cove, and down past Garden Island to get to Woolloomooloo. While he felt safe with weapons tucked into the back of his trousers, he had second thoughts and caught a taxi. Better to be early. He could have a beer at the pub to pass some time and maybe catch some of the lads at the pub. The taxi only took ten minutes to get to the pub and he spotted the lads sitting at the same table as the night before.

At ten to six, one by one, the lads and Geoffrey left the pub. Better to have five targets than a group. They made their way up to the Astor in Plunkett Street, arriving bang on six o'clock and Geoffrey again noticed the black cop car on the Bourke Street corner. *This'll be interesting,* he thought. When the two vans pulled up in front of them, the cop drivers got out but said nothing. They left the motors of the vans running and walked towards their lift.

Geoffrey had told the lads they were off to Manly. He drove the lead van and Christiano was at the wheel of the second van behind. They would meet up with Nick and Rusty, split the money bags and the armoury, and abandon the hire car. It was about a forty-minute drive to Manly and as they double-parked beside the hire car, Nick got out and quickly greeted them. A couple of minutes later, they split up—three men per van. Rusty and Geoffrey would drive the vans out of Sydney as they were both savvy with Sydney traffic. The vans were full of fuel, so they headed off on their long trip back to Tweed Heads. Two lads were in the back seat of each van busily setting up their guns and ammo, ready for action. The New England Highway was a lot quieter than the Pacific Highway, so they were more vulnerable if attacked. The only positive was that they were travelling with the comfort of knowing that everything had been done to cover their tracks with their change of route back home to the Tweed. They planned to stop at Armidale, a medium-sized country town, for a fuel and piss stop.

They were travelling only half a kilometre apart because of the remoteness of the highway and had switched their two-way radio frequency to a different band, keeping the radio chat to a bare minimum. If they were going to be attacked, their radio would be a vital piece of equipment in defending themselves. They caught up at the pit stop in Armidale, going in to pay for the fuel one at a time to provide cover if required. Then they headed north, again with a small gap between the vans.

It was a pitch-black night, no moonlight. The entire group was still on high alert, keen as ever to get home in one piece. Rusty and his lads were in the lead van. Suddenly, there was a yell from Rusty over the two-way: 'Red alert, red alert, pull over.' Geoffrey looked at the car clock. Two-thirty-five. Who on earth would be on the road at this time of night except truckies and potential trouble?

'Geoff, we're under heavy fire! Looks like around half a dozen gunmen firing at us from behind two trucks parked at the rest area on the side of the road.'

'What do you want us to do, mate?'

Geoffrey was now about four hundred metres away and could now hear the noise from the offensive. "Are you intact, mate?'

'Yes, at this stage, but under heavy fire. Can your lads leave the van, go out wide, and smash them with grenades?'

'Copy that.'

'Mate, hurry. This is fucking full-on. Our van is undrivable.'

Geoffrey pulled over, his two lads stashing as many grenades as they could fit into their flak jackets.

'Okay,' Geoffrey said, 'Christiano, you take the left flank, and you, Nick, take the right.'

They nodded and knuckled up as a sign of let's-fuck-ing-do-this, and in a flash they were gone into the darkness. They planned to distract the attackers to give Rusty a chance to recover. He was clearly in grave danger. Geoffrey pulled out both his pistols and stayed with the money bag, opting not to move his van any closer to the action, just in case his lads were totally overrun. He didn't have to wait long before he saw the first grenade explode behind a parked truck. Rusty was right; the distraction got the attackers firing in Nick's direction. Then there was another blast, this time from Christiano; then Nick again. The battle had now gone to a whole new level. Geoffrey saw return gunfire … Rusty's lads. *Fuck, these lads are good.* Then two more grenade blasts.

Geoffrey got back on the radio. 'What's your status?'

'They're back into it, but I'm down a man.'

'Okay, I'm going to get involved. Look out for me, mate. I'll make my way up to your van.'

As he crept closer, Geoffrey noticed the attackers' firepower seemed to have diminished. As he got closer, he heard one of the trucks start its engine. Then another grenade blast. At this point, the truck cab lit up as it completely exploded, a cry coming from the other truck. The gunfire completely stopped. None of them knew what the casualty count would be. Geoffrey yelled, 'Okay, you pricks, put down your weapons, put your arms in the air, and walk towards us!' There were three of them left. 'Cover them, Nick,' Geoffrey yelled.

'Got 'em.'

'Okay. Sitrep?'

Rusty was the first to call out. 'Here, but I've been hit in the thigh.'

Then confirmation from Christiano and Billy. That could mean only one thing. Peter was in trouble. 'Keep those bastards covered, Nick.'

'I've got 'em, mate. One move from any of them, they all die.'

Geoffrey made his way over to Rusty, who was propped up against a tree. Billy was on the ground, blood streaming from his arm. Geoffrey ripped off his own belt to try to staunch the bleeding.

'How are you, mate?'

Rusty winced. 'I think my leg's in bad shape. But I'm more concerned about Billy here.'

Geoffrey tried to think about what to do next. He'd spotted a few onlookers turning their cars around on the highway from both directions. There was no chance of escaping unnoticed. For the first time in his life, he was at a loss about what to do next. He walked over to where Nick was still covering the three remaining truckies behind their trucks. He noticed Nick was shaking, a look of absolute fury on his face. Pete was on the ground near him, his body a hell of a mess. Glowering at the three men, Nick yelled, 'Mate, these blokes are our worst enemy.' He spun around and let go with a blast of his weapon. It was all over.

Geoffrey was in a daze. *Fuck!* 'Nick, go and get the other van. It's just down the road.'

They had to assist Rusty into the middle passenger seat of the van. His vehicle was simply undrivable. They pulled out the money bag Rusty had been carrying, stacked it into the back of the working van, and slid Peter's body between the two bags. Geoffrey sat against the passenger window, and the other lads squeezed into the back seat. Billy seemed okay, but very quiet. The van was overloaded, but they had to get as far away from the ambush spot as quickly as possible. Nick was behind the wheel and drove a few metres before stopping the van.

'What's up?' Geoffrey said.

'I'll be back.' Getting out of the van, Nick pulled out his last grenade and ran back to the disabled van, pulled the pin, and blew it to pieces. On his return, Geoffrey said, 'Good work, mate,' and they were off. Again, total silence in the van. Everybody was on a knife's edge, not knowing if they would make it back to the Tweed or be arrested by the police and spend the rest of their lives in gaol. Nick was pushing the van to its limit. Rusty had collapsed from shock, but his pulse was steady. At this rate, the balance of the trip would take about four hours. Geoffrey tried to keep Rusty awake as best he could. Being jammed into the front of the van was good because it kept Rusty's leg stable, but he kept drifting in and out of consciousness. The crew in the back seat were very quiet

Finally, they were only half an hour from the Rusty Nail. How the hell they'd made it back without being pulled over was beyond Geoffrey. He thought that the only way that this could have happened was that their cop connections must have been protecting them. They arrived an hour late, and as they pulled up at the cannery gate, Kev Skinner half-trotted his way towards them. It wasn't hard for Kev to assess the situation, and he quickly opened the gate to let them into the cannery. As it was Sunday morning, there were no workers around to witness what was happening to their employer Rusty, who again was unconscious. They parked near the cannery building to unload the van.

Before they opened up the back, Geoffrey warned Kev that Peter was dead. Then to their absolute horror, they realised Billy had died too.

'Fuck! Who the fuck did all this?'

'Who do you fucking think, mate? You think *we* look in poor shape? You should see what we left behind.'

'Okay, okay, get them out, and we'll hide their bodies in one of our chillers. We'll take the money bags down to the vault at the Nail, but for now, put them into the chiller until we have Rusty sorted out.'

Kev said he'd drive up to the monastery to ask Father O'Reilly for his help. 'While you lads sort out the van, I'll go and get things set up for Rusty's arrival. Maybe with the help of the nuns, Rusty can be given the care he needs urgently.'

Between the ins and outs of consciousness, Rusty muttered, 'Get Ann, she'll know what to do.'

Kev ignored Rusty's request and carried on with his plan to go up to the monastery and rally the nuns into action. Kev had forgotten that it was Sunday, and as he approached the monastery's gates, he heard Father O'Reilly giving mass. Kev entered the church and tried to get Father O'Reilly's attention. As a failed Catholic, Kev was uncomfortable about entering a church, but Rusty's life was at stake, so he decided not to mess around. He stood by the rear pews and waited until Father O'Reilly noticed his presence. Father looked up and saw the panic on Kev's face. He calmly asked someone to stand in and take his place, indicating to Kev to meet him outside. 'Father, I'm sorry to interrupt your service, but something has happened to Rusty.'

'What has happened?'

'He's been shot.'

'Where?'

'In the left thigh.'

'Can he be taken to hospital?'

'No,' Kev replied.

'Oh, I see. Bring him to the back entrance. I'll organise the nuns to get a private room ready. Where is he now?'

'He's over at the cannery. I can get him here in ten minutes.'

'Okay, let's get this done before the end of mass so as not to raise any suspicions. I'll have everything ready for his arrival and the back gate will be open. Just drive in. Can you bring enough manpower to get Rusty upstairs?'

'Yes, I'll bring another three men.'

'All good.'

Kev asked Father O'Reilly if he would phone Ann to let her know the situation, excused himself and hurried back to the cannery. Rusty was still unconscious, and it was difficult to get him into the back of the empty van. After a big effort from some exhausted men, they stretchered Rusty up to his room at the monastery. The nuns swung into action with warm water and bandages. As Geoffrey had the most first aid experience with gunshot wounds, he gave Rusty's wound a thorough going over. The bleeding had stopped, and it was clear that the bullet had gone all the way through, severely damaging his thigh muscle. Fortunately, his femur looked intact. What he needed was a surgeon who could stitch up his damaged muscle and that expertise was beyond Geoffrey. Geoffrey knew that infection would kill him if Rusty didn't get the correct medical treatment. He thanked the lads for their efforts, and Kev took them back to the cannery. Two of them were to stay at the apartment, and Kev was taking the other one back to his home. Geoffrey stayed at the monastery while Rusty was vulnerable. The sisters took Geoffrey to another room down the hall from Rusty, where there was a fresh change of clothes and towels, and he could have a shower. He absolutely ponged of stale sweat after their ordeal last night. Sister Loretta asked him to join Father O'Reilly for lunch in his study at midday. He said yes, of course. Father O'Reilly would be a perfect sounding board for resolving Rusty's problem.

Geoffrey's shower was unforgettable. He must have used all the hot water. It was half past eleven, and he thought he might just lie down for a rest. Rusty was sleeping and stable. He set his watch for half an hour and collapsed. When he heard organ music coming from the church and the tower bells sounding noon, he quickly dressed. He went and checked Rusty's pulse and temperature. All okay. He knew he'd have to find a medico, sooner rather than later. The difficulty of it all was finding a doctor who they could trust. If the lid was lifted on last night's operation the press would get hold of it and their goose would be cooked. It would create such a blow-up that even Tunner would not be able to keep them safe.

Father O'Reilly greeted him at the door of his study. Geoffrey had never been inside these walls before. Father's study was beautifully decorated; the timber panelling reminding Geoffrey of his apartment back in Balmain, and Issey jumped into his mind momentarily. He wondered if he'd be able to get back to her ever again.

'Take a seat. Sister Loretta will bring us lunch in half an hour, so we can get our chat sorted.'

'Thank you, Father.'

'Now, Geoffrey, I don't need to know the nuts and bolts of what has happened to Rusty. I just need to know how I can help our dear friend.'

'Well, he needs a specialist doctor. Can Rusty and I stay here until we get him sorted?'

'Of course.'

'Father, the trick is, the medical person has to be able to keep a secret. The costs of a "friendly" doctor will not be a problem.' Father sat back in his dark red leather lounge chair and thought for a few minutes. Geoffrey stayed quiet. Then the priest came up with a suggestion. One of his most prominent parishioners was a specialist surgeon at the Tweed Hospital. He was also an acquaintance of Rusty. 'I'm sure he will help; he knows what a great local man Rusty is. I trust him, Geoffrey, especially if I was to give him the call. Perhaps he could set up a makeshift theatre here, and the sisters could assist him. Shall I call him before lunch to get things rolling?'

'Definitely.'

'Good, I have his home number, so I'll call him now.' He picked up the phone and dialled. 'Hello Ted, it's Father O'Reilly. I apologise for disturbing you on your day off, but I wonder if you could come down to the monastery to have a look at someone you know. It's a delicate situation, Ted, as I need your word that you'll keep things private.' There was a pause. 'It's Rusty McCloud. Bring your medical bag; you're going to need it.' Another pause. Then, 'Thanks, Ted. Can you come around to the back garden gate? I'll have one of the sisters waiting to take you up to Rusty.'

Father O'Reilly turned back to Geoffrey. 'Ted is the best person to sort out Rusty and he will be totally discreet.'

There was a knock, and Sister Loretta entered, pushing a wooden food trolley. Geoffrey hadn't eaten in twelve hours or so, and roast lamb and all the trimmings made his stomach growl. While they enjoyed their lunch, they didn't talk any further about the situation. Geoffrey was offered dessert but apologised, thanking Sister Loretta for the meal. She asked if he'd be staying.

'Yes, but I don't know for how long, if that's okay?'

'That will be no problem.'

He found his way up to Rusty's room where Sister Marion was cleaning Rusty's wound again to stop the infection from taking hold. Geoffrey watched her. *Fuck, that's a nasty wound.* Her gentle care calmed his head, and he started to think more clearly about the big picture, including the major offensive by the six gunmen last night. He was back in the same frame of mind he was fifteen minutes earlier, just fucking pissed off again that Mack had attacked them and taken another two lives. He snapped out of his angry state when an elderly well-dressed man carrying a largish black leather bag entered the room accompanied by sister Loretta. There was no acknowledgement. The doctor went straight over to Rusty's side and held his hand. 'Mate, how are you feeling?'

Rusty answered, 'Hello, Ted. Thanks for coming mate.'

'My pleasure. Now let's have a look at your wound.'

While the doctor started his evaluation of Rusty's wound, Geoffrey asked Sister Loretta if Ann had been contacted. She said Kev had gone up to the house to give her the bad news, and that Jacob was already on his way to them. Geoffrey was feeling quite exhausted and asked the doctor if he was okay to have some sleep. The doctor didn't say anything; just gave him a solemn nod.

Sister assured him that she would make sure that things were sorted, and that Geoffrey needed to get sleep to function properly.

Geoffrey went to his room and put his head on the pillow. He didn't remember anything more until he heard the soft ringing of bells coming from down the hallway—breakfast. As he went past Rusty's room, he looked in and was given a half-smile by the patient. He walked over and put out a gentle handshake.

'Mate, well done,' he whispered.

'How many did we lose?'

Geoffrey hung his head. 'Two. Peter took a head shot and Billy died on the way back here. Their bodies are being cared for by your undertaker, Grant.'

'Fuck, mate, how did Mack know that we were taking the New England Highway?'

'I don't know, mate, but my gut tells me it was either one of our cop mates that saw us leaving the Astor, or Mack had both highways covered.' Then it hit him: 'Ricky! Fucking Chinaman Ricky. Those fucking walls are thin between the rooms at the Astor and maybe Ricky heard us when we were going through our plans. I'll bet that Ricky passed on our highway swap plan to Mack. It's a small world around Woolloomooloo and I'm sure Ricky would have been paid more than twenty dollars for the info.'

'Oh, God.'

'What about the money?'

'Yeah, it's all good, but your bag's looking a bit worse for wear, several bullet holes and all. The money's stashed in the vault over at the cannery. Have you seen Ann yet?'

'Yes, she and Jacob only just left. You were unconscious so they said they'll come back for lunch.'

'Are they okay, mate?'

'Yes. Ann was very upset, but Jacob will give her the support she needs. I've doubled the security now that Ann has gone back to the house.'

'Thank you.'

'Has the doctor done his patch-up?'

'Yes, he's done his best. I'm waiting on a visit from him shortly. I'm as sore as all fuck, but I know I'm lucky to have all of this care.'

Geoffrey hesitated and, with considerable emotion, looked at Rusty and said, 'Mate, you're king around here and never forget it. Even though most people know that you bend the rules a bit, you always have others in mind. This show of support is from their hearts, mate. Savour the moment and get well again. I'm flying back home to Sydney on Wednesday morning. Before I leave, I'll have a rough plan to go back and avenge our fallen and also take over that arsehole's business. Rusty, just focus on healing and let Jacob sort out the day-to-day running of the business. I imagine there is another coke shipment due.'

'Yes,' Rusty said. 'Talk to Kev. He's sorting out the delivery and pick up and we'll go from there.'

'I'll contact Sergei and bring him up to speed.'

'Thanks, Geoffrey. He's probably a little concerned. I reckon your success in grabbing Mack's transport is the key for us to all go forward. Last night was an example of how vulnerable we really are. We would not have to get involved at a hands-on level if we owned our own trucks. Trucks and good men will sort it.'

'You're right. We were lucky that any of us survived last night.'

'What happened to the three survivors on Mack's side?'

Geoffrey answered, 'There were no survivors.'

'Fuck,' said Rusty. 'We probably did well.'

'Rusty, if it wasn't for Nick and Christiano with their counterattack with grenades, we would have all been killed.'

'Geoffrey, you go back and do what you have to in order to get control of Mack's business but know that you will not be alone. Send the bastard broke with brutal force. Keep good contact with Sergei and his cop mates. Oh, and with that other fellow Jimmy Spillane, you know the bloke who has all the pull with the cops running the truck delivery business? There must be good money in that delivery business.'

He winced before continuing. 'They have everything to gain from you becoming a major player in the transport business. Be ready to pay a fire sale price to his liquidator. I'll back you financially. I'll also get Jacob to set up a line of credit at our bank for two million dollars. I can carry your repayments for six months. That'll give you enough time to get on top of your cash flow. Try to take over as many of his old contracts as possible to keep the business legit. Sergei will rest easier when he knows that his regular coke supplies are assured. I think that Mack has to have a miserable end after you have taken over the business. He will not be a happy camper and will stop at nothing to get square. You'll have to kill him so that you get a fair go and start afresh. Do your best not to employ any of his past heavyweights.'

'Thanks, Rusty. Paying a fire sale price does give the business a legit start, without the risk of more loss of men.'

'Oh, don't forget Peter and Billy and the funeral director. What's the director's name? Grant Fletcher—he's a good man and will give the lads a good send-off.'

'Okay.'

'I'm sorry I can't be there. Ask Kev when he gets time to contact the lads' next of kin. We'll make sure that they get looked after. Now mate, I'm going to have a fucking big cry. The pain killers are wearing off and the pain is unbelievable.'

'Oh, mate.... See you later in the afternoon. I'm staying just down the hall for security.'

'Thanks. Shut the fucking door, mate, so that I can get on with it.'

As the door lock engaged, a deep scream of pain came through the door. Doctor Ted was hurriedly walking towards Rusty's room, followed by Sister Loretta.

CHAPTER TWENTY-FIVE

Geoffrey went to his room and rang Kev from his room phone, asking Kev to bring him a pair of weapons and some ammo.

'How are the lads going, Kev?'

'They've been mostly sleeping since they got back.'

'Won't hurt them, mate; they've been to hell and back.'

Geoffrey gave Kev an update on Rusty's progress. Deep inside of him, he knew that Rusty might have to be moved to Tweed Hospital. He went back down the hallway and hovered around Rusty's door until the doctor came out. An hour or so later, Rusty's door opened, and Doctor Ted said, 'Rusty is in a bad way. The infection has taken over, and he needs urgent hospital care. Now I've stitched and dressed the leg it looks less like a gunshot wound.'

They agreed that Rusty's wounds could possibly be put down to a farming accident to avoid a police investigation.

'Okay, let's call for an ambulance.'

'Doc, is there any way that I can set up in the same ward as Rusty or maybe in an adjoining room to protect him?'

The doctor nodded. 'I reckon we can fix that. After Rusty leaves in the ambulance, you go down to the Rusty Nail and get Kev to call you an ambulance. Tell him to say he thinks you're having a heart attack. I'll be at the hospital to make sure our plan comes together.'

As the ambulance wailed its way into the entrance of the monastery, the doctor excused himself. Geoffrey decided to make himself scarce. If he was going to make a trip to the hospital himself in an ambulance in an hour or so, he needed not to be identified. He explained the situation to Sister Loretta, who just gave him a nod of okay. He slipped out of the back gate and found his way back to the cannery and found Kev in his office.

'Hello, mate,' said Kev. 'How're things?'

'Shitful. Rusty has to go to hospital, or we'll lose him to infection. But we've hatched a plan to keep him safe.' Geoffrey explained the plan, suggesting Kev could accompany him to the hospital in the ambulance wearing the pistols Geoffrey needed to guard Rusty.'

'No worries.'

Kev made the emergency call and five minutes later Geoffrey was being placed in the back of the responding ambulance with Kev sitting at his side. The Tweed Hospital was only five minutes away and their doctor was on the job. After running a series of tests, Doctor Ted admitted Geoffrey to hospital 'for observation'. Kev, of course, found an excuse to accompany Geoffrey to his room which, through no coincidence was next to Rusty's. There was a lot of activity, staff moving in and out of Rusty's room.

'Kev, have Jacob and Ann been brought up to speed?'

'Not sure.'

'Probably best they stay away from the hospital at this point. The less fuss made around Rusty, the better.'

Now that Rusty had a better chance of surviving, Geoffrey was happy to sit tight. He secreted the two pistols that Kev had slipped him in the bedside locker.

'Good thinking,' Kev said. 'By the way, I've been in touch with Tunner Meskle to get an update on the shootout on Saturday night. Tunner was a bit short with me and said that a lot of political shit was going down. But when I told him Rusty was in hospital, he said he'd do whatever he could to protect the hospital from attack. So, I assume the building's now under police surveillance.'

This made Geoffrey feel more comfortable. He needed sleep, so he thanked Kev and said he'd be okay, bidding him goodnight. 'Thanks for your help today. See you tomorrow?'

'Yes, mate, hopefully.'

Geoffrey started turning this over in his mind. The next day was Monday, and he was thinking that his return trip on Wednesday was starting to look doubtful; it would all depend on how Rusty went in the next twenty-four hours. He finally dozed off to sleep amid the flashing and beeping heart monitors.

Geoffrey woke to a young nurse asking him if he'd like a cup of tea. He accepted, carefully concealing his two pistols under the blankets. He and Rusty were on the fourth floor which had a great view looking out over the Tweed port area. From his bed, he could see Rusty's entire empire, from Rainbow Bay beach round to the trawlers, the monastery, the Rusty Nail. In the far distance to the west, he could see Rusty and Ann's home on the banks of Terranora Lake. He could not think of a better outlook for Rusty to wake up to every morning during his recovery.

The nurse checked the spaghetti of leads and explained the doctor had authorised their removal. 'But don't be in a hurry to move around too much yet,' she cautioned.

'My mate's next door. Any idea how he's doing?'

'He's had a blood transfusion and is starting a long journey to recovery.' 'That's great.'

'Feel like some breakfast?' she asked.

'Yes, please.'

After breakfast, he decided to walk up and down the hallway to stretch his legs. There was nobody around, so he opened Rusty's door and put his head in to see if he was awake. He was greeted with a half-smile.

'Hello stranger,' Geoffrey said.

Rusty sighed deeply. 'Yes, mate, it is a bit like that.'

'Rusty, before you try to ask too many questions, all you need to know is that every one of our bases are covered, and I mean every one.'

Rusty settled and gave a short sigh of relief.

'You just need to stay here and recover. Apparently, you were given a blood transfusion last night. Your colour looks a lot better. How's your thigh?'

'Fucking sore as. Hey, why are you in pyjamas?'

'Ah, Doc Ted helped me wangle my way into a bed next to you. I *may* have had some heart trouble.'

Rusty smiled.

As they were talking, a nurse came in and asked Geoffrey what he was doing in Rusty's room. He explained that by coincidence they had both ended up in hospital and that they were good friends, and of course he was concerned about Rusty's situation. He said he only intended to put his head around the door and look at him, but Rusty caught him out and asked him to come in. 'So here I am.'

'You really shouldn't be in here.'

'I know that. I'll leave in a couple of minutes.'

'Okay, just a couple.'

Geoffrey smiled at her, and she left them in privacy.

'Well, mate,' he said jokingly. 'This is another nice mess you have got us into.'

'Yes mate,' Rusty replied. 'Sometimes I wonder why the fuck I'm putting myself through all this drama. I'm too old for it.'

'What are you getting at, mate?'

'Well, for a start, all my businesses are thriving legitimate and profitable businesses. And the coke scene is getting the better of me.'

Geoffrey could tell that he was serious and let him continue to unload.

'I have enough money to last ten lifetimes, so what's it all about? When I'm at home with Jacob and Ann, I'm a different man, without the pressure of gun fights, money laundering, looking over my shoulder, and now this. I'll probably be dragging this fucked up leg of mine for the rest of my days.'

'Sounds like you're getting cold feet, mate.'

'Geoffrey, I don't want you to take this the wrong way, but the biggest reason I would be going on would be to see you sorted in the transport business.'

'So, what is the answer, mate?'

'The answer is that you go back to Sydney, I set up the two-million-dollar line of credit, I keep the lads on the payroll for six months and I keep the coke deliveries coming for that period. You and Sergei really get to know each other. Then at six months, and you being successful in your take-over of Mack's business, we set you up as the importer of the coke from his Colombian dealer. The only change will be that the drop-offs at sea would not happen here at Tweed, but at some other port that suits the operation. You'll have trucks and you will be in the box seat with getting the product to Sydney undetected.'

'Mate, that wasn't what I expected to hear from a dying man,' Geoffrey chuckled.

Rusty smiled. 'Mate, it is what I have been wanting to say for the entire time you have been in Sydney, and I know that's a lot for you to take on board. When are you planning to head back to Sydney?'

'I'm booked to fly out at ten on Wednesday morning. I've leased an apartment in Balmain which suits me to a tee. I have met a young woman, a student doctor, and my plan is for us to live in Balmain. I was going to keep its location secret while I secure the transport company, but I guess not much would change if we went ahead with your plan.'

Rusty agreed. 'You were always going to be shipping the coke, so why not ship it for yourself? The only difference would be the shitload of money that you'll make!'

Geoffrey nodded. 'Hmm, I guess I was hoping to focus on the distribution side via the fleet of trucks.'

'Anyhow, mate, you go back to Sydney and meet with Sergei. When I'm well enough, I'll contact him. If you like, you can run it past him to get his view.'

'Okay, thanks Rusty. I'll stay next door tonight to ensure that your security is good.'

'Thanks, mate. I know I can always rely on your loyalty; that's why I'm entrusting this business over to you. What I must insist on, though, is that you kill that fucking arsehole, Mack.'

'Don't worry, mate. He's dead meat as we speak. You get some sleep, Rusty, and I'll do the same.'

'I'll sleep a lot better knowing our plan, mate.'

'All good.'

Geoffrey went back to his room and got back into bed. *If I'm in hospital, I may as well take advantage of the situation and do what people do in hospitals.* He planned to lie in bed and be waited on hand and foot. He also had plenty to think about with Rusty's plan for him to take over the coke trade aspect of his business. The more he thought about it, the more churned up his stomach became. His gut said, 'Go for it, but also have a plan. Just like Rusty, get in and get out.'

When he'd made enough money to get his freight business fully operational, he could get out, and maybe it would be Nick's turn to step up. He had shown great loyalty and had a good business head. Geoffrey decided he would make a call after lunch to Sergei to set up a meeting for Friday. He would also call Jimmy Spillane, the truck sales king, for a meeting early next week to get to know him a lot better. Jimmy struck

Geoffrey as a man that knew everything and everyone in the heavy truck business. He might also give Geoffrey a few clues about the transition of Mack's business, how to link with the truck-driving cops. He'd quietly bring the right people into his life to secure the future of his freight business. He had learned one thing from Rusty—it's not what you know, it's who you know and trust.

Lunch was memorable—a large red-hot saveloy in the middle of a big plate with cabbage all over it. Geoffrey had never been a processed meat person, because who knows what the fuck is in those red rubbery fuckers? He came up with an excuse and said he was vegetarian, asking if he could have a salad sandwich.

Geoffrey had a couple of hours of sleep and then started making calls on the room phone that Ted had arranged. His call to Sergei was brief, and the Friday meeting was on. Not on his ground; they were meeting at a spot in the middle of Farm Cove at the Opera House end. Geoffrey also contacted Jimmy Spillane and they were on for lunch next Tuesday. Jimmy insisted on going to his favourite restaurant in Surrey Hills called Angela's and he sounded very keen to get together.

Geoffrey took advantage of the quiet time to reflect on the next five years. He believed five years was an achievable target for him to be a primary mover and shaker in the transport business, incorporating the cocaine transport initially then expanding to transporting other, less dicey cargo. And with the loyalty of Sergei and Jimmy, they would all make a lot of fucking money and hopefully stay alive to tell the story. It was certainly going to be very fucking interesting. Geoffrey planned to manage the business like Rusty, run silent and run deep.

Geoffrey left his room at about five o'clock and paid a visit to Rusty's room. To his surprise, Rusty was sitting up and looked a lot better and had started an early dinner. 'Hello mate!'

'What have you been up to, Geoffrey?'

'Well, I made a couple of calls to both Sergei and to Jimmy Spillane to let them know that I'll be back in Sydney for a meeting on Friday with Sergei and Tuesday with Jimmy. They both sent their regards.'

'Oh good.'

'You're looking a lot better, mate.'

'Yes, it is amazing what drugs can do to your brain to stop you from feeling pain. Doc Ted has been outstanding. I don't think I would have made it without him.'

'I believe that as well, mate. You were certainly in a bad way.'

'Jacob's coming up shortly with Ann.'

And right on cue, the door swung gently open and there were Ann and Jacob. Ann tearily hugged Geoffrey and thanked him for looking after her man. Rusty also teared up, and it was time for Geoffrey to leave them alone to catch up.

Ann and Jacob settled into the big vinyl armchairs on each side of Rusty's bed and smiled at each other. Jacob said, 'Dad, I have some news that I know will make your day.'

'What's that, son?'

'Well, I've decided to get married. I had intended to tell you last Sunday morning, but things took a different direction!'

'Yes, son, I'm sorry about that. Who's the lucky girl?'

'Lisa, Lisa McNab.'

'Oh, the beautiful young oyster board member?'

'Yes, Dad, that's her.'

'You dark horse. How long have you been together?'

'Oh, about three years but we've managed to keep our relationship under wraps.'

Ann was in tears again, but she was smiling as well, reflecting on her own covert romance with Rusty all those years ago.

'Dad, my other news is that Lisa is pregnant. We're expecting our first child in about six months.'

'Congratulations. When's the wedding?'

'Well, of course, with a baby coming, time is of the essence, so we thought that we'd have a private ceremony in the garden at the monastery and ask Father O'Reilly to marry us, but the date will now be set around your recovery, Dad.'

'That's a wonderful plan, Jacob. Great incentive to get well again.'

Ann was gently rubbing Rusty's hand, beaming at him. *God, I love her*, he thought. His decision to leave his drug trading life was timely, especially with Jacob and Lisa's new baby coming. A grandchild—boy or a girl—didn't matter.

'Well, while we're sharing things, you should know that our lives are going to take a new direction soon.'

'What do you mean, Dad?'

Rusty told them about his plans to get out of shady dealings and concentrate on their family businesses. This brought Ann undone again; this time, she was hugging him and kissing him gently on the cheek.

'Jacob, tell Lisa how happy I am with her becoming my daughter-in-law.'

'Thanks, Dad. Now just keep resting here. Kev and Jacob have everything under control.'

'I knew they would. How's the oyster farm going?'

'Well, the move to form a controlling board of management is working well. Of course, Lisa will stay on as a board member. The farm is her passion, and our kids will all be brought up around saltwater, thanks to you, Dad.'

Ann gave Rusty another soft kiss and they left him to rest.

Content and dreamy, Rusty drifted back to that special day at the Rusty Nail—it was the blessing of the fleet—when he claimed Jacob as his son. He needed his son in his life and also the woman he loved. He and Ann had wasted twelve years of their lives after she had fallen pregnant with Jacob. It wasn't just his decision to have Jacob brought up by the church; in those days a nun falling pregnant to the owner of the local pub was a scandal. Ann had not been ready to leave the church, and there was no middle ground: you're either in or you're out of the church, and Ann wasn't ready to leave her faith, which he now understood. The way things were now turning out was remarkable. Jacob's early upbringing by Mrs Kelley was a credit to her. Feeling deeply sentimental, Rusty wept himself to sleep. He was woken several times for a dressing check on his thigh. But with the news Ann and Jacob had given him, he was starting to feel stronger by the minute.

Geoffrey caught up with Rusty before he was discharged from hospital with a clean bill of health.

'Hi Geoffrey – you're looking well! I've been thinking and I'll move forward with the line of credit that we spoke of. Can you send me a monthly budget for you and the lads for the next six months? I'll take that money out of the golden egg and get it to you through Kev.'

'Thanks, mate.'

'I'd like it if we had minimum contact from here on. The less I know, the easier it will be to get on with my new direction. I'll get Kev to deal with the coke deliveries for the next six months with Sergei. Can you bring Sergei and Jimmy up to speed? I'm sure they'll agree.'

'Thanks, Rusty. Seems strange to think about going our separate ways after what feels like a lifetime together where we've never had a bad word or any mistrust. Like you said, Rusty, mates can be in business together. You and Hecky have been so good for me, and I thank you for the opportunities, mate. Who would've known a Nimbin boy could come so far?'

CHAPTER TWENTY-SIX

Kev picked Geoffrey up from the hospital, stopping off at the cannery to pick up the thirty grand that Rusty had promised him, along with some casual gear—shorts, surf shirts and thongs.

Geoffrey signed a docket that said he had paid each of the surviving lads thirty grand and that thirty grand was also on its way to Peter and Billy's mothers. The two young men had been laid to rest at a Tweed cemetery in a private service. The lads apparently gave their own military salute for Peter and Billy and then went to Fingal Head, where they set up a five-gallon wood keg and got well and truly pissed. Kev had no idea where the lads were now.

'That's okay Kev. They've earned a holiday, and they know the importance of security. I've made arrangements with Nick to meet him with the others in two weeks' time in Woolloomooloo, where we'll regroup for an assault on Big Mack.'

'Make sure you make the prick suffer, mate.'

Geoffrey confided in Kev, briefly outlining Rusty's plan to hand over the baton to him. 'But can you act surprised when he tells you? I don't want to insult Rusty.' Kev was actually delighted with the plan. 'I'm thinking it'll be a five-year plan, Kev. Any longer in the drug trade and things start turning to shit, if you know what I mean!'

'So, what's your plan?'

'I reckon six months to close Mack's doors, set up the new venture, and start my journey to becoming super-rich. I'll stick to my original plan of bringing Nick into the business so that he could be groomed to take over in about five years' time.'

'You think Nick's got great promise, eh?'

'Yep. My goal is to have Nick become a high-ranking Transport Workers' Union member. Our good friend Hecky Parker is very influential in the Australian Labor Party, which is at the core of the union movement in Australia. I reckon Hecky will know the "shortcut to grandma's house" when the time's right for our move into the national transport business. I want to be in the know when the opportunity arises to bid on both state and federal freight contracts. I'm gonna give it everything I've got, and I plan to live up to the high standards that Rusty's set for all of us heading to Sydney to make their fortunes.'

'You've really thought this through. Let me know the delivery date of the next marine drop-off so we can sort out the money with Sergei.'

'Okay, I'll arrange for a secure telephone when I get back to Sydney so we can stay in touch. Let's keep using our usual security password. I'll call you at the cannery at five every day until my phone's hooked up.'

'Have you thought about getting one of new mobile phones?'

'Oh, the bricks? Maybe.' Geoffrey didn't see himself as an early adopter of new technology – wait till they'd ironed out all the wrinkles.

They had to shout over the racket of three semi-trailers being loaded by forklifts. The cannery was now a huge business.

'Where does all of this canned seafood go, Kev?' Geoffrey yelled.

'All over the world, mate. Most of it to Melbourne and then it is shipped to many parts of Asia.'

'And the canned oysters. How are they going?'

'They were slow to start with, but now that the oyster leases are producing a bigger product, they have really taken off. Most of the canned oysters go to Japan.'

'Japan, hey?' He pictured Issey. 'What's the deal with the oysters?'

Kev explained that they used several other tray-back semi-trailers to bring spatted-up timber oyster frames from the Hawkesbury area just north of Sydney.

'Why is that Kev?'

'Well, the water there produces more oyster spats.'

'Spats?'

'They're baby oysters that attach themselves to the bitumen-coated timber frames. Because the Hawkesbury is only ten hours away from the Tweed, the spats survive out of the saltwater, and we get them into their new watery homes up at Terranora lakes as quickly as possible. It works well.'

Geoffrey wasn't only informed but impressed. *The power of money*, he thought. And the possibility of his new transport business requiring substantial freight opportunities. He was starting to get excited about the potential interstate and overseas freight businesses.

Kev dropped Geoffrey off at the departure terminal at Coolangatta Airport. It was a typical country airport, very casual. He was pleased he'd changed his clothes; he fitted in well. He wanted to look as nondescript as possible, carrying thirty grand in his overnight bag. He was also armed with a pair of side arms tucked into holsters, one on each side of his chest tucked under his shirttail. As he waited for the call to board, he was on high alert, looking out for anything suspicious that could mean a threat to his safety. He was flooded with relief at the call to board his flight. As he got up and headed to the gate, he tensed as he saw a police officer walking to the same gate. He was unsure of what to do, so with no other option, he just kept walking toward the gate. The cop didn't give him a second look. In fact, he actually pushed in front of Geoffrey to get through the gate! Geoffrey told himself to stay calm. Then he started worrying that he'd be sitting next to the cop on the plane. Fuck, that would be interesting!

As they made their way through the plane, the copper slid into the front row—first class. Luckily Geoffrey had only booked economy class, and he didn't draw even a look.

He started to settle as the aircraft blasted its way towards Sydney, his thoughts slowly drifting to his upcoming night with Issey. He planned to ask her over to his Balmain apartment on Saturday night in an effort to show her that he was a man of substance.

He had time to reflect on the events of the past months, and what he had achieved. His veteran soldiers had managed to counter all of Big Mack's attempts to remove Rusty from his throne as king of the Northern Rivers. Then there was the disappointing loss of their three mates, Stevo, Billy and Peter. He was on the lookout for three new highly skilled team members, looking forward to training them before starting his assault on Big Fucking Mack.

PART FIVE

CHAPTER TWENTY-SEVEN

Three years later

After a successful convalescence, Rusty withdrew from direct involvement with any of his businesses. With more time for reflection, his thoughts turned to his old mate, Hecky Parker. Even though he was older, Rusty had come to regard Hecky with a great deal of respect, almost as a mentor. He was certainly the spiritual moral compass Rusty would refer to when confronted with challenges in some of his less savoury activities. Rusty had seen Hecky grow from an innocent, naive young man into a canny and successful entrepreneur who used his wealth for philanthropic ends. Hecky and Rhonda had made a difference to the lives of orphaned children, homeless men, and the cyclone-ravaged residents of Port Moresby. Hecky's legacy would certainly benefit people for years.

Rhonda had eventually succumbed to ill health and when she died, it seemed a big part of Hecky died too. He was quite unwell. It meant that Rusty and Ann had now become heavily involved with the orphanages. Rusty also kept his finger on the pulse of his own businesses which were building from strength to strength under the leadership of Jacob and Lisa who now had two infants, Benjamin Hector McCloud and Rhonda Lisa McCloud.

Then, late one night, Hecky rang Rusty, asking him to come up to Brisbane as soon as possible. Hecky didn't elaborate on the urgency, but he said something about witnessing his last will and testament.

On their last visit to Hecky, Rusty and Ann had noticed that Hecky's old mistress, Leonie, was back on the scene and seemed to have a keen interest in Hecky's affairs. She was always hanging around and Rusty couldn't get any private time with Hecky to suss out why Leonie was suddenly back. Leonie was very proprietorial with Hecky: 'Hecky needs this' and 'Hecky wants that.' It was as if Hecky no longer had brainpower or choice. She treated him like an old fool. Rusty knew that Hecky was a very wealthy man and felt that Leonie hanging around could only mean trouble. Ann had similar concerns. Rhonda and Ann had been close friends, so Leonie making a late move on Hecky was unacceptable in Ann's mind.

The next day, Ann and Rusty made an early start, organising a driver to take them to Hecky's house for lunch. When they got there, everything looked normal. The ground floor of his home was buzzing with activity. Because his fortune was based mainly on a massive blue chip share portfolio, Hecky needed the support of a crew comprising a stockbroker, an accountant, secretaries, and a banker to manage his affairs.

Hecky was becoming less mobile and had installed a small lift to enable him to shift between his carpark and his lounge room. Rusty's bad leg was also very appreciative of this luxury. When the lift reached the first floor, Ann and Rusty were greeted by Hecky and—of course—Leonie.

Hecky was watching cricket on the television and was quick to point out that Australia was playing the West Indies. Rusty let go a big laugh and so did Hecky. It brought back memories of the Gabba many years ago. Leonie was very distant, making Rusty feel quite uncomfortable.

Once lunch was over, Ann and Rusty wanted to get down to business. So, Rusty asked Leonie if he and Hecky could have a private chat. Leonie stood up and carried on about not being included in their conversation. Rusty didn't back down, telling Leonie that it was none of her fucking business if he wanted to have a private conversation with an old mate.

Leonie settled a bit, hopped into the lift, and they did not see her again that day. Rusty and Hecky went into his office while Ann made them some tea.

'Hecky, what the hell is that fucking bitch doing in your life? Seems to me she's only here for one thing, and that's your money.'

Ann brought in the tea tray and left them to chat. Rusty noticed Hecky's hand was shaking as he attempted to sip his cup of tea. 'Rusty, I know what you're saying. In fact, I think Leonie and my staff might be ripping me off.'

'What?'

'I'm figuring they've stolen about twenty million from me.'

'How do you know that Hecky?'

'Well, she and another supposed *friend* convinced me to invest in an apartment development up in Caloundra and I think the development costs were hugely inflated'.

'How much have you loaned them?'

'About twenty-eight million dollars.'

'Fuck! Twenty-eight million? How many apartments are being built?'

'Twelve.'

'Fuck, mate, twelve? That doesn't sound right. Can you get out of the deal?'

'No, I can't,' Hecky said. 'I've tried to, but it's all gone too far.'

'How can I help, Heck?'

'Well, I want to set up a new will so that I can get back some control of my finances.'

'Please, Hecky, don't tell me that fucking bitch Leonie is involved in your will.'

'Unfortunately, mate, she is. Rusty, it gets worse. I've been diagnosed with early-stage dementia. Leonie has somehow become my power of attorney which apparently means that she can do whatever she pleases in the day-to-day running of my business. Rusty, believe me, I had no idea what I was signing when it was put in front of me… all of those smart arses downstairs that are supposed to be working in my best interests… I am sure that Leonie has them all working in *her* best interest.'

'So, what do you think I can do, mate?'

'Well, I am quite okay mentally when Leonie's not here. I think she must be drugging me somehow. Now that she has my power of attorney, she can come and go as she pleases.'

'What does your doctor say about your condition?'

'Well, that's another story. I think he is in it with the rest of them.'

'What do you mean, Heck?'

'Well, he's the one prescribing me the heavy drugs and he's authorised Leonie to give me shots. So sometimes after she has been here, I wake up and I've been asleep so long that I have pissed and shit myself. That's her rationale why I need a carer.'

'Fuck, mate. The best I can do for you is to go and see my lawyer and get some direction on what he can do to help you. Ann and I'll head back to Tweed, and I'll make an appointment with him asap. Is Norma still working here as the housekeeper?'

'Yes, she is. I think there's no way that Norma would be involved in this scandal.'

'Is she here now, Hecky?'

'Yes, she's been living out the back since her Herb passed away.'

'Good. You stay put here and watch the cricket. Ann and I will go around the back and have a quiet word to her about your situation.'

Ann had met Norma many years ago when she and Rhonda were establishing the orphanages here in Brisbane, so Norma knew that whatever Ann and Rusty had to say about Hecky's situation would be kept confidential. She started to cry when Rusty started to get down to Leonie's involvement in Hecky's affairs. Through her sobs, Norma tried to make the point that Hecky was not suffering from dementia and that he was only in a state of mental unbalance when Leonie spent time with him.

Rusty was now worried and asked Norma to do whatever she could without Leonie realising they were onto her. He explained they'd go back to the Tweed and seek some legal advice.

The driveway from Hecky's carpark to the main road was about two hundred metres long. Halfway down the drive, they met another car coming towards them. Rusty got his driver to shift over and let the other car pass safely. As the small car approached, it stopped beside Rusty's car window. It was Leonie who started yelling obscenities at Ann and Rusty.

'Keep your fucken nose out of our fucken business!' she yelled.

'Charming,' Ann muttered.

Rusty responded with, 'Hey, Leonie. I will be back.'

Rusty gave their driver the word to move on. They needed to come up with a plan to stop that bitch from taking over Hecky's empire.

CHAPTER TWENTY-EIGHT

When they got home, Rusty was straight on the phone with his lawyer, Richard Thomas. Rusty was not only Richard's best client but was also a trusted close friend. Richard knew Hecky through business deals that they'd done together over the years, and he knew Richard would give him a realistic option without taking years to get to court.

They teed up an appointment for ten o'clock the next morning. Then Rusty went to his study and made notes on what he and Ann had witnessed at Hecky's home earlier that day.

When Rusty related everything that had transpired the previous morning, Richard was furious that Leonie had moved in on Hecky's emotions after Rhonda's death. 'She is such a fucking lowlife. Bet she's using their illegitimate son as a lever to get at Hecky's heartstrings. If she's got a crooked doctor on board, then your mission to regain control of

Hecky's affairs is going to be very difficult to achieve in the short term. If that doctor deems Hecky has lost decision-making capacity, and Leonie has power of attorney, then it will take a considerable amount of time to get a court order to get rid of Leonie and her gang of intruders. Do you think they're conspiring to get rid of Hecky and appoint themselves as board members on Hecky's companies? Isn't he worth around three-quarters of a billion dollars?'

Rusty took a long look at Richard and said, 'Mate, it gets worse. I think Leonie is trying to murder our old friend.'

Richard looked horrified. 'Look, give me time to get some senior counsel legal advice. I promise to call you when I have a plan.'

Rusty went down to the Nail to have a bite to eat and catch up with everybody. The second level they'd added to the Nail had made a great difference to the tavern. The entire ground floor was now just dining, and patrons had a choice of three different types of food, mostly fresh seafood. The Nail also had an award-winning takeaway fish and chip outlet.

The auditorium on the upper floor was a world-class space where lots of famous acts performed. Rusty didn't know many of the employees who now worked at the Nail since Jacob had taken it to the next level and beyond.

As Rusty sat down at his favourite table out on the river deck, he saw Jacob, Lisa and the kids heading toward him. He adored those kids and made a big fuss of them.

'Lisa, the oyster farm is looking better than ever.'

'Thanks. Kev Skinner's son is now the chief biologist at the farm, and he's developed a new oyster species.'

Rusty was impressed, sat back, and felt somewhat emotional. Sensing his dad's mood, Jacob rounded up the kids to give their pop a big family hug. The lunch was a good reprieve from what was to come with the Hecky story up in Brisbane.

Richard called Rusty about a week later and invited him for a meeting at his office. Rusty sat in disbelief as Richard gave him the bad news. He confirmed that Leonie had gained the power of attorney over Hecky's affairs and not much could be done about it. Richard had checked the authenticity of the deed and it was all legal.

'Rusty, the only solution is for a new will to be drawn up. That will stop her. Leonie's job as the attorney is to ensure that the last will and testament of our mate Hecky be settled in strict accordance with the *intention* of the will.'

'Yes, Richard. Go on.'

'Well, one hitch. We'll need a specialist doctor to vouch for Hecky's capacity. Leonie's power of attorney would have been invoked when his current doctor deemed him as lacking capacity.'

'Shit, do you know anyone?'

'Sure do. One of my clients is a renowned geriatrician. Dr Barney Mezger. You may have heard of him. He's also the chair of the Southside Grammar Old Boys' Association.'

'Southside, isn't that where Hecky—'

'Exactly.'

'Well how about I draft a new will and POA and we'll grab Doctor Mezger and go up to Hecky's place?'

'Good idea, Richard. It'll be a challenge, but if we can get Hecky on his own, then we might have a chance.'

'Is there anyone we can trust to help us get Hecky alone?'

'Yes, Norma still lives there. She can let us know when Hecky is alone.'

'That'll work, Rusty. How about you phone Norma and let her know that we want time with Hecky? Tell her we'll need about three or four hours alone with him and don't tell her why. Just say that we are catching up as old friends. I'll get in touch with Barney. Hope he'll be able to squeeze us in.'

When Rusty got onto Norma, she said that Wednesdays were still tennis days. 'A lot of Mr Parker's old friends drop in to smash a ball or two and have a beer and a sandwich. Leonie always leaves Hecky alone with his tennis mates so you guys could just blend into the afternoon.'

'Sounds perfect,' Rusty said. 'What time do you think we should be at the house, Norma?'

'Well, tennis starts at two, but Leonie leaves the house at one sharp.'

'Thanks for helping us with this, Norma. Is that the only time she leaves him?'

'Yes. She's always by his side. She seems to be in charge of giving him regular injections. I asked her what the shots were for, but she said she was just following the doctor's orders. Leonie and the doctor seem to spend a lot of time together lately.'

'Is that so, Norma?' Rusty responded. 'Okay, Norma. We'll aim for next Wednesday, about one fifteen.'

'Okay, but don't bother if it's raining as the tennis will be cancelled.'

'Oh, so can I call you on Wednesday morning around nine to confirm everything?'

'That'll be fine.'

'Oh, and Norma, mum's the word.'

'I understand, Rusty.'

Rusty called Richard who said he'd contact Barney and hopefully they'd see Hecky the following week. Rusty relaxed a bit, reassured that he was doing something positive towards preserving everything that his lifetime friend Hecky Parker had worked for since Rusty had met him as a young eighteen-year-old lad at Rainbow Bay.

Richard picked Rusty up from the Nail at ten on Wednesday morning. Barney Mezger was in the passenger seat. Spotting Rusty's limp, he quickly hopped out, shook hands with Rusty and nimbly jumped into the back of Richard's car. Their trip to Brisbane was enjoyable, talking about old times and deals that were good and deals that were not. Barney could see the common respect they had for each other which had taken a lifetime to achieve. Rusty had checked with Norma that tennis was still on. She said Hecky was really looking forward to seeing them.

'So, all is good for our meeting?'

'Yes, see you then, Rusty.'

They arrived spot on quarter past one and when they took the lift up, there was Hecky, standing in his dressing gown and slippers. He was unshaven and looking scruffy.

There was a strong odour of urine about him. Rusty was not used to seeing him in such an untidy state and felt embarrassed for him. He introduced Richard and Barney to Hecky. 'Do you remember Richard, Hecky? And this is Barney, an old Southie boy.'

'Sure do. Hi Barney.'

They firmly shook hands and slowly made their way through to the living room and into his office. It was in chaos, and they had to clear a space on Hecky's desk for Richard to lay out his documents.

Richard sat quietly as Rusty chatted to Hecky. Barney observed, throwing in a few pertinent questions to help him assess Hecky's mental state. Rusty expressed his concerns about Leonie getting control of Hecky's estate. 'I'd go so far as to suggest, mate, that it's not in Leonie's best interests to have you around.'

Hecky looked down, a beaten man. Then he shook his head. 'Rusty, how could I have been so fucking stupid, mate? She's pumping me with this green juice all the time, I feel like shit, and now she's running all my affairs. Seems I've been deemed incompetent! It's humiliating.'

It was time for the three visitors to show their hand. They outlined their plan.

'Are you okay with that, Heck?'

Hecky did not hesitate with his agreement. 'Where do we start?'

By that point, it must have been around two and they could hear a bit of yelling and laughing going on. Tennis must have started.

'Okay. We'll leave you with the doc. Barney, wave us back in once you've finished your assessment.'

Rusty and Richard went out to watch some tennis.

Finally, Barney called them in. 'Set to go, Richard.'

Rusty said, 'Richard's prepared a list of questions for you to answer, Hecky. I need to tell you that you cannot include either me or Richard as beneficiaries in this new will nor anybody that either of us are associated with.'

Hecky nodded. As Richard carefully worked through building the new will, Rusty was a bit taken aback by the size of Hecky's estate. He was not surprised to hear that generally, the money was all to go to various charities. The only unusual request was that he wanted to leave his brain to dementia research. Neither Richard nor Rusty questioned Hecky on his organ donation. It was *his* last will and testament, not theirs. But if they'd looked, they would have seen a wry smile on Doctor Mezger's face.

Two hours later, and it was done. Rusty reached over and put his hand on top of Hecky's and said in a loving tone, 'Feel better, mate?' Hecky was shaky and emotional but overall, he was happier. Richard asked Hecky if there were any of the tennis players that could witness his signature on the will. Hecky said, 'Go out on the back deck and call out to Graham and John. They'll happily sign, I'm sure.'

The tennis was paused while Hecky explained to his close mates that he had just completed an updated will and asked if they would witness his signature.

'Thank you, boys,' said Hecky. 'Who's winning?' he asked.

John responded and said that he and Bobby were all over it. He jokingly added that one of the opposition had to leave early and would Hecky like to back Graham up for a game of doubles. Hecky gave a beautiful smile and accepted. John and Graham were both taken aback by his acceptance to join in a set of doubles.

'I'll be out when I get dressed,' Hecky called out.

Not long after, the yelling and swearing continued, but by this time somehow Hecky had got his tennis whites on and was holding his favourite Slazenger racket standing with Graham at the southern end of his home court on the net. Barney was stunned by Hecky's determination to get on the court while Rusty and Richard watched their old mate have what was possibly his final tennis match. Hecky's teammate was putting in a great effort covering both sides of the court while his opponents at the other end were doing what they could not to dominate this moment in Hecky's life. On a couple of occasions, Hecky actually hit a couple of winners playing on the net. They came off the edge of his racquet, but they all counted. Much to their amazement, the final score was Graham and Hecky six, Bobby and John two. When they all went up to shake hands at the net, Hecky started to dispute the score. He quite firmly claimed that the score was six-one. Well, Bobby and Rusty, of course, played it up a bit, but in the end, agreed that maybe there was a bit of a mix-up and gave him the extra game. Hecky propped himself against the bench to enjoy a beer and called out a thank you to Richard, Rusty, and Barney for their backup. 'Safe trip back!'

On the way back to their car Rusty muttered to the others, 'Not a bad effort for a man dying of dementia!'

Several weeks later, Rusty got a call from a nurse at the Brisbane General Hospital. When Rusty acknowledged that it was him on the phone, another voice took over. It was Hecky, begging him to come to the hospital to pick him up because—in his exact words—'They're going to kill me. Please, mate, come and get me.'

Then the phone went silent, and Rusty was in shock. He immediately telephoned the hospital and asked to speak to the sister in charge. She said that she would look into it and then phone him back. He never got that call and regrettably, the next call he got was from Norma, in tears. She informed Rusty that Hecky had died in his sleep at two that morning. There was no explanation for his death. Only that he had died in his sleep.

Rusty was shaken by the news and said he'd be up in the afternoon to see if there was anything he could do to help with the funeral arrangements. Norma suggested that he wait until things settled down and promised to keep him posted. Leonie had taken over the arrangements.

Rusty worried that Leonie would have a field day if she found the will that Richard had prepared for Hecky before he was killed. Rusty was going to use that word—killed—as he truly believed that is what happened to his dear friend.

Rusty was sure she'd either destroy the latest one or change it with codicils to her advantage. Richard held the other two signed copies of Hecky's last will. So Rusty called

Richard to advise him Hecky had died and asked him to contact the funeral parlour to ensure they were advised of Hecky's wishes to donate his brain to dementia research.

Rusty tried to contact Leonie to get involved in Hecky's send-off, but to no avail. He was surprised when he got a call from her two days before the scheduled funeral, where he was sure there would be mourners from the Prime Minister down. She asked Rusty if he would be a pallbearer on Hecky's casket. He had to bite his tongue and not tell her to go and fuck herself. He accepted the offer but did not thank her. That old saying of 'Keep your enemies close…' rang home to him. She explained the time and place where Rusty and the other coffin bearers would gather prior to Hecky's casket arriving at Oliver Plunkett Catholic Church. He had a quick thought as he was finishing his discussion with her. 'Leonie, can you organise for me to go to the funeral parlour and pay my respects to my dear friend? I will be able to grieve better if I can sit with Hecky and go over some "unfinished business".' Leonie said she thought that was unusual, but she agreed and gave him the contact details of the funeral directors. She even said she would call them in the morning to give her consent to his request. Rusty managed to squeeze out a thank you and they said their goodbyes. *Fuck, this will be interesting,* he thought. Rusty was on the telephone the next day to the funeral parlour and asked if eleven o'clock the next day was suitable. Yes, the man agreed; eleven would be fine.

Tomorrow could not come around quickly enough for Rusty. He was up early, had breakfast with Ann and explained what he hoped to achieve by viewing Hecky's body. As Rusty's old gunshot injury got very sore when he drove long distances, he got his driver to take him up to Brisbane. The trip up was a time of reminiscing about all the kids and all the people who had been taken care of by Hecky's commitment to them. This common man was a true hero of his time and Rusty thought the world of him. His humour under fire was fantastic and Rusty loved his philosophy: 'Try not to worry; it's always darkest before dawn.' Rusty never forgot those words.

The driver parked just outside the main entrance to the funeral home. He sat and chatted for a short time with the undertaker who asked if Rusty was comfortable with seeing his friend in that situation. Rusty explained he was all ready and braced himself for the next step.

The undertaker took Rusty to a beautifully decorated room. In the middle was Hecky's coffin. Soft piano music was playing in the background. It was now time for him to take a final look at his old friend and he asked the undertaker to leave them alone. As he stepped up to view Hecky's body, he took a deep breath. He could see Hecky's face was heavily made up, some of the white silk coffin lining strategically arranged to cover the top of Hecky's head at the hairline.

Rusty drew in a deep breath. He quietly said his goodbyes and shed a tear as he gingerly pulled back the silk covering.

'Wow...' he whispered. 'Well, well, well, you cunning old fox.'

With a quiet chuckle, he mused, *This is going to be interesting.*

EPILOGUE

It was nine o'clock on Easter Monday morning. A knock at the door.

'Leonie May Edwards?'

'Yes.' She felt her stomach drop.

'My name is Senior Sergeant Michael Farrell.'

'Yes, how can I help you, sergeant?'

'Leonie Edwards, you are under arrest for the murder of Hector James Parker.' He went on to caution her, 'You have the right…'

Leonie was startled when the assisting policeman took her by the arm, turned her one-eighty degrees, and placed handcuffs on her wrists. 'Please come with us back to headquarters. You'll be given the opportunity to call your lawyer from there.'

Leonie was taken out onto the footpath where a police car silently waited. As they travelled down her street, she felt like a sentenced criminal taking her last steps to the gallows. There was a large gathering of press milling on the footpath outside, camera operators jostling for space to catch some good footage. Someone within the newspaper community must have been tipped off.

ABOUT THE AUTHOR

Allan 'AJ' Holland was born in Brisbane 1951. His heritage is Kurtijar and European. He is an emerging author, self-publishing *All Will be Well*, a moving tribute to his family, in 2021.

Driven by a new-found love for writing and passion to write a tribute to a dear friend, he started writing *Money, Power & Greed* in 2022.